DEAD Pretty

By Robyn Nyx

2022

Praise for
Robyn Nyx's work

Never Enough

"Nyx's debut is an entertaining thriller with two well-realized heroines. But readers who can handle the gory content will find it well balanced by plenty of romance and copious amounts of sex, as well as a solid cast of supporting characters and some insightful handling of contemporary social issues." *Publishers Weekly*

"If you are a sucker for fast paced, gritty crime thrillers that will make you neglect your household chores and read way past your bedtime, well fellow book lover, this is certainly the story for you." *The Lesbian Review*

The Extractor Trilogy

"Nyx balances the task of developing emotionally complex characters and creating a plot that is well paced and full of action on a grand scale. The story is captivating, and the best part is that it's the first in a fantastic trilogy." *The Lesbian Review*

"I genuinely couldn't have predicted what did happen though, and urge everyone to read this trilogy if not for the imaginative story, then for the intensity of how people's actions affect not only their own lives but the lives and feelings of others. So good! Robyn has perfectly captured all that moral uncertainty between doing the right thing legally and then doing the right thing morally." *LesBiReviewed*

"The redemptive power of love is a huge take-away from this book. There were more than a few times where I found myself on the verge of tears while reading some of Landry's conversations with her best friend Delaney." *Victoria Thomas*

Music City Dreamers

"Fans of the show Nashville will love Music City Dreamers by Robyn Nyx, for its angsty drama involving megastars and aspiring singers, songwriters and record executives. This is also not the stereotypical Nashville of bros and whiskey you often see on CMT." *NPR*

"I really enjoyed this story and I am so glad Ms Nyx made this foray into lesbian romance. She has captured the passion and intense emotions of the two women, as well as weaving a fascinating story." *Kitty Kat's Book Blog*

The Golden Trinity

"Ms. Nyx tells an awesome story with real characters, and that to my mind is the goal of a good book." *Lesbian Reading Room*

"What an excellent book and I demolished it in one go! I had such a great time reading Uncharted and would be happy to pick it up again tomorrow. The pace was perfect and felt like I was on the adventure with Chase and Rayne. For the last 30% of this book, my heart was in my chest with all the excitement." *Les Rêveur*

The Copper Scroll

Holy hotness, batman!! Chase and Rayne's sexual and emotional chemistry flows onto the page. This isn't an experience you want to miss. Just make sure you read the first book before this one. It's just going to make the experience all the better. This book really is jam-packed with action, adventure, and romance. I really hope this isn't the end of the 'The Chase Stinsen' books because I am not ready to let these characters go just yet. *Les Rêveur*

Nyx has the ability to get you into the heads of her characters, and Chase and Rayne are no exception; and I loved that she showed us that not everything in life is always black and white. I've already re-read it twice. I thought The Golden Trinity was good, it had my heart racing, and I was awash with adrenaline in places, but The Copper Scroll surpasses it. I'm just waiting for Book 3 and the film series. *The Lesbian Review*

LesFic Eclectic Volume One

Robyn Nyx has put together a fantastic collection, and brought to us some amazing new talent as well as stories from some of our already loved and established authors in the genre. Engaging readers with new writers is always fantastic, and the new writers included in the Lesfic Eclectic are all absolutely brilliant." *LesBiReviewed*

LesFic Eclectic Volume Two

"I have read the seasoned writers before such as Anna Larner, Robyn Nyx, Brey Willows, Jenn Matthews and Anne Shade as always blew me away with their storytelling. A little something for everyone is the tagline across the cover, and I couldn't agree more. I highly recommend grabbing a copy of Lesfic Eclectic, a bottle of vino and taking one story at a time." *Les Rêveur*

LesFic Eclectic Volume Three

"Having read the previous two volumes, I wondered if volume three would still achieve the same delightfulness as its counterparts but, truth be told, it's the most magical one yet." *Queer Literary Loft*

By the author

The Chase Stinsen Adventures

The Golden Trinity (Book One)

The Copper Scroll (Book Two)

Music City Dreamers

The Extractor Trilogy

Escape in Time (Book One)

Change in Time (Book Two)

Death in Time (Book Three)

Never Enough

Edited by Robyn Nyx

LesFic Eclectic Volume One

LesFic Eclectic Volume Two

LesFic Eclectic Volume Three

DEAD Pretty

ROBYN NYX

Words for women who love women

By Robyn Nyx

2022

BUTTERWORTH BOOKS

Butterworth Books is a different breed of publishing house. It's a home for Indies, for independent authors who take great pride in their work and produce top quality books for readers who deserve the best. Professional editing, professional cover design, professional proof reading, professional book production—you get the idea. As Individual as the Indie authors we're proud to work with, we're Butterworths and we're *different*.

Authors currently publishing with us:

E.V. Bancroft
Valden Bush
Michelle Grubb
Helena Harte
Lee Haven
Karen Klyne
AJ Mason
Ally McGuire
James Merrick
Robyn Nyx
Simon Smalley

For more information visit www.butterworthbooks.co.uk

Dead Pretty © 2022 by Robyn Nyx. All rights reserved.

This trade paperback is published by Butterworth Books, UK

This is a work of fiction: names, characters, and incidents are the product of the author's imagination or are used fictitiously. Any resemblance to actual persons, living or dead, business establishments, events, or locales is entirely coincidental.

This book, or parts thereof, may not be reproduced in any form without express permission.

Cataloging information
ISBN: 9781915009128
CREDITS
Editor: Jan Stone
Cover Design: Robyn Nyx
Production Design: Global Wordsmiths

Acknowledgements

First, I must thank my editor, Jan. You pick up all the things I think are on the page but are still in my head; I couldn't do this without you. Thank you to my wonderful team of ARC readers for their lovely comments and for taking their precious time to read my words. And of course, thanks to my readers, new and old; I hope you enjoy this story. I love you all.

Dedication

For the center of my world, Brey.
You are my everything, and
I love sharing this writing
dream with you.

Chapter One

"I'M JUST WRAPPING UP this final case. The new team will take everything from there." She closed the fridge door, took the top off the beer, and headed for the living room. Her final case here was almost settled, and she felt like celebrating.

"It's been six months, Daniella."

Dak shook her head and dropped onto the couch. Her mom was prone to exaggerating, but maybe the time apart felt longer for her. Either way, using her first name had always signified her mom's seriousness. "I miss you too, Mom." It *had* been too long, and Dak didn't quite know how the cold cases she'd been working on had managed to suck so much of her time into a seemingly bottomless vortex. However it had happened, she hadn't been able to get home. She didn't have the heart to tell her mom that she only had two days before she would have to head to Seattle for her next case. "How's Ward doing?"

"Your brother is fine. He's always fine. Don't change the subject. When will you be home?"

Home. It hadn't felt like home for a long, long time. The familiar vice-like grip tightened around her heart, and Dak closed her eyes to concentrate on breathing away the pain. How was it still so raw after almost twenty years? And why did it feel that way when her mom and brother were still there? She took a long slug of her ice-cold beer. "Like I said, Mom, I've got a few things to finish up, then I'll pack up the truck and drive home." She used the word though it lacked the resonance she wanted it to hold. She'd gotten so good at hiding it, her mom wouldn't pick up the difference. Or if she did, her mom had gotten good at hiding her awareness of Dak's distancing too.

"That old truck is going to give up on you with all these long-distance trips, honey. Maybe it's time to think about buying a new one."

Dak laughed. "No way, Mom. Betty's got years left in her." Her truck was the last vehicle she and her dad had worked on before he died. She wouldn't replace it until the engine gave up on her. Sure, with a top speed of sixty-five downhill with a following wind, she was no use in a car chase, but that's why she usually traveled in her partner's car on the job.

Her phone vibrated to indicate call waiting. She checked the screen and saw it was her current temporary partner, Hamilton. "I'm sorry, Mom, the precinct's calling. I'll let you know when I'm coming home." Yep, it sounded genuine enough, she was sure.

"Make sure you do, honey. I love you."

Her mom ended the call without waiting for a response, and Dak switched to Hamilton. "You're calling to tell me you have him in custody and he's already confessed."

"Huh. Impressive, Special Agent Farrell. Yes, we do, and yes, he has," Hamilton said. "But that's only part of why I'm calling. The captain wants you to come in. There's been another murder that looks like that surgeon from a month ago. Male victim in his thirties."

Dak sighed when she realized what Hamilton was really saying. She'd flicked through the case file and given the captain her thoughts. She'd suspected it was the first of many to come, but that had been four weeks ago and there'd been nothing new. The killer had been careful so there hadn't been much to go on. Still, it was an open investigation, and Dak was only working cold cases. If it was a serial murderer though, the case would be huge. This kind of thing didn't happen in Salt Lake. The public would panic, and the department would be under enormous pressure to solve it fast.

"You've got this, Hamilton. You don't need me." Dak grabbed the TV remote and pulled up the local station. Sure enough, the scrolling news banner screamed about a murder and a possible connection to the surgeon in East Bench, whose body had been carefully arranged postmortem. No one could ever be considered lucky to be murdered, but this victim had been lucky his injuries were inflicted *after* he'd been murdered.

Dak blinked away the visceral images of the crime scene photos, imprinted on her mind as they always were. She only had room in her head for one psychopath at a time, and until the Rat Bucket case was fully closed, she didn't want another one.

"The captain wants you to come to the crime scene. Maybe you can see something we can't," Hamilton said. "Come on, Farrell. The Rats case is all but closed now that Atkins confessed. Just give us your thoughts and then get back to packing."

Dak scanned the living room. There wasn't much to pack. The house came furnished, and she traveled necessarily light. Clothes, books, tools. It wouldn't take long, and she could be on the road by tomorrow afternoon. She could consult long distance if the captain really wanted her to, but Hamilton and his team had everything they needed really…though this case would be intriguing if it was the beginnings of a serial murderer.

"Where are you?"

"2295 South Benchmark Circle. Body's still here."

Dak smiled at Hamilton's unsubtle carrot dangling. It had been a while since she'd been to an active crime scene. She checked her watch. Rush hour hadn't kicked in yet, but Hamilton was at the north end of the city. She rolled her neck and the ensuing cracking made her grimace. "It's going to take me over an hour to get there."

"That's because you insisted on living in suburbia, dumbass."

"Shut it, city boy." But there was no point to arguing. When she learned she'd been loaned to the Utah PD for at least a year, finding a suitable place to live had been paramount. Living in any city that long wasn't an option for fear of suffocation. "Sure you want to wait?"

"CSU and forensics are here. Mosley says the guy's been dead two days. An extra hour ain't gonna matter to him."

Dak sighed at Hamilton's persistence, a trait of his that she usually admired but had no time for today. Burnett had clearly put a bug up Hamilton's ass, and he wasn't taking no for an answer. Best that she analyze the scene to appease him.

"Okay. I'll be there when I can." She hung up, pulled on her jacket, and slipped her phone into her pocket before she headed for the door. She stopped at the family picture on the bookcase—always the last thing she packed—and held her fingers to her dad's face. This line of work wasn't exactly what they'd had in mind when she applied to join the police after 9/11, but he'd still be proud of her. She was still making a difference.

"I miss you, Dad." Dak drew back. She didn't have time for maudlin thoughts now or any other day, but the grief always slammed her hard right after speaking to her mom or her brother. It was a good enough reason to limit contact, but she couldn't shake the feeling she was punishing her mom too, which was totally unfair. When she lost her husband, in some respects, she lost her daughter too. But no matter how many times Dak tried to find her way home, emotionally more than physically, she couldn't quite do it. Home just wasn't home without her dad.

Chapter Two

"THEY'RE NOT RENEWING?" CJ reached back for the arm of her chair, a support, something, anything to keep her from falling into the gaping wide abyss of failure that appeared as quickly as her agent spoke the words. She *had* spoken the words CJ didn't want to hear, right? She hadn't just misheard, and this would simply be a moment they joked about in years to come.

"Don't worry, Callie." Paige caught her forearm and guided her into a chair. "They're making a huge mistake."

CJ pushed at the bottle of bubblegum-colored gin on the table beside her. Someone at last night's party had bought it. He made a show of telling CJ how expensive and exclusive it was. She didn't care last night, and she didn't care now. Expensive or not, it wouldn't dilute the bitterness of Paige's bombshell. "Why not?" she whispered though the desire to shout burned at her throat. Yelling at Paige wouldn't change anything, and it wasn't her fault anyway. Somehow, somewhere along the line, CJ had messed up. She hadn't smiled enough, or she'd rebuffed the advances of one too many executives. But it couldn't be her work, she was sure of that.

"Oh, honey. It's not you." Paige sat on the seat beside CJ. "Do you mind?" she asked as she poured herself a gin without waiting for an answer. "The network wants to try something new. Some YouTube sensation that won't last beyond the pilot, most likely." She knocked the gin back in one swallow. "They'll be knocking on your door soon enough, but by then, it'll be too late."

"Too late because I'll be on the streets and no one will want to employ me?" Defeat wasn't something CJ gave entry to easily, but the familiar specter of failure sat on the countertop leering at her.

Paige shook her head. "Don't be silly. I mean that we'll already have you ensconced in another network." She poured herself another gin and put two fingers' worth in a second glass. "Drink this. It'll make you feel better."

CJ eyed the pink liquid. She doubted Paige's wisdom but took the glass anyway. "I don't see how another network is going to take the show. And it's not like I can do anything else." And she liked this life she'd been leading for the past three years. She couldn't imagine going back to daily life in a silent morgue. No lights. No camera. No action. Who was she if she wasn't fronting *Dead Pretty*? Just another small-town mortician with a talent for rewinding the visual effects of death. And she wasn't likely to see the kind of deaths back home she'd gotten used to seeing, macabre as that thought was. More than that, she couldn't go home and face her parents. How unimpressed would they be when she turned up with nothing but her Ferrari to show for three years of her life? She could already see the disappointment in their eyes. Her father might appreciate the car through his disapproval. At least that was something.

"This is their loss, not yours. They'll be back with their tail between their legs and an offer so big, you'd pee a little if you hadn't already signed the deal of a lifetime for their biggest rival." Paige clinked her glass to CJ's and knocked her second serving back before picking up the bottle to study it. "This might be the best gin I've ever tasted. Who gave it to you again?"

"One of the network executives." She sniffed it and put her glass down without tasting it. "Looks like it was my severance package. I can't believe no one had the balls to talk to me at the wrap party. Everyone smiling and patting me on the back. 'See you next season.' Did anyone else even know?" CJ leaned back into the soft Italian leather chair and sighed. She didn't own a stick of the fancy furniture she was surrounded by. How had it come to this? The devil on her shoulder laughed. Three years of partying hard and saving nothing, that's how.

"I don't think so. You weren't being taken for a fool, if that's what you're worried about, CJ. This is Hollywood. Everyone is your best friend until they're not." Paige plugged the gin with its rubber cork and pushed it away as if it was tempting her to finish the whole bottle. "You'll be back. I have no doubt there'll be an online petition to bring the show back as soon as the public finds out you've been canceled. Plenty of shows have had multiple seasons following audience pressure." She placed her hand on CJ's knee and squeezed. "The best thing for you to do would be to take a break while you can. Go home. See your family. Relax and do nothing while I field all your offers and turn them into something worth coming back for." She tilted her head slightly and pursed her lips. "A little down time will be good for you. Recharge your batteries and flush your system."

"I'm not a car, Paige." But CJ knew what her agent was hinting at. Paige was inclined to act like CJ's mom on occasion, something she didn't fully appreciate since her actual mom hadn't been around all that much when she was a kid. She'd taken care of herself then, and she could take care of herself now. If CJ wanted to party, that's what she'd do… Which was why she had the Italian sports car she'd always wanted, enough clothes to wear a different outfit every day for six years, and a houseful of transient friends eager to party with her.

And little else. How was she supposed to have known the ride would come to an end so abruptly?

"Maybe not, but you're not invincible either. Some time away from this scene will be the best thing for you, trust me. And your absence will make the networks want you more. Going home for a few weeks will be gold for your career and your health."

CJ raised her eyebrow. "Says the woman who just knocked back a quarter bottle of gin in the middle of the day."

Paige smiled and flashed her perfect teeth. "Years of training, CJ. It's do as I advise, not do as I do." She gave CJ's knee another gentle pat and got to her feet. "I'll call you when I have something solid put together," she said as she headed out of the room. "Call your mom."

Paige underscored her words with a gentle-ish slam of the front door, tempting CJ to throw the stupid gin after her. What was it about older people that made them think they had the right to dictate what anyone else under forty should do? Experience. Wisdom. Knowledge. Fuck all of that.

This was all her fault. All she was really good for was a crappy little mortuary back home. How stupid had she been to think otherwise? She stood and studied herself in the ridiculously large gilt mirror above the ornate fireplace made from the finest Italian marble. She hadn't removed her make-up yet, but how much longer would it hide her true face anyway? And if she stripped herself of that facial armor, she doubted her ability to brave this shallow environment anymore.

Paige was right, as she irritatingly often was. Home would be a good place to hide from all her faux friends who'd disappear once they realized the party was over. She could recover from this unexpected blow and hope that Paige would work her magic and convince another network that they needed *Dead Pretty*, that they needed Callie Johnson to draw in all those people obsessed with the ugliness of death and her talent to undo it. She might be a fraud in all other aspects, but she *was* good at her job, that much she knew. She had her last paycheck to come. It was peanuts if she stayed here, but back home, it would last a couple of months. And that'd be all Paige would need to get CJ back on TV.

She picked up her phone and scrolled through to her dad's cell. No use calling the home line. They were bound to be out somewhere, possibly even in another country, God willing. She pressed call and waited. Swallowing her pride had a taste more bitter than those stupid kale health shakes her personal trainer made her drink. She'd miss everything else about Hollywood, but she wouldn't miss those.

Chapter Three

"WHAT'D I TELL YOU? It's either a copycat or a serial killer, isn't it, Farrell?"

Dak half smiled at Hamilton's enthusiasm, which she'd say was misplaced if she didn't feel exactly the same way. "Classic or spree?" She was leaving town and wanted to know if her training had actually made a difference to him.

"Too soon to tell…"

Dak noted the rising pitch of his voice, indicating his lack of certainty. "Are you asking me or telling me?"

He straightened up and ground his cigar butt into the pocket ashtray he carried with him. It was another one of the things Dak liked about him. He took the integrity of a crime scene as seriously as she did.

"Telling."

"Explain." She motioned to the male body displayed on the wall. *Displayed* was the right word, though it would seem incongruous to anyone outside the force. This was artistry. Misplaced artistry, for sure, but artistry, nonetheless. She looked back to Hamilton and waited for his rationale.

"This is only the second body, and while the way the body has been mutilated and arranged matches the victim from a month ago, it's not clear what the motivation might be behind the killing. On both victims, the penis has sustained multiple lacerations, but they seem carefully drawn almost, rather than manically or angrily slashed at, so the murder doesn't appear to be sexually driven. The first victim was moved from wherever he was murdered, and this one appears to be the same. That implies the murder was premeditated rather than impulsive, which would infer a spree serial killer."

Dak smiled. It was almost like listening to a voice recording of her own observations. She'd trained him well and couldn't help a short blush of pride that blossomed in her chest. She pushed it away as quickly as it tried to rise. She didn't want Hamilton, or anyone else, thinking she was a soft touch.

"You're impressed, aren't you?" He gave her shoulder a firm shove. "I can tell. All those sessions with you paid off, huh?"

"Don't get ahead of yourself." She punched his shoulder to deflect from how easy it'd been for him to read her expression. "Solving the case would impress me so I don't have to pick it up in five years when the trail's gone cold."

He snorted and scribbled something in one of the little leather notebooks he now carried since they'd started working together. Imitation *was* the sincerest form of flattery, wasn't it? She self-consciously touched her own notebook in the pocket of her jacket but didn't pull it out. This wasn't her case, so she didn't need to write anything down. The visuals would be with her whether she wanted them or not.

"Do we know the vic's profession?"

"He was a financial advisor."

Dak paced a semi-circle to get a complete picture of the front of the guy's body. "And this is his home?" When Hamilton nodded, she moved closer and used her gloved hand to pull him away from the wall slightly. "Has forensics taken photographs?"

"Yep. We were waiting for you to check it out before we pulled him down to check the rest of him—"

"For wings?"

"Yep."

"And that detail wasn't released to the press last month?" She asked the question despite already knowing the answer since she'd advised Captain Burnett not to do so.

Hamilton shook his head then motioned the four beat cops waiting by the door to come over. "Take the body down, guys."

"And be careful." Dak stepped back. It'd take them a while to complete the task. The victim's bindings were elaborate, as was the rope tree construction he was secured to. Whoever their killer was, they were extremely skilled in the art of shibari and had taken the ancient Japanese practice of knot tying to a whole new level. She gestured toward the large glass container on the floor to the side of the victim's body, almost full of the victim's bright red blood and topped off with a cork like it was an expensive bottle of wine. "Looks like a full ten pints again."

Dead *Pretty*

"We can discount a vampire as our killer." Hamilton squinted at the bottle. "Why do you think he does that?"

"Could be any number of things, but I'd bet that our killer doesn't want the mess." She pointed to a puncture wound on his chest. "Looks like he inserts a sharp knife here to cut through the aorta." Then she pointed to a second stab wound in his abdomen. "And he drains the majority of the blood through his stomach. Once his victim is fully drained, he gets to work on the incisions." She stepped away. "He takes his time. There's no sign of a hurry here at all."

"Which implies that he knew the victim's schedule well enough to know he had all the time he needed to do his thing without being interrupted."

Dak nodded. "Exactly right."

Hamilton straightened his tie and rolled his neck. He had something to say and wasn't sure how to put it, that was clear. She'd spent enough time with him to learn his body language, though he was a pretty straightforward human being, which she was always grateful for. Playing games had never been her thing. It reminded her too much of the people she hunted for a living.

That said, she wasn't about to make it easy for him, especially since she had a nasty sense of foreboding. She tapped the travel ashtray he still clutched in his hand. "How can you be so obsessed with going to the gym when you're always shoving those sticks of Satan in your mouth?"

He laughed loudly, causing everyone in the room to look their way. "Man, I love the shit you come out with sometimes." He pulled out a double cigar tube and motioned to the front door. "Take some fresh air with me?"

Dak followed him gladly. The body had been there a couple of days judging by the putrescent smell, and her tolerance for that had long abandoned her. She hadn't been this close to a relatively fresh kill for over ten years, and it wasn't something she missed. "Fresh air is a bit of a misnomer if you're just going to fill up your lungs with carcinogens."

He sucked on his cigar then grinned. "It still smells better than that guy."

She moved upwind of the misty fog escaping from his mouth in exaggerated circles to evade the memories of her dad that cigar smoke would bring forth. Hamilton seemed too young to smoke cigars, and his brand was a helluva lot cheaper than the ones her dad celebrated each birthday with. She blew out a short breath. This was exactly why she tried not to talk to her mom while she was away. Her concentration shifted into a past she couldn't change, and it took a while to slip back into gear. "I'll give you that. I could never get used to that smell. It was a motivating factor for my career change."

Hamilton pulled the cigar from his mouth. "Yeah, right. Had nothing to do with your special brain power, huh?"

He tapped her forehead lightly, and she shoved his meaty fingers away. Had anyone else done that, she might've broken their offending digits, but there was something about Hamilton that reminded her of her little brother, and that gave Hamilton a pass for way too many things he was happy to take advantage of.

"Speaking of, what's your special brain make of this?"

Here it comes. She didn't want to be right. As much as she wasn't looking forward to going home, that didn't mean she wanted to stay in this city much longer. One week back home to make sure everything was in order, and then she'd be back on the road and on another cold case in another city. The problem with staying too long in one place was exemplified in the man standing in front of her right now—personal relationships. "I work cold cases only, Hamilton, you know that. This isn't my area of expertise."

"Sure it is. Dead people, you're great with 'em." He snickered. "Not so great with the live ones, but I guess you can't have everything."

"Funny. You should be on SNL."

"And you should be on Saturday Night Dead."

Hamilton's obnoxiously loud laugh got the attention of the line of reporters gathered behind the police cordon. A photographer aimed his camera their way and the flash nearly blinded her. She turned away, conscious that plenty of journalists could read lips so they could get their exclusives. "Maybe we should go around back, away from the vultures. You don't want the city panicked by the papers scare-mongering."

Dak led the way around the side of the large house and through an open side gate. The alley opened into a yard with an Olympic-sized pool in its center. "Looks like the finance business was treating your victim well."

Hamilton cleared his throat. "Speaking of…"

She rolled her eyes at his clumsy segue into whatever was on his mind. She still held a sliver of hope that she'd be wrong about what that might

Dead *Pretty*

be.

"What if he was *our* victim?"

Dak held up her hands. "I've been at the house all afternoon packing, officer. And before that, I was helping the old neighbor with his vintage Mustang. And I couldn't tie a knot if my life depended on it."

"Now who's being funny?" He tapped the inch long ash from his cigar into his pocket ashtray and stubbed it out. "Burnett wants you on the case if this guy has wings on his back."

Hamilton slipped his cigar back into the tube and into his pocket as if all he'd needed it for was to give him courage to pass on his captain's wishes.

Dak ran her hand over the back of her head, irritated that she'd supposed right. "It doesn't matter what Burnett wants. I've got another assignment in Seattle."

Hamilton adjusted his tie again and made an apologetic face.

"You're not serious?" No one from the office had called her—probably because they knew she'd give them shit if they tried to make her stay. "Burnett went straight to Walker, didn't he? He didn't even have the courtesy to ask me outright."

"Burnett pulled in a big favor to get you to stay, that's what I know. You should be flattered. The captain hates owing anyone anything. And to be fair to him, he probably didn't ask you straight up because he knows you would've said no. And not politely either."

It usually didn't hurt that she had a reputation as a hard ass who wouldn't bow and curtsy to her superior officers but going over her head to bypass that issue wasn't appreciated. "That doesn't make it okay, Hamilton."

"I know, I know. But on the bright side, you get to knock my ass into shape some more, and I get to continue my instruction under the hand of the master."

"You're being an asshole." Though she did appreciate his attempt to appease the situation, it wasn't Hamilton she had a problem with. Why would Walker okay Burnett's request without talking to her directly? Her work was important. There were nearly a quarter million cold cases in the country, dammit. The FBI shouldn't be using her time on new kills when this police department had a perfectly capable homicide squad. Hamilton was right though, her ego was nourished by Burnett's desire to have her work this case.

13

"I'm trying not to take your stance as a personal rejection, Farrell."

Dak glanced back at Hamilton. Damn those puppy dog eyes he turned on whenever he needed to. It wasn't the first time she wished she'd had a sister instead of a brother. "You know it's not about you. Don't be one of those people who makes everything about them." Quite when she'd started caring so much about Hamilton and his *feelings* she wasn't sure, but she'd been almost as powerless to his youthful charm as she was to a lady with long hair...or short hair...or, who was she kidding? She liked every kind of woman, and their hair length didn't factor in much at all, but there was something *extra* special about the feel of long hair trailing over her naked body.

She re-focused on Hamilton. She wasn't usually prone to wandering thoughts when she was on the job, but her last hook-up had been a while. And if she was being forced to stay in this city to help catch a serial killer, she would need to blow off some steam soon. "You've got this. You don't need me."

He tugged on his tie again. "I appreciate your confidence, but it's what the people in charge want, and they usually get what they want. I'll bet the captain doesn't want the mayor breathing down his neck over these murders, and your expert profiling skills are second-to-none whether the case is cold or brand new. They'll both want this case solved before the city turns to panic. That's where you come in, whether you like it or not."

She ran her fingers over her brow to smooth away the possibility of a tension headache creeping in. Hamilton was right. The decision had been made, and she could do nothing but obey the orders. And her dad wouldn't have been impressed by her lack of a "team player" attitude. Maybe she'd get lucky, and there'd be no wings carved into this guy's back. Then again, a copycat would mean two killers on the loose, and Walker would still want Dak to stick around until the case was solved.

One of the beat cops opened the sliding door at the back of the house. "Wings," she said and pushed the door all the way open, as if to beckon them back in.

Dak's hope of getting on the road the next morning slipped away with the last of the daylight. "Wings." An unexpected rush of adrenaline raced through her veins. If she had to stay, she'd catch this son of a bitch before he made too much of a name for himself.

The hunt was on.

Chapter Four

SALT LAKE CITY, I have not *missed you.* CJ pulled over on the corner of Elm Tree and Bridge, questioning her decision to drive nearly seven hundred miles from LA to home in a car her dad would probably fawn over more than her. It'd give them something to talk about, she supposed. She couldn't really remember ever having a conversation with him that lasted longer than six sentences, but they did share a love of fast cars. The only quality time she'd ever spent with him were the occasional moments under the hood of his 1967 Shelby GT500. He probably wouldn't be impressed with her choice of an Italian sports car over an American muscle car, but he might still be able to appreciate its beauty.

She gathered her courage, and her prepared reasons for coming home, and turned the corner. The old Shelby was in the driveway with two legs sticking out from under its nose. She'd always questioned her father's choice of color in Wimbledon White—grease seemed unnaturally attracted to the bodywork—but he said it was his homage to Ken Miles, the British driver of the Shelby Ford at Le Mans in '66. It was a detail she'd rather forget, but years of that race being the highlight of her father's summer had imprinted the useless information onto her brain. It also ensured she'd never buy a white car: sport, muscle, or electric.

CJ parked alongside it. She left the top down—anticipating the need for a swift escape after thirty minutes, tops—and switched out her sneakers to three-inch heels. She stepped out, expecting her father to scramble out from under his car and investigate the intruder with the foreign car on his property. The Saturday poker nights he and his buddies spent guessing car makes from short sound clips of their engines had kept her up way past her bedtime too many times to count. And they were made all the more memorable by her confusion that he had time to spend with them and never any time for her. She curled her toes in her heels. She hadn't thought about her childhood in years, and she didn't want to start now. Her impending proximity to her parents made reflection inevitable. So be it.

Her unwanted thoughts were nicely interrupted by the person who emerged from beneath the car. She was unexpected, to say the least. Unexpected in a very, very good way. What was it about a tight white T-shirt straining across a muscular chest, its sleeves desperately trying to stay stitched over strong, bulging arms? Teamed with greased-up old jeans, a thick belt, and engineer boots, it knocked the whole appearance of this woman into another stratosphere of sexy. Oil on her nose and cheek, hair just long enough to run her hands through and flop lazily onto her forehead—it was like she'd just stepped out of a lesbian calendar shoot. CJ didn't want to dwell on the fact that the woman had just emerged from underneath her father's car. For a blissful moment, she was transported into a fantasy world where this impossibly handsome woman would look under *her* hood and take her for the ride of her life. Okay, she wasn't impossibly handsome. There was no such thing. But she *was* incredibly good looking, and CJ found herself hoping her car wouldn't start.

"Hi," CJ said, affecting a breezy tone to hide her visceral reaction to the woman in front of her. "I'm CJ, Roger's daughter."

The woman held out her hand then pulled it back quickly. "Sorry, they're all greased up. I'm Dak." She jerked a thumb toward the property next door. "I live there…for now."

The addition of Dak's words made her even more intriguing—though what kind of a name was Dak?—but it partially explained her presence in the driveway.

"Calista?"

Great. He still liked to drop her formal name. She'd hated it since it became synonymous with that ditzy TV lawyer. She turned and faced him, smile plastered in place. "Hey, Dad."

"Did you rent that at the airport?"

He walked toward her with his arms open—surely he wasn't expecting a loving embrace?—then pulled her into an awkward hug. CJ kept her arms by her side, unsure how to react. Maybe he was just playing the doting father for the benefit of his mechanic, whose presence was still a mystery since she'd never known him to pay for professional help. CJ peered over his shoulder to see Dak wiping off her hands on an old rag, seemingly looking anywhere but at the two of them. She was clearly as embarrassed about his show of affection as CJ was.

Dead *Pretty*

"What? No hug for your old man?" he asked.

He partially released her from the unwelcome contact but still held her at arm's length. CJ took a step back from his grasp and rested against her car door, choosing to ignore the question. Family laundry wasn't for the entertainment of strangers, no matter how sexy they were. "I own the car, Pops. I didn't rent it." She heard the petulance in her voice and saw Dak's reaction in a fleeting twitch of the eyebrow. CJ couldn't tell if Dak was amused or distinctly unimpressed. She'd make a good poker buddy for her father. Maybe that's how they knew each other.

He whistled then tsked. "Did you *have* to go Italian?"

She ignored that question too. It was more of a prod than a question anyway. "Is Mom home?" It seemed like the thing she should ask since there was no sign of her rushing out the door to hold her only daughter tightly and welcome her home. Like that had ever happened. Of course she hadn't made an effort to be there.

"She's playing golf. She's got a tournament coming up soon."

Her father circled CJ's Ferrari like he was stalking the damn thing, which she might've made a pithy comment about had she not been completely blindsided by this new information about her mom not only taking up a sport but competing at it. How did she have time to knock a tiny white ball around a fancy park in between all the oh-so-important corporate meetings she had to juggle?

"Do you need a hand with your bags?"

Dak's gentle question drew CJ's attention back and she sighed. Barely back home and she'd already slipped back into old insecurities. Hadn't she spent a fortune on therapy wading through all this shit? *I won't let my past shape my future.* She repeated the tired and clichéd mantra a few times while she gave Dak her best TV smile. No, not her TV smile. Her real smile, if she could find it. Dak seemed like the kind of person who'd see straight through her being disingenuous.

And she wanted Dak to carry her bags up to her old room too so she could watch her ass as she climbed three flights of stairs. "You wouldn't mind?" CJ popped the trunk and tried for another genuine smile. "I'd really appreciate it." Of course, she could slip out of her heels and back into her sneakers and carry the bags upstairs herself. Her father certainly wouldn't give her a hand.

"It'd be my pleasure." Dak held up her hands and grinned. "All clean now."

CJ bit her lip lightly at the sight of Dak's strong hands. Could she carry CJ up the stairs? She might not have been able to when CJ lived here as a teenager, but now she was Hollywood skinny, and Dak's muscles certainly made her look capable. Her grin was super cute too. CJ wouldn't mind seeing more of that over the next few weeks. The hot neighbor next door would make for a far more bearable stay than she'd anticipated, especially if she was going to spend her weekends working on the Mustang in full view of CJ's window.

She could hope.

"And I thought I raised an independent woman."

Her father's chiding comment was almost impossible not to respond to. *You didn't raise me though, did you?* was the first retort to come to mind, but she swallowed it down, not wanting to make a scene or make Dak uncomfortable.

"The strongest women know when to accept help," Dak said and winked.

Her father came around the car and patted Dak on the shoulder like she was the son he'd never had, and CJ swallowed down the threat of a repeat of the Caesar salad she'd had for lunch. Well, they'd labeled it as a Caesar salad, but it'd tasted more like Caesar's sandal.

"Then I'll let you two ladies get to know each other while I get on with dinner." He gave Dak's shoulder another squeeze and ambled back into the house.

CJ stared after him. "Get on with dinner?"

"Sorry, what?"

Crap, she'd said that out loud. She shook her head, not quite able to process what she was seeing and hearing. "Did you ever see that old show, *The Twilight Zone?*"

"Which version? There've been a few."

"Oh, yeah. Well, it doesn't matter—they were all the same kind of thing. I feel like I'm in an episode where my parents have been replaced by robots or aliens…or something, but they're not mine."

Dak moved to the trunk and pulled out her two pieces of luggage like they weighed nothing. "Ah, I see what you mean. People change. How long has it been since you were last home?"

Not long enough. She didn't say that, of course. She was doing a lot of self-censoring already, another thing she thought she'd stopped doing. She took a long, cleansing yoga breath. Things would settle down after a few days, and she'd go back to being her usual self. She'd done too much work on herself to be triggered so easily. "A while."

Dak half-smiled. "Same for me."

Common ground. That was promising. She already wanted to know more of Dak's story, beginning with her name. Short for Dakota, maybe.

"Lead the way," Dak said.

"Of course." CJ headed to the house, feeling slightly guilty that she was only carrying her handbag. "Can I take one of those?"

Dak grinned and shook her head. "One in each hand balances me out."

CJ appreciated the gallant gesture and accepted it, though she'd ended up leading instead of walking behind Dak, and that needed to be rectified. Her father had left the front door open, so CJ stepped to the side and gestured for Dak to enter. "Up the central stairs, all the way to the top."

Dak paused and the corner of her mouth quirked in a small smile as if she'd cottoned on to CJ's voyeuristic motive for having her go up the stairs first, but she said nothing other than a quiet, "As you wish."

Dak's jeans were nicely snug around her ass, making CJ very happy with the view she'd engineered.

"When you've taken your luggage up to your room, come and help me make dinner, please," her father called, presumably from the kitchen.

CJ rolled her eyes, glad that Dak couldn't see her. She seemed quite at ease with CJ's father, and CJ wondered further about the nature of their relationship. "Have you been living next door for long?" she asked when they reached the top of the staircase. She walked around Dak and pushed her old bedroom door open, assuming Dak would go in.

But she didn't. She placed CJ's suitcases on the floor and smiled again. This time, CJ noticed a small, adorable gap between Dak's front teeth.

"If you're okay with them from here?" Dak asked and gestured to CJ's luggage.

CJ raised her eyebrow. Was Dak shy or just being chivalrous? Or had CJ misread the situation and Dak was simply being polite? CJ's gaydar had zinged all the way across the rainbow when their eyes met. She glanced at Dak's hand but saw no wedding jewelry. And it wasn't like she was luring Dak into her room to seduce her. She decided to let it go. She had a couple of weeks to see where her initial attraction might lead, and even if Dak wasn't interested, she seemed like an easy person to have dinner or coffee with. She looked older than CJ but close enough to her age to be a better bet to spend time with than her parents. That said, the corpses at the local mortuary would be preferable to her parents. Maybe she'd get a temporary job, after all. A few moments with her father had spiraled her into the past, so what would she be like when her mom showed up from her *golf practice*? Yep, she'd need more of a distraction than she'd realized.

"So, you're good?"

Ah, she hadn't answered. "Sure. Thanks." CJ kicked off her heels, putting her gaze at Dak's chest. She looked away before it might've become obvious she was staring and tugged one of the cases into her room. When she returned for the second one, Dak hadn't moved.

"Over a year," she said. "You asked how long I'd been here."

CJ yanked her suitcase in then stepped into the corridor and closed the door behind her. "And you're not planning to stay much longer?" She started down the stairs and Dak followed.

"It's temporary. I move around the country for work, but something's come up here that means I've got to stay a while longer. How long are you here for?"

CJ huffed. "That depends on how hard my agent is working."

"Your agent? Are you an actor? That explains the sweet ride outside."

CJ checked that off as a potential carrot to them spending time together, but it didn't stop the sting of her father's lack of pride in her work. "Daddy dear didn't tell you what I do? You two seemed quite pally—you must be for him to let you under the hood of his true baby." There was that childish petulance again. "I'm sorry, ignore that. Sort of. He makes me crazy." And that was too much information. Self-censoring might be a good thing to stick to when she was around Dak. "Did he really not tell you what I do?" She glanced at Dak and saw her cheeks had colored slightly, clearly embarrassed for her father's disinterest in his own daughter. "I suppose it doesn't matter. Out of sight, out of mind." Her father hadn't paid that much attention to her when she was a child. It was stupid of her to assume she was part of his conversational repertoire now she lived in another state. But she didn't want to focus on that. She wanted to know more about Dak. "What do you do that involves so much travel?"

"I'm an FBI agent."

CJ stopped at the base of the stairs and looked at Dak from tip to toe.

Dead *Pretty*

"You don't *look* like an FBI agent."

"Really? And what does an FBI agent look like?"

Dak's cute and quirky smile made it clear she wasn't offended. CJ pointed to Dak's outfit. "Aren't you all supposed to be buttoned-down stiffs?"

"All my trouser suits and Oxford shirts are at the dry cleaners."

CJ flicked at a non-existent piece of fluff on Dak's T-shirt. "But are they nice suits? I thought you all had wash and wear clothes."

Dak straightened the hem of her shirt and tucked it behind the buckle of her belt. "I can't tell whether or not you approve of what I'm wearing."

CJ clenched her jaw to stop an escaping sigh and twisted a strand of her hair to stop herself from pulling Dak in by that very belt and kissing her, wild and hard. "Oh, I approve."

"Are you staying for dinner, Dak? It'll be the only proper meal you'll get until next weekend."

Great timing. CJ gazed up at Dak, certain she could see her desire mirrored in Dak's eyes. It didn't matter that they'd just met. Attraction didn't have a time constraint. CJ wanted her to stay for dinner. It was an easy way of spending more time with her. She also *didn't* want her to stay. She didn't want Dak to see the worst parts of her, which would inevitably rise once she was captive at the dining table with both parents.

But then, no wedding jewelry and no "proper meal" other than whatever her father was heating in the microwave hinted that Dak was alone on her work travels. And that opened up interesting possibilities for her brief stay at home.

Dak took a sidestep around CJ. "I wouldn't want to intrude, Roger."

The sub-text and undertone were clear. *You should want to spend time alone with your daughter.* CJ smiled at Dak's sweet naivety. However long Dak and CJ's father had known each other, it was clear that she had no idea who the real Roger Johnson was and how little he valued time with his only child.

"Ah, I see what you're saying, Dak," he said. "Thank you. I'll come around with a plate later."

"What the—" Her quiet indignation drifted away when Dak winked and touched her arm gently.

"People change," she said. "See you again."

CJ simply nodded and kept her eyes firmly on Dak's butt as she left. Maybe this enforced vacation wouldn't be so bad after all.

Chapter Five

DAK CLOSED THE FRONT door, leaned against it, and sighed deeply. Roger had been holding out on her. He'd mentioned his daughter a few times and said she was working in Hollywood but had neglected to say exactly what she did. Next time she had a chance to talk to him, she'd definitely ask. What was CJ doing that he wasn't the usual kind of "Dad proud?"

She grabbed a light beer from the fridge and sat at the kitchen table. She flipped open her laptop and googled "famous actresses from Salt Lake City." Dak questioned her immediate leap to actress, but CJ was certainly beautiful enough for the movies. A little too much make-up and a little too thin for Dak's taste usually, but that was what Hollywood demanded mostly.

Over five hundred hits came up, which surprised Dak. She scrolled down through the first fifty, *not* surprised that she didn't recognize any of them. Somehow, this place didn't seem like a hotbed for Hollywood talent. Maybe she wasn't an actress. All sorts of people had agents. She could be a screenwriter, or director, or musician. Dak went back to the original search and changed it to "CJ Calista Johnson Hollywood."

"There you are." CJ had her own Wikipedia and IMDb page. She half-closed the laptop and shook her head before she leaned back in her chair and unscrewed the bottle top. "What are you doing?" She hadn't asked CJ what she did for a career. Shouldn't she just do that instead of this light stalking? Dak pushed her chair back and wandered over to the den, beer in hand. She knew she should eat something but just one beer would be okay, and Roger always came through with meals when he promised them.

She flipped on the TV, sank into the sofa, and put her feet on the table. She left them there for less than thirty seconds before she heard her mom's voice in her head telling her to have more respect. She kicked her boots off and relaxed again before flicking through to the Disney channel and selecting a Marvel movie, needing something easy to watch. It wasn't just the sexy neighbor she didn't want to think about too much, it was the murder case she'd been thrown into unwillingly. The fugitive squad were busy rounding up witnesses and anyone close to the victim, particularly those who might be suspects, so she could relax a little for now. But come Monday, she'd be hip-deep in all of it, and this weekend was precious adjustment time.

She'd had her rant at Hamilton. Now, she just needed to get on with it so they could close the case and she could get back to her usual work. There was little point in spending time and energy bemoaning the situation. The high-ups had made their decision, and they weren't going to change it. Her mom's saying about life and lemons was one Dak repeated in her head when things like this happened. She was a professional, just like her dad was, and she'd always behave as if what she did might make him proud even though he wasn't around to see it.

Family was a third thing she didn't want occupying brain space right now, either.

As the opening credits on the movie rolled, Dak stopped trying not to think about CJ. Aside from not being impressed with herself for doing a little cyber-stalking, there was no reason she *shouldn't* think about CJ. Roger didn't seem like the type to gatekeep his daughter's private life and considering the way he'd greeted her, there was clearly some tension between them. Dak had only relatively recently begun to spend any real time with Roger—prior to his Mustang's engine trouble, their exchanges had been short—but she didn't think he'd care all that much about who his daughter dated.

Dak took a swig of beer. Dating. She hadn't done that since college, and it hadn't worked out so well then. Once she joined the FBI, her ambition took center stage, and relationships and family faded into the background. That was a thing her dad *wouldn't* have approved of.

The boxes scattered around the room reminded her she'd have to call her mom. She definitely wouldn't approve of the new development in Dak's job situation, and Dak didn't want to face that conversation just yet. She put her beer on the table beside the sofa, laid down and closed her eyes. "Alexa. Lights off." She blinked away the images her brain had captured of the victim and focused on the ebony darkness of her eyelids, willing the blackness to envelop her thoughts and pause her overactive mind.

Dead *Pretty*

***

The banging that woke her sounded more like someone pounding on her door than knocking. Dak opened her eyes and focused on the TV through hazy eyes. The screensaver cycling through available films signaled that she'd missed Captain Marvel saving the world. She ran her tongue over her teeth and reached for the beer to make her mouth taste a little less like the bottom of a birdcage. She grimaced when she felt the bottle was lukewarm. How long had she'd been asleep? She took a long pull anyway and swished it around like mouthwash.

The knocking persisted so Dak raised herself from the couch and headed to the front door. CJ waved through the glass as Dak approached. In her other hand, she held the plate of food Roger had promised to bring over. Dak ran her hand through her hair as she glanced in the hallway mirror and wished she'd bothered to take a shower and change her clothes before she flaked out on the couch.

"Special delivery," CJ said after Dak opened the door. "Dad kept it on the stove so it's still hot if you haven't eaten."

This was a question of etiquette. Roger usually dropped the food off and left without expectation of an invitation into the house. What would CJ be expecting or wanting? "Thanks, that's very kind of him." She took the proffered plate from CJ and waited for a cue. When none came, Dak lifted the foil from the plate and peeked under it. "Ah, ten bean chili. One of your dad's specialties."

CJ's raised eyebrows provided further evidence that their father-daughter relationship didn't include recipe swaps.

"He has specialties?" CJ looked distinctly unimpressed. "It did taste great, but I thought he might be a one-hit wonder."

"Nope, he's quite the chef. He said he was practicing this one for you because you'd gone vegetarian."

Another high eyebrow raise indicated CJ's confusion over Roger's behavior. Dak was beginning to sympathize. It was clear they had a complicated relationship, and she wasn't sure she wanted to be in the middle of that…but damn, CJ was cute.

"Would you like to come in and have a drink?" Dak stepped aside and opened the door fully.

"Are you sure? You don't want to eat in peace?" CJ was already in and closing the door behind her as she spoke.

Dak smiled at her boldness. "I rarely eat alone."

"Always out with the ladies, are you? Or is it the guys?"

Dak laughed hard at the implication she might be into men. She hadn't been mistaken as straight since she'd chopped all her hair off for a bet in college and never grown it back. Though it was about so much more than hair length, Dak felt certain the rest of her presentation made her sexuality pretty obvious to anyone interested. Which, it occurred to her, was why CJ had asked the question. Dak hadn't been sure whether CJ was just being charming or whether there was a spark. Now she knew.

"Always out with work colleagues. It's not often I get to sit and actually enjoy a meal. Most of the time, I'm just eating to keep moving." Dak walked down the hall to the kitchen and placed the plate next to her laptop on the table. "What can I get you to drink?"

"Do you have green tea?"

Dak shook her head and opened the refrigerator door. She turned back to CJ and motioned to the shelves. "I have organic beer. Will that do?"

CJ seemed to hesitate. She nibbled on her upper lip and looked up to the ceiling, like that might help her answer the question.

"Or don't you drink?" Dak hoped she hadn't put CJ in an awkward position. Had she come home after a spell in rehab? Dak pushed the thought out of her mind. It'd been so long since she'd had this kind of conversation with a woman, she was reverting to thinking the worst and treating CJ like work.

"Oh, I drink," CJ said. "I just don't know if I should when I'm not training twice a day."

Dak allowed her gaze to travel the length of CJ's body. "Is that how you maintain your physique?"

"It's one of the *many* ways." CJ pulled at her blouse. "I'm not naturally this skinny, I'm afraid. I have to work hard to be camera-ready."

Dak pulled out a beer and held it to her forehead. She should cool down. They'd gone from just meeting to heavy flirting alone in her house in the blink of an eye. Okay, so Dak didn't have time for relationships, but she wasn't used to meeting women outside of bars, and Roger might come knocking on the door to see where his daughter was, any minute. This was the point where she should ask questions about CJ's life so she wasn't tempted to investigate her online. She glanced at her laptop, still partly open on the table. It would've gone to sleep at least an hour ago. CJ wouldn't accidentally discover what Dak had been up to.

"You're an actress then? You didn't answer when I asked earlier." Dak unscrewed the bottle cap and offered the beer to CJ.

She took it and smiled. "You're an FBI agent—aren't you supposed to be a good influence?"

Dak got another beer and a fork from the drawer before sitting at the table. "I figure you're old enough to make your own decisions."

CJ laughed. "You sound like my dad. You can't be that much older than me."

"How old do you think I am?" She'd circle back to the actress question again, which both daughter and father seemed reluctant to share the answer to.

"I'd never ask a lady her age."

Dak chuckled. "You're not asking. You're supposed to be telling, and do I *look* like a lady?"

CJ held up her hands. "It's not my place to define who is or is not a lady. Presentation and internal representation are very personal things that shouldn't be social constructs."

"But you can judge what an FBI agent looks like?" Dak waved her fork toward CJ. "That's an okay social construct?"

"That's different."

"How so?"

CJ pulled out a chair and sat opposite Dak. "An FBI agent is a profession. Being a lady—or not—is an internal thing."

"I think you're grasping. So how old am I?"

CJ shook her head. "Why don't you just tell me?"

"Why don't you just tell me if you're an actor or not?"

"I'm not an actor."

"Then why do you need to be camera ready? Are you a journalist?"

"Do you always ask so many questions?"

"Is three questions a lot?"

"When they're fired off like I'm being interrogated, yes, three questions is a lot." CJ took a small drink and placed the bottle on a coaster. "I'm in a reality TV show."

"Interesting. What's it about?" Dak clinked her bottle neck to CJ's "And I'm thirty-eight."

CJ's eyes widened. "Really?"

"You sound surprised. Were you thinking higher or lower?"

"Lower, by five years minimum."

"It's the moisturizers I use."

CJ gave a short laugh. "I thought you said you weren't a lady?"

"Face care products aren't just for ladies, they're for everyone. What's your show about?"

"Has anyone ever told you you're relentless?" CJ frowned.

Dak nodded. "That's why I work the cold cases. What's your show called?"

"It's called *Dead Pretty*—I make dead people look better than they did when they were alive. I'm a creative with cadavers."

"Huh. Nice tag line. Is that on your business cards?"

"No, but it should be, thanks for the suggestion. Who *are* you? Because you didn't seem like this when we met a few hours ago."

"Like what?"

CJ gestured in circles toward Dak's face, but it didn't help her explanation. "All smooth and sharp, like you've got an answer for everything."

Dak took a breath, realizing what CJ meant. It was a big change from her usual persona. Truth was, she didn't know what had come over her. She hadn't had this much fun talking to someone in ages. Other than her family, she hadn't really talked to anyone outside law enforcement in ages either. Maybe that was it. "Sorry. I'll shut up and you can lead the conversation."

"No, don't stop. I like it...I like you."

Dak's confidence fell away instantly. She peeled the foil from her plate and had a forkful of Roger's chili. "Did you like the meal your dad prepared for you?" There was that raised eyebrow again. CJ seemed able to express a whole gamut of emotions with the most minuscule part of her body.

"So, thirty-eight, going on seventeen?" She smirked and took another drink of her beer without taking her eyes from Dak's.

"Fine." Dak placed her fork on the table, taking a moment to revel in CJ's undeniably attractive sass. "I like you too. Now what?"

"You're asking me? You're the older woman. Aren't you supposed to have all the answers?"

Dead *Pretty*

"Wait—how young *are* you?"

"Not young enough for this to be an age-gap romance," CJ said, motioning her finger between the two of them.

Dak rubbed at the back of her head. "I have no idea what that means. Are you saying you like me, but I'm too old for you?"

CJ laughed. "No. I'm saying I like you, and I want to do something about it, but you were talking about chili and my father, so you're kind of ruining my mood."

Dak blew out a breath. She had no idea what she was doing, but why the hell not? "How about we go out on a date?" She hadn't been on one of those for years either. What kind of spell had this beautiful woman cast on her in the space of a few hours?

CJ tilted her head slightly and grinned. "You're one of *those* kind of butches? That's sweet."

"First of all, what's 'one of those kind'? And secondly, who are you calling butch? I was dancing around the house in my heels before you interrupted me. That's why it took so long to get to the door."

"Really?" CJ reached over the table and ran her hand through Dak's hair. "Looks to me like you were sleeping. That's bed head, right there. And you can still wear heels and be butch, you know? Things are a lot more fluid than they used to be in your day."

My day? How young was CJ? "Huh, *this* butch can't."

"You admit it?"

"I'm not ashamed. Butch and proud, baby."

"I bet you were rocking those heels though. Were you watching *Drag Race*?"

"The only drag races I watch involve cars." Which wasn't true. She'd watched and thoroughly enjoyed her fair share of drag queen shows. Who didn't appreciate the pageantry of such a noble artform?

"Liar."

"I'm not sure I can date someone who is so clearly ageist. Are you even old enough to drink that beer? I'm a Federal Agent. Plying a minor with alcohol would destroy my career."

"Relax, Agent Dak, I'm thirty-one. My moisturizers are good too."

With CJ living out of state and obviously not close to her parents, Dak couldn't imagine that Roger would have a problem with the two of them spending some time together. She wasn't about to bring him up now since

CJ had already cautioned her for doing so, and Dak didn't want to ruin the conversation they were having. She hadn't had this much fun talking to someone…possibly ever. Dak was stuck here for another few weeks. What little downtime she'd get during the murder investigation would otherwise be wasted eating take-out and watching Marvel movies. What harm could possibly come from spending that time with the sexy girl next door?

Chapter Six

"DOUBLE SHOT, SKINNY AMERICANO, please. No, sorry. Make that a double shot latte." She'd work it off later. CJ couldn't have been more grateful for the presence of an artisanal coffee house in her neighborhood. She'd only been home for two days, and the 2.0 version of her parents was already driving her insane. They'd shown more interest in her in the past forty-eight hours than in her whole childhood, and they'd even shown some empathy for the situation with her show. And that was okay, she continued to tell herself. Costly therapy should equal a Zen-like acceptance of the new situation.

Except it didn't. At every turn, they were acting the exact opposite of the mom and dad she knew and sort of loved. Not the TV family brand of love, but enough love to keep her from disowning them completely. And she had to get out of the house. This comfy little coffee place was going to be seeing a lot of her in the coming weeks if she didn't get a job. Agent Dak would be good as a distraction too, but her time was limited given the case she was working on.

"Callie Johnson?"

CJ turned to the source of the voice she didn't recognize but immediately put a name to the woman standing in front of her—her best friend and first girl-crush from high school through college. ""Emily? Oh wow, it's so good to see you."

Emily pulled CJ into a bear hug. "I saw you from across the street and thought I was seeing things. How long has it been? What are you doing here? Are your mom and dad okay?"

CJ eased out of the embrace. Reigniting past flames wasn't on her agenda for this enforced trip. "Hold those thoughts. Do you want coffee?"

"Does a bear poop in the woods? Of course I want coffee."

CJ smiled, remembering her friend's discomfort with curse words. She made a mental note to watch her language. Emily placed her order with the barista and after a short back and forth about who was picking up the

Robyn Nyx

tab, CJ paid for their drinks. They chose a booth at the front window and slipped onto the scarred leather benches opposite each other.

"It's only been three years, Em," CJ said.

Emily took CJ's hands and squeezed them gently. "Three years too long. I watched every episode of your show. It's fabulous. You're so talented."

CJ soaked up the compliments. After news of the show being canceled and Paige effectively sending her out of Hollywood, it was nice to get some praise. Especially when it was coming from Emily Woods. CJ glanced at Emily's hand—no sign of a wedding ring. Was she still Emily Woods? That couldn't be true of the most popular girl at college.

"Nothing's happened to your parents, has it? You're not here because of anything bad?"

CJ shook her head and smiled. "They're fine. Better than fine, actually. I think they've had a complete personality transplant. I don't really recognize who they are."

One of the baristas brought their coffees to the table, and Emily released CJ's hands. CJ wanted the contact renewed, but Emily wrapped her hands around her mug and gave a sigh of appreciation after taking a deep inhalation of the coffee scent. That was about right. Emily had always loved coffee more than most other things.

"What's with your parents then? You were never that close, were you? Are you staying with them, or do you have a hotel nearby?"

CJ laughed. "Still the same old Emily with a million questions."

Emily covered her mouth dramatically. "I'm sorry. It's just that it's so good to see you and I've missed you."

CJ had missed that pout, the one that got Emily everything and anything she wanted. CJ always felt like such a duff around her in college. But CJ was a successful woman now with a TV career—a stalled TV career—and Emily was still in her hometown. "I miss you too." She said the words but didn't feel the sentiment. Getting out of Salt Lake had been long overdue, and she and Emily had already been drifting apart before CJ left. It was good to see her though, and it would be nice to catch up. "My parents are being weird but in a good way. Sort of. It's complicated."

"Weird how?" Emily asked then placed her hand over her mouth again as if to stop any further questions from escaping.

"Well, they're around a lot more for starters. And I know that makes sense because it turns out they've semi-retired—something they hadn't told me—but Mom's playing golf and Dad's taking cooking lessons." CJ paused and ran her finger along the rim of her coffee cup. What would her therapist say about this change in situation? That she should embrace it and live in the moment not in the past, no doubt. That was pretty much her takeaway from years on the couch: *live in the moment.* And that had been working for her very well in Hollywood. But coming home was severely testing that philosophy.

"Has one of them had a health scare, do you know?"

CJ shook her head. "I really don't know. I haven't been keeping in touch."

One of the baristas approached and placed a plate of gooey-looking mini brownies on their table.

"We didn't order those," CJ said.

Emily drew the plate toward her and wiggled her eyebrows. "But we'll eat them, won't we?"

The barista nodded toward the door. "They're from that woman who's just leaving."

CJ looked over just as the woman turned and waved. Agent Dak. CJ didn't know why she couldn't just call her Dak. Agent Dak sounded more playful, and she *so* wanted to be playful. CJ returned the wave. Dak held up a tray of two coffees and a paper bag and gestured outside. She was obviously working and had just zipped in for a caffeine hit. "Thanks." CJ picked up a brownie and gave Dak a thumbs up. A thumbs up? How embarrassing and totally uncool. She put the sticky treat back on the plate. Her trainer wouldn't be impressed if she went back to LA with an extra five pounds of cake weight. Dak left and went around the corner, out of sight.

"Who's *that*?"

Emily gave CJ the "spill everything" look before she took a brownie bite. It was just like being back at college, except then, it had usually been the other way around. "She's an FBI agent living next to mom and dad."

"FBI? Is she on a case or did she just randomly move in? I suppose they have to live somewhere."

CJ laughed. "That's a strange thing to say."

Emily gently touched CJ's hand. "You know what I mean. You don't generally think about where FBI agents live, do you? Aren't they all in

DC?"

"I guess I'd never had reason to think about it, but don't they have offices all over the country?" CJ shrugged. "She did say she had to travel a lot though."

Emily tapped CJ's hand again. "She's kind of handsome. Do you have anything going on with her? I've seen all those photos of your wild nights out with plenty of women who look like that."

CJ frowned. Damn those paps and the internet. "You shouldn't believe everything you see on celebrity sites. They do a lot of Photoshop crap to tell the story they want to tell."

Emily raised her eyebrows. "I was talking about your Instagram."

"Ahh." CJ popped a brownie into her mouth. One wouldn't hurt if she did some training later, and it stopped her from incriminating herself any further.

"Hey, no judgment here, honey. I'd be doing just the same if I were a famous TV star."

CJ didn't respond while she enjoyed the little burst of heaven tantalizing her taste buds. God, it'd been so long since anything that naughty had passed her lips. "We're supposed to be going on a date."

"Supposed to be?"

"She's working a new case, so her schedule is messed up. It may not happen." CJ sighed, realizing how bad she wanted it to happen. Emily wasn't wrong about the kind of women CJ liked, and Dak fitted her requirements pretty much to the letter. But other women did it for her too. Women like Emily, for instance. "What about you? Is there a Mr., Mrs., or Mx. Woods?"

"Why? Are you interested in applying for the position?"

Heat shot up CJ's neck and flushed her cheeks. "What? What do you mean?"

Emily pressed her lips together and shook her head slowly. "Don't play coy, Ms. Johnson. I know you had a thing for me in college."

CJ focused on the coffee in front of her and the fancy little tree the barista had fashioned in the milky top. "You never said anything."

"There was nothing *to* say. You were my best friend, and I didn't want to ruin that. Anything we did would just have been an experiment or experience for me, but you were looking for something real. I couldn't give that to you."

"That went real deep real fast." CJ looked up and laughed, though the sudden seriousness of their conversation shocked her a little.

"I'm sorry we've drifted apart, Callie. Is that the reason?"

CJ started to shake her head but stopped herself. Her unrequited crush *was* the reason she'd distanced herself from Emily after college. And now that she thought about it, that sucked. "Will you hate me if I said yes?"

"I could never hate you. You were my best friend, and I missed you, but I understood."

They both sipped on their coffee and sat in silence for a few moments.

"I've done a lot of growing up in the past few years *and* a lot of work on myself. Maybe we could try being friends again, and I won't be such an absent flake."

Emily put down her cup and took CJ's hand. "That'd be great. I've had some poop in my life recently, and I could do with my best friend to talk it all through."

Heaviness settled in the pit of CJ's stomach and a blanket of melancholy wrapped around her. Emily had been the only one CJ had ever been able to talk to, and she'd lost that when she'd pushed Emily away. The past three years of her life had been filled with people professing to be friends, but she never felt lonelier than the nights when there were multiple women in her bed. "So, is there a Mr. Woods?" she asked, needing to lighten the mood.

"Not at the moment. Like I said, there's been some unpleasant stuff happening in my life recently, most of it centered around my cheating fiancé."

CJ closed her mouth before she gaped like a fish. "*He* cheated on *you?*" That didn't sound right at all.

"See?" Emily gestured to CJ. "This is why I need you around. *This* is why I've missed you. Only you can carry off the right amount of indignation at Jason's infidelity. I come off sounding too arrogant."

"Jason? High school quarterback Jason?"

"Of course. Although I wasn't so much of a cliché that we've been high school sweethearts all these years, but you know that. We got together just after you left… Does it make my heartbreak your fault if I fell into Jason's arms because I was bereft when you left?"

"I only think it would be my fault if we'd been sleeping together and Jason was your rebound man. But since we've just established that women aren't your thing, no, I don't think you can blame me at all."

Emily pushed out her bottom lip and pouted. "Are you sure? I was really lonely after you left."

CJ shook her head. "Definitely not. But I can't believe that you gave that idiot a chance. He never could keep it in his pants."

"I thought I'd be enough for him. I suppose that was naïve or stupid, whichever you prefer. Anyway, we were engaged to be married and now he's left me for someone from his factory."

"Factory? His football dreams didn't come true then?"

"Pfft. He couldn't make anyone's dreams come true." She wiggled her pinky finger.

"Is that bitterness talking or was he that bad in bed?"

Emily rolled her eyes. "Bitterness, of course. Whose side are you on?"

"Yours, of course, but I don't want you going all Miranda Lambert crazy and—"

"Miranda who?"

"Really? You don't remember Miranda Lambert? It was all I used to play on our road trips."

"Oh, her. You know I'm not a big country music fan. I had to put up with your choice of music because it was your car."

"Anyway, my point is that you don't let one stupid guy ruin you for the next great guy who's bound to come along any minute."

"Boundless optimism. Another reason I need you around." Emily picked up another brownie then shoved the plate toward CJ. "You need to eat some of these. Don't make me eat alone." She raised her eyebrow. "And you could do to put a little weight on. I can almost see your whole collarbone."

CJ raised her hand to her chest instinctively to cover up.

"You've gotten skinnier with each season. Do they make you lose weight? Is it part of your contract to be thinner than a meth addict?"

"Ouch. And again with the multiple questions!"

"Sorry." Emily chewed on the sweet treat and pushed the plate closer to CJ.

"Fine." She ate another one. "But I'd already had one."

"Pah, these are so small, you could snort them. One barely counts."

"My personal trainer would disagree. There's probably two hundred calories and fifteen grams of fat in each of those."

"So, do they insist on you being a certain weight?"

"It's not in my contract, but when you're surrounded by skinny people, it's impossible not to strive to be one of them. And the camera really does add ten pounds." It sounded weak, and she knew it. She'd fallen victim to the ideal that Hollywood peddled—well, not so much fallen as was pushed toward to it by countless snide comments and *helpful* suggestions on how to lose weight and a wardrobe for the show that was two sizes too small. "It might not matter anymore since the show's been canceled. That's why I'm home. My agent forced me to get away while she supposedly works her magic and gets the show commissioned by another network." In a somewhat masochistic way, it felt good to finally say it out loud.

Emily placed her hand on CJ's forearm. "That's terrible. Why would they cancel you? It's a popular show, isn't it? Have your ratings fallen?"

CJ widened her eyes and pressed her lips together.

"Sorry. I'm doing it again." Emily did a little dance in her chair. "I really am so excited to see you again though. You're home."

"Not for too long, I hope. But I need a temporary job to keep me out of the house during the day, just until my agent finds me something new. I'll get used to my improved parents but exposure has to be in slow bursts." CJ pulled the local paper from her shoulder bag and opened it to the page she'd folded over. "The Bryan's Funeral Home is advertising for a mortician."

Emily's expression changed immediately, and she looked sad. "His wife died six months ago. Old man Bryan's been advertising that job for a couple of months now. Nobody wants to work with him because he's so grumpy."

CJ smoothed out the page and shook her head. "He's harmless. I did my apprenticeship with them. I'm sorry Iris died." She took a sip of coffee to give herself a moment. She should've come home for Iris's funeral, but her filming schedule hadn't allowed it. Bernie—Old Man Bryan—said he understood, but she'd heard the disappointment in his voice. "They were so good together. It was sweet to see them still so in love despite—" She stopped herself from completing the sentence. Love and romance didn't just belong to young people. "It's little wonder he's grumpy. She was his life. He was devastated, and I don't suppose that goes away in six months. I can't imagine how hard it must be to be around all that death when you're grieving yourself."

"Then maybe you'll be able to cheer him up some."

CJ checked her watch. "I've got a meeting with him in ten minutes. I better go." She gathered her things and stood. Emily joined her and pulled her into a long hug.

"It's so great to see you. Make some time for me while you're here?"

"Of course." And she meant it. They'd slipped so effortlessly into best friend mode that CJ wondered how she'd coped without Emily over the past few years.

Emily broke away and held CJ at arm's length. "Promise?"

"Promise."

"Bryan's is all the way across town. You're not walking, are you?"

CJ pulled the car keys from her pocket and dangled them in front of Emily's face. "Nope."

Emily's eyes lit up. "Do you have that keyring because you *want* a Ferrari, or do you have that keyring because you've *got* a Ferrari?"

CJ winked. "Text me your address, and I'll pick you up another day with the answer to that question." She turned and headed toward her car parked in the rear lot of the coffee house with a light spring in her step. Getting up three hours later than her usual morning schedule, a relaxed chat with an old friend, and a plate of brownies from a possible romantic interest: she'd been expecting none of those things but had enjoyed each of them in very different ways. Coming home might not have been her idea, but it was turning out to be far more bearable than she'd thought it was going to be.

Chapter Seven

"WHO WERE YOU WAVING to?" Hamilton asked as he tore open the paper bag and pulled out a sticky, sugary donut.

"Why do you want to know?" Dak asked and took a sip of her coffee. It was a little cooler than burn your lips off hot, but not far from it. She wouldn't be able to taste anything for a few hours, that was guaranteed. And her tongue tingled but not in a good way… not the way it might tingle if—nope, she wasn't going down that road while she was on duty. Her laser focus and concentration were two of her most powerful tools, and she'd need them if she was going to get this case solved before the city started panicking. She hadn't appreciated Burnett's monologue to the team this morning. It was supposed to be motivational, but it came off as accusatory and anxious. The chief of police had obviously taken a bite out of his ass about this possible serial killer.

"Because she looks familiar. And because I'm a good police officer, and good police officers ask questions." He bit into the donut and the jam squirted out all over his tie. "Aw, crap." He lifted his tie and licked it.

"Oh, man, that's so gross. How can you be so meticulous at a crime scene but eat the way you do?"

"Practice." He grinned and revealed gooey red teeth. "Sorry, Farrell," he said and looked contrite enough. "I enjoy my food, what more can I say?"

Dak put the car in drive and pulled away. "So, the cameras in the area yielded nothing?"

"Not yet. The ones in the vic's house had been disabled and wiped. Marks and Williams are looking at the footage from some of the other houses on the street, but that's going to take a while. Davis and Earl are interviewing all the neighbors but so far, they've come up with nothing. Seems like everyone minds their own business and keep to themselves."

Dak briefly thought about her hometown and how her mom had complained it had changed so much from when her father was around.

"Another neighborhood that's forgotten how to be neighborly."

"I'm not sure anyone remembers how to be neighborly anymore. Everyone's too frightened to get involved in anyone else's business in case it comes back on them. Just goes to show that money can't buy you meaningful connections."

Dak gave Hamilton's shoulder a not so gentle shove. "That's deep coming from you."

Hamilton snorted. "I can be deep." He shoved the rest of the donut into his mouth and more jam spewed out.

"Deep-throated, sure." She concentrated on the road and switched focus. "And we're heading to the sister?"

Hamilton grunted, his mouth still full.

"Don't answer that. I don't want donut spit all over the windshield." She followed the GPS, and they'd gone a few blocks before Hamilton washed the last of his breakfast down with a swallow of coffee.

"The twin sister, yeah. She's the only surviving relative that we can track down. Everyone else in the vic's family is dead."

Dak knew why Hamilton, and lots of cops, preferred to refer to the homicide victims on the cases he worked as just that, but it didn't work for her. Using their name personalized them in a way that motivated her without her getting involved or emotionally attached. "What's his name?"

The low sigh coming from the passenger seat reinforced her supposition.

Hamilton reached into his pocket, pulled out his leather notebook, and flipped through until he reached the correct page. "Arnold, Wallace Arnold. No tattoos or scars. Thirty-eight years old." He closed the book and tapped it on the dash. "His clothes were neatly folded and placed on a chair nearby. A very nice Giorgio Armani suit, made-to-measure in Sydney on a recent business trip. Davis interviewed his boss, who said that Arnold had synchronized the trip to coincide with Armani sending their tailor to Australia. Apparently, they only do that once a year." He shrugged. "I'm pretty sure that's not pertinent to the case at all. It just made me jealous. I'm thinking of asking his sister if she'll let me have it."

Dak shot a look toward Hamilton then saw the grin on his face. "You can be such as asshole."

"To be fair, he was more your size. You'd probably look better in it than he did."

"And you're a terrible ass-kisser."

Dead *Pretty*

"Don't be so sure. Ask my girlfriend." He straightened his tie and fussed with his hair in the pull-down mirror.

"Your girlfriend? There's a woman out there willing to be *your* girlfriend?"

"Huh, you joke, but I think you can see the attraction even though I've got the wrong junk to appeal to you."

She laughed. It wasn't the kind of thing she spent any time thinking about. She barely had time to think about the people who *did* appeal to her. "Also—gross. What makes you think I want to ask your imaginary girlfriend about your lack of sexual expertise?"

Hamilton grumbled and muttered something that Dak didn't catch. She'd been working cold cases for five years, and in all that time, she hadn't met anyone she riffed with quite as easily as she did with Hamilton. His similarity to her brother notwithstanding, his personality had made it damn near impossible *not* to like him quite as much as she did despite her desire to stay detached.

They drove the rest of the way in relative silence which Dak felt no need to fill. The peace gave her time to think about the case and reignite her familiarity with working something current. There was so much more pressure to solve live cases, let alone with the chief's interest increasing in line with his panic over PR and public safety with each murder. And every police captain was obsessed with their department's clearance rate, desperate to be higher than the national average. With the violent crime rate across America catching the new president's attention, the spotlight on PDs was more focused than usual. This wasn't gun crime, which seemed to be the president's main focus, but Dak saw this kind of murder as just as concerning even though the number of victims would likely be less than a single mass shooting. Gun crime, for the most part, was driven by rage or greed. Their killer was a far more dangerous beast. Calculating, diligent, and brutal. And their killer was making a statement, creating an exhibition they wanted the world to see. Their killer was icy-calm and controlled.

She pictured Wallace Arnold secured by the killer's carefully crafted shibari rope tree. In the killer's head, might it be an act of love? Did they see what they were doing as preserving their victim's perfection at its peak? Both the surgeon, their first victim, and Arnold had been in excellent physical health with exceptionally low body fat and impressive muscular definition. They were fit in a way they must have worked hard to achieve and maintain. Strong too, which would have made them hard to overwhelm…unless they knew their killer and were strung up willingly. She hadn't seen the tox report on the surgeon, and the one on Arnold would take at least a month. Both victims could have been drugged.

"Earth to Farrell, come in, Farrell." Hamilton accompanied his words with a shoulder punch. "You just missed the left to the sister."

Dak tuned back in and swung the car around. "Aren't you supposed to tell me before the turn comes up?"

"I could just drive, you know. Then you could go off in your head and solve the case for us without having to worry about silly little things like driving."

Dak tsked and put her right blinker on as she slowed for the missed turn. "I feel like your reverence for me has vastly reduced since I was assigned to this case."

"No way. But you're one of us now, at least until the end of the case. I'm just enjoying that."

Dak shook her head at Hamilton's honesty. She'd never met a cop so open about showing his respect before. Most cops she'd met treated her with something akin to suspicion and were happy to keep her at a distance. Hamilton had made no attempt to hide his admiration of her work and had followed her around, writing notes in his books, from the very start of her assignment there. Maybe it was that unabashed almost-adoration that appealed to her ego and had thus broken through her usual barriers rather than any resemblance to her brother. He'd also never seemed bothered or threatened by her presentation. A lot of cops steered clear and let her get on with her work. Whether her being a few inches under six feet and nearly a hundred-and-sixty pounds had anything to do with it, she didn't know. Most of the time, she didn't care. She knew when she took this promotion that it was going to be lonely and that was okay. She hadn't taken the job to enhance her social life, she'd taken it to get away from family expectation and responsibility, to try to forget. Up until Salt Lake, it had proven to be as solitary as she'd expected.

But now she'd met Hamilton *and* CJ. Granted, she'd only just met CJ, but there was no denying the instant attraction.

Dak pulled up to the sister's house and killed the engine. "What does the sister do? And what's her name?" She was out of the car before Hamilton had time to pull out his notebook. She closed the door and leaned over the roof of the car. Hamilton did the same.

"Mrs. Nina Jones. She's a stay-at-home mom. Davis said she was hysterical, demanding to see the body, but you saw what he looked like. There was no way she could identify him, and she shouldn't have to see him like that. But she insisted."

Hamilton flipped his notebook and came around the car as Dak headed up the driveway to the front door. "Take the lead, Hamilton."

He looked slightly puzzled but didn't question her instruction. Dak's lack of contact with relatives who had just started the grieving process made her slightly cautious as to how she might handle it. She expected Hamilton would simply assume it was more training, and she wasn't about to disabuse him of that logic. It was partially true.

A short woman with strikingly similar features to Arnold opened it before Dak pressed the bell.

"Mrs. Jones?" Hamilton asked gently.

Despite not having visited a newly grieving family member for quite a few years, Dak recognized the effects instantly. Puffy, red eyes, tissue clutched tightly in her hand, trembling lips, and an overall appearance of barely being able to stand upright, the weight of the grief heavy on her shoulders.

She nodded, stepped aside, and waved them in. "Please," she said, her voice breaking.

Dak motioned for Hamilton to go in before her, and she followed him after a quick visual sweep of the surrounding neighborhood. Nothing seemed out of the ordinary or out of place. Mrs. Jones ushered them into a front living room and sat on a sofa opposite the one she pointed to for them to sit down. She pulled another tissue from the ornate wooden tissue box on the table and dabbed at her nose. A pure white cat joined her but settled on the adjacent cushion. Just like a cat to be emotionally distant even when their owner was grieving. It was another good reason to prefer a loyal dog over the feline version of mean girls.

"We're sorry for your loss, Mrs. Jones," Hamilton said.

The gentleness of his voice impressed Dak. She hadn't seen him in this kind of situation before but was reminded again of why he'd been tapped to join homicide from vice. His investigative skills were already top notch, and his people skills clearly matched them. It'd been a pleasure to mentor and train him, and she might even miss him when she finally moved on to her next assignment. Even though he'd joked about the dead man's suit, his respect and empathy were the highest standard of professionalism. He was the perfect cop, if there was such a thing.

Mrs. Jones took a deep breath, as if gathering enough strength to use her words. "Do you know who did this?"

Hamilton shook his head. "Not yet, but we will, we promise you that."

Promises. Dak stretched out her legs. It was always so tempting to make promises like that, but it was a rookie mistake and also gave hope where there might be none. Dak had seen so many unsolved cases where the vein of hope that family and friends tapped into had simply been tapped out. "We're doing everything we can, Mrs. Jones," Dak said. "We were hoping you might be able to tell us about any friends or lovers that Wallace had, particularly recent relationships."

Mrs. Jones straightened her back and appeared to stiffen. The cat stretched and looked as disinterested as before. "I hadn't heard from him for a couple of days, which was unusual. He'd been over for dinner on Sunday like always. He came every week. He seemed fine."

Dak glanced at Hamilton and saw he was diligently scribbling notes so she left her own pad in her pocket. She'd remember everything that was said anyway. She only took notes in an effort to stop her brain storing every little thing it heard. It had yet to work.

"Did you call or text each other during the week?" Hamilton asked.

"Mostly texts, just checking in. He liked to keep tabs on the kids." She glanced at an array of frames on the fireplace and took another deep breath. "He wanted his own but his career came first, and he never really stayed with anyone long enough to make a family."

Now they were getting somewhere. Short-term relationships were often envisaged as short-term from one side only. But a spurned lover wouldn't explain the near-identical murder of the surgeon unless the killer was for hire and wasn't a traditional serial killer per se as much as an assassin with a particular modus operandi. But there was so much care taken to prepare the body. This was a killer with something to say, and he wanted an audience. Of course, she had no way of being certain the perpetrator was male, but over ninety percent of them were, and the dexterity with which the bodies were arranged indicated a strength beyond the average woman. Serial killers didn't tend to be average people, however, so Dak certainly hadn't disregarded the possibility of a female murderer.

"Did you meet any of the people he was involved with?"

Dak liked the non-gendered phrasing of Hamilton's question. No assumptions, no judgment, just plain questions that should help their investigation.

"Not really. He didn't want the kids to get attached to them before he'd decided he was serious. But that day never came." She gestured to her cellphone on the table. "I have to admit to watching his Instagram feed to see who he was spending his time with."

"Would you mind showing us his account?" Dak asked softly.

Mrs. Jones nibbled her lower lip and remained otherwise motionless and silent for a few moments. Neither Dak nor Hamilton pressed her. Finally, she picked up her phone and unlocked it before she passed it to Dak.

"I can't..." Mrs. Jones closed her eyes briefly and leaned back into her couch.

Dak understood the woman's reservations. She couldn't bear to see photos of her brother in one piece and enjoying himself just yet. No doubt she was still reeling from seeing Arnold at the morgue. Dak opened the app and searched for his name but nothing came up. "Sorry, Mrs. Jones, do you recall what his username was?"

Her jaw clenched, probably against Dak's use of the past tense. It always took a while for those left behind to change from "is" to "was."

"Aces underscore high with a capital H."

Dak glanced at Hamilton and quirked her eyebrow. A gambling habit might lead to a whole other pool of suspects, a hard-to-track-down pool given the hardcore illegality of gambling across the whole state, but that made any potential associates law-breakers. And law-breakers often moved in vicious circles. Hamilton nodded almost imperceptibly and made a note. She'd bet he was already thinking of crosschecking the surgeon's after-hours activities. Whether it was in an underground casino or online sites, it could be a meaningful connection between the two victims.

She tapped in Arnold's username and began to scroll through his posted photos. They'd need to check his account more thoroughly and look at his followers too, something they could do from his phone *if* it was found at his house. "Do we have Mr. Arnold's cell, Hamilton?"

He nodded. "Yeah, Earl is working his way through it after the techies got through the security on it."

Dak handed the phone back to Mrs. Jones and offered a small smile, hoping it looked like an apology for their presence and gentle interrogation. "Do you know if your brother liked to gamble?"

Mrs. Jones laughed softly. "He was a financial adviser. That was his job."

Dak widened her smile and nodded. "Of course. And did he use his skills for pleasure?"

"Are you asking me if he broke state law?" She reached out for the cat and gave it a slow stroke from its head to its tail. It inched away from her and fended her off with a casual paw flick.

Typically defensive behavior for both cat and human. Dak needed to back off and calm Mrs. Jones down. She held up her hands. "No, of course not. Not at all. We're just trying to find out what circles he moved in so we can identify potential suspects, Mrs. Jones."

"We need to find this guy before he strikes again," Hamilton said.

Fuck. His usual competence made Dak forget he was still a homicide rookie. They didn't need the city panicking about a potential serial killer. It gave the killer too much power, too much motive to kill again. Which was a double-edged sword, of course, because if he rushed into another murder for the publicity, he was likely to make mistakes and they might catch him sooner.

Mrs. Jones jumped to the edge of her seat. "This bastard has killed before? Who? Did Wallace know the other person? Do you know who the murderer is? Did Wallace know him?"

Her voice increased in pitch with each question until it was so high, the cat leaped from the sofa and sauntered away, looking thoroughly unimpressed with its owner's show of emotion. Dak briefly thought of her dad's dog, Sam. *That* was an animal in tune with his master. He'd stayed by her dad's side through everything, right to the end. Dak swallowed hard and controlled her reaction to the memory before she responded. "We don't know any of that yet, Mrs. Jones. We're just trying to get a picture of Wallace's life."

Mrs. Jones eased back onto the couch and placed her hands in her lap. She slid one of her manicured nails beneath another one on her other hand and flicked at something. Dak didn't imagine there was dirt underneath them. Mrs. Jones looked as spotless as the interior of her house *and* her indifferent snow-white cat.

Dead *Pretty*

"I understand," she said quietly. "If Wallace was involved in any gambling, he didn't share it with me. He went to the gym a lot and ate out almost every night. He had a very healthy social life with lots of young ladies. High income, no dependents. So he had plenty of disposable income and he enjoyed himself. That's not something he should be murdered for."

"No, it most definitely isn't, Mrs. Jones." Hamilton's calm, professional tone returned. "Do you know the name of Wallace's gym or any of his favorite restaurants?"

Mrs. Jones began to reel off names that meant nothing to Dak, so she tuned out for a moment and concentrated on her visual memories of the crime scene, or at least, where they'd found him, elegantly strung up like performance art. The house had been as clean as this one. The murder itself had taken place in the basement but that was void of even the odd cobweb. Everything seemed to have a place, and nothing seemed out of that place. No sign of a struggle. He'd posted plenty of photographs with the interior of his house in the background, and those would be pored over and compared to photographs taken of the house by forensics. The killer was meticulous. They could have moved items around on shelves to cover up anything missing, or broken, or damaged. She could hope for that. It would give them something to search for. But as she surveyed the scene in her head, she could see nothing physical that might be a useful clue, nothing to lead them directly to their killer.

Hamilton signaled the interview had come to a close, and Dak rose, thanking Mrs. Jones for her time. As they strolled out into the fresh air, Dak resigned herself to a long haul investigation. This wasn't going to be an open and shut case. There was no jealous or jilted spouse to slot neatly into a crime of passion mold. The killer had left nothing behind except his exhibition, and that was the biggest clue of all. The killer didn't want their attention anywhere other than on the body, on his work of art. Maybe that's where the killer had left a signature that would lead her to him.

"Do you want some good news?" Hamilton asked after Mrs. Jones closed the door after them.

"Always."

"The first victim, David Quentin, and Wallace Arnold both frequented the same gym. I've got the name and address." Hamilton waited by the driver's side.

"Bury the lead, why don't you?" She shoved him out of the way, unlocked the door, and climbed in.

"Next stop?"

"Sure. Maybe we'll get lucky and find a dude with a locker full of shibari rope and a grudge against rich guys with amazing bodies." Hamilton puffed out his chest and flexed his arm. "This killer's making me grateful that I'm on a meager cop's salary or I could be his next victim."

Dak laughed. "You're about twenty pounds too light and nowhere cut enough to fit this guy's type."

Hamilton clutched his hand to his chest. "That hurts, Farrell. And how could you know? You've never seen me naked."

"Praise the Lord." The image of her hot new neighbor dropped, uninvited but not unwelcome, into her mind. Naked CJ was an entirely more interesting prospect. She gunned the engine to drive the thought from her mind. It was only Monday, and their date was five days away.

Enough time to catch this killer? She seriously doubted it.

Chapter Eight

"MORNING, HONEY. I JUST made a fresh pot of Texas pecan coffee. Would you like some?"

CJ placed her iPad on the countertop, rubbed her eyes, and looked again. No, her eyes didn't deceive her. Her mom was at the stove top making what smelled like pancakes, really good pancakes, like the ones she hadn't been able to eat in three years. Like the ones she used to make herself when she was a kid, because no one else was around to make them for her. "No. Thanks." She opened the fridge and pulled out the bottle of fresh OJ she'd picked up from the store. "I always start the day with some juice."

Her mom stopped what she was doing, got a glass from one of the cupboards, and placed it on the counter. CJ couldn't decide if it was passive aggressive or a caring gesture. She did know that her lack of certainty on the matter spoke volumes about their relationship. Pushing that aside, she poured some juice and sat at the breakfast counter while her mom went back to making pancakes that promised heaven in her mouth.

"I'm making your favorite." Her mom glanced over her shoulder and smiled. "I've been practicing."

CJ pinched the bridge of her nose. Her parents were making huge efforts to try to make amends for her childhood. Understanding what was going on wasn't rocket science. But she didn't need them to do anything. She'd spent thousands on therapy so that they didn't have to change. *She'd* changed. She no longer needed their approval or time. She was as at peace as she could be and was doing her best to put her childhood behind her and simply accept them for the people they were. They did their best, and it wasn't ideal. Boo hoo. Thousands of kids had it a lot worse than she ever did.

But she wasn't sure her therapy had covered how she was supposed to deal with her parents suddenly being engaged, interested, and caring. Pushing them away would make her the asshole, but weren't they supposed to explain the turnabout? Didn't they want to talk about why they were trying to make up for their epic failure as parents? Her therapist would certainly encourage that. Maybe CJ didn't want to talk about it. She'd come home for a break, not to reconnect with her family. She would've gone anywhere else in the States if she'd had the money. *People change.* Dak's words echoed in her head unbidden. Now *she* was the kind of distraction she needed on this break, but it was two more days to Saturday and their date—if it happened. She'd watched enough TV crime shows to know that an FBI agent's job was rarely nine to five.

"Can I tempt you? Or are you still on a Hollywood diet?"

CJ looked up at her mom. "Huh?"

"The pancakes I made for you. Would you like some? I got some Canadian maple syrup in too."

Her mom looked so hopeful, her eyes almost pleading for CJ to say yes. She checked her watch to make sure she had time. "Sure, I'll try one." One pancake wouldn't hurt if she used it to fuel a quick Shabam workout in the garage before she headed off to work.

Her mom plated her creation and placed it in front of CJ, along with a fork and a bottle of pure maple syrup. "So are you on a strict diet while you're here?"

CJ shrugged. "Kind of. I don't know exactly when I'm going back yet. I can't pile on the pounds, if that's what you're asking. Why?"

"Just taking an interest in my daughter's health. That's okay, isn't it?" Her mom took a seat at the edge of the breakfast bar.

CJ ignored the syrup—a sacrifice to the hope that she *did* have to stay camera-ready—and forked a mouthful of pancake into her mouth to avoid answering her mom's question with snark. Her taste buds rejoiced, and she couldn't stop a low moan of appreciation. "Can I taste hazelnut?"

Her mom grinned. "My special ingredient. Do you like it?"

CJ was reminded of mornings at Emily's house after a sleepover and how Em's mom wouldn't rest until both she and Emily were properly fed. At the time, she'd envied it. But nearly fifteen years later, and coming from her own mom, it seemed out of place and too little too late. "Yeah, it's nice." She finished the rest of it far quicker than she wanted to and downed the rest of her juice. It was too early in the morning for this to get any deeper.

CJ pushed her plate away and got up. "I'm going to get in a quick

Dead *Pretty*

workout before I leave."

"I don't understand why you're working there. Aren't you supposed to be taking a break and relaxing?"

"Old Man Bryan needed my help. He hasn't been able to get anyone to replace his wife, and he's nowhere near the artist she was." An unexpected pang of melancholy had CJ reaching out for the countertop to steady herself. Iris had been more than an employer. She'd been almost like a mom and seeing Bernie without her was like seeing half a person. He looked hollowed out, almost, like Iris had taken his lifeblood with her.

"We went to the funeral," her mom said. "It was terribly sad, but it got us thinking about death. It was quite the catalyst for your father and me. Bernard is pushing seventy, but Iris was our age."

Ah, now everything made sense. Her parents hadn't been friends with the Bryans, but they knew them through CJ's apprenticeship. And there was nothing like death hovering close by to make someone reassess their life.

She glanced at her watch again. No time to engage in an existential conversation with her mom now. "Maybe we can talk about it later." CJ grabbed a bottle of cold water and headed to the garage with her iPad without waiting for a response.

She set up the workout and started warming up. Through the side window, she spotted Dak walking down the driveway. CJ hit pause and knocked on the glass to get Dak's attention.

"Hey." Dak came through the gate in the fence separating their properties and smiled.

"You weren't kidding about the trouser suits and button-downs." CJ emerged from the garage and motioned to Dak's outfit. She looked nothing like the black-suited stiffs on TV. In fact, CJ hadn't seen someone look that good in a suit and jacket probably ever. The sharp navy tie and sky-blue shirt was both professional and incredibly sexy, and the combination had CJ imagining a post-dinner date scenario where she'd only partially undress Dak and go down on her, Dak's shirt open and tie still on.

"But you like it?"

Dak quirked her eyebrow knowingly, and CJ would've blushed at being caught staring if she'd been any kind of shy, but she wasn't, so she simply gave Dak her best come-on smile. "What makes you think that?"

"I don't know. Maybe the way your expression makes it look like you want to devour me right here, right now." Dak took a step closer.

"You can see that from my expression?" CJ said, matching Dak's move and bringing her within touching distance. God, Dak was tall. Why was tall such an attractive quality?

"Then you're not denying it?"

CJ shook her head slowly. "Why would I try to deceive an officer of the law? Nothing good ever comes of that."

"You've got that right." Dak shifted her jacket and put her hand in her pocket, revealing the FBI badge on her hip.

She'd be "packing heat," no doubt. Why was *that* sexy too? CJ wasn't a gun person, but the thought of Dak with a firearm brought a different kind of heat to her body. "Is it Saturday yet?"

Dak grinned. "Is something happening on Saturday that you're looking forward to?"

"It's the end of the work week, for starters."

"Why would that register for you? Aren't you on vacation?"

CJ wrinkled her nose. "I'm helping out for someone who helped me when I needed it." She thumbed toward the house. "And it's getting me out of the house. Win-win."

Dak's expression turned from sexy to serious, making CJ wish she hadn't mentioned her parents. It seemed like a hot button topic for Dak, and she wanted to know why. Dak and her father hadn't been friendly for all that long, so it couldn't be that.

"Still finding the change difficult?" Dak asked.

The change? What did Dak know about how her parents had changed other than her passing reference to the *Twilight Zone*? Seemed like her father had talked more to Dak in a few months than he had to CJ in all the years she'd been alive. But just like the conversation with her mom moments ago, it was still too early for something so deep. And deep conversation with Dak wasn't really what interested her. Ignoring the fact that CJ had gotten a job, she *was* on vacation, and she fully intended to indulge in a vacation fling. And she was damn sure that didn't involve analyzing and dismantling her relationship with her parents.

CJ tugged at her tank top. "Speaking of getting out of the house, I need to finish my workout before I head off to work."

Dak blinked briefly, clearly registering CJ's disinterest in talking about her parents. "What kind of workout are you doing?" she asked.

"Nothing like the ones you do, I'm sure." CJ's gaze flicked to Dak's biceps, easily filling the sleeves of her jacket. Strong arms like that must come with some serious stamina.

"Do you ever just answer a question?"

"If it's a question I want to give a straight answer to, yes. I'm doing a dance workout, if you're really interested."

Dak frowned. "Why wouldn't I be interested? I could learn some new moves." She swayed her hips a little.

"Do you dance?" That nugget intrigued CJ. She loved music and dancing.

"You can be the judge of that when Saturday finally arrives."

"What are the odds you'll be pulled away for work?"

"We should be fine unless another victim shows up. Oh, hold on." Dak pulled her phone from her pocket as it rang. She mouthed an apology to CJ and turned her back before walking away.

CJ checked her watch again. Her workout window was rapidly disappearing, but if she continued to miss them *and* eat brownies and pancakes, her personal trainer would have to perform a miracle to get CJ camera-ready. She looked back at Dak. How long was CJ supposed to stand there and wait for Dak to finish her call? She hadn't had much time to ponder the question when Dak walked back toward her.

"I'm sorry. I have to go." She leaned in, rested her hand lightly on CJ's hip, and kissed her on the cheek. "Until Saturday?"

CJ nodded and watched her leave before she touched her cheek where Dak had kissed her. That had been unexpected, old-fashioned almost.

"She's a solid prospect, Calista."

CJ twisted around to see her father standing at the garage side door. "I'm not panning for gold, Dad, and you shouldn't be spying on me." A rather extreme accusation, possibly, but he'd caught her off guard, sharing a private moment.

"I'm not spying on you." He chuckled, apparently unfazed by her reaction. "I'm just making an observation. Dak has a solid career ahead of her and she's a very nice person. That makes her good wife material."

Wife material! How did he jump from them meeting a few days ago to thinking about them getting married? And why the hell was he thinking about who she should marry anyway? She'd only just entered her thirties. There was no rush to settle down—and no reason to, either, with the plethora of prospects back in Hollywood. "I'm pretty sure I don't need your help choosing a wife, Dad, but thanks for the 'observation.'" She went back into the garage, grabbed her iPad, and headed upstairs. She'd do a quick core workout in her room and take a cold shower though her father's appearance had already acted like a fire hydrant on her ardor. She switched her focus back to Dak and smiled. Each time CJ saw her, the sparks surprised her. Saturday couldn't come fast enough.

Chapter Nine

"BOTH VICTIMS WERE MALES in their late thirties. Affluent. Unusually fit for their age and in well-paid occupations. Wallace Arnold was single, but David Quentin was married. Both were heterosexual."

Dak held up her hand to stop Hamilton continuing. "You're making a pretty big assumption there that would close down a potential avenue of investigation."

"You don't think they were straight?" Hamilton took his feet down from his desk and sat up in his chair.

She shook her head. "I'm not saying that's what I think, but it's something that we don't know for certain. Arnold's social profile showed him with plenty of women, maybe too many women. Maybe it was for show. And when you were working vice, how many 'straight' married men did you bust for getting blowjobs from rent boys in alleyways?"

"Shit. Getting a blowjob from a guy doesn't make you gay, does it?"

For a brief moment, she thought he was being serious until he broke into a wide grin.

"I got you that time, didn't I?"

She stood and pushed her chair back. It smashed against the wall, and the rest of the office looked across at them. "I'm asking the captain for a new partner."

Hamilton's expression changed from joker to hangdog puppy in record time. "You wouldn't? The dead surgeon popped my cherry and now it's a serial killer. I don't want to have lost my murder virginity and then get bumped from the case."

Dak scoffed and dropped back into her chair. "And I got you."

Hamilton blew out a long breath and put both hands on his head. "Shit, Farrell. You're a cold bastard."

"I've heard worse." She leaned back in her chair and motioned to Hamilton's notebook. "You were saying?"

Hamilton flicked to the next page of his notebook. "We spoke to most of the gym staff and a few other people at the gym they both attended, and there's nothing to suggest they knew each other. They didn't lift or train together, and for the most part, they went to the gym at different times." He pointed his pen toward Dak. "But that doesn't mean that our killer doesn't work at or attend the gym."

Dak nodded. "Exactly. We should start with background checks on the staff and see if there's anyone worth bringing in, anyone with a criminal record or a hint of trouble. See if any of them went to Quentin's hospital or better yet, had surgery under him or his team."

"Or any of their family, especially if it went wrong," Hamilton said.

She shrugged. "The family, yes. But malpractice? That's a bit of a long shot. If anyone had a grudge against Quentin, they'd be pretty stupid to slice him up. Our killer isn't stupid, or he would've slipped up and we would've caught him already. We're still waiting on the tox screen, so we don't know if our victims were drugged."

Hamilton flipped back and forth through his book. "There was no sign of needles or puncture wounds on either of the victims."

"But that doesn't discount the victims ingesting an incapacitating drug. Which means we should also be looking at their regular hangouts and seeing if there's any crossover."

"Because our killer could be a barman, waitress, or bouncer?"

"Any of those, and anybody else who works at any establishment they were both seen at, even if it was only once. Serial killers hide in all kinds of professions, and a lot of their killing is about opportunity. Maybe we're looking at a late-night Uber driver." Dak paused. As much as this was about solving the crimes and finding a serial killer before they struck again, it was also an important teaching moment for her rookie to learn the trade. "Talk to me about motivation."

"From the Uber driver?"

Dak nodded.

"The victims are both good-looking guys with money. Our killer's motivation could be sexual. Our driver likes the look of them and he's into some kinky shit. These aren't sex games gone wrong, though. It's all too tidy for that. This guy is neat beyond neat, but some of that could come from knowing he's got to cover his tracks."

"Yep. Forensics hasn't found anything at the crime scenes that doesn't belong to our victims. The usual DNA on toothbrushes, bedding, and combs but the actual places of death and display were pristine. What else?"

"If it's not sexual, it could be wrath—"

She gave a short laugh at his word choice. "Biblical."

"My parents' fault, Farrell. I'm a good Christian boy."

Dak arched her eyebrows. "I doubt that but keep going."

"Rage. The driver picks up our guys, maybe a few times and always with different women. Maybe the victims ask him to pick them up in a few hours, and our driver is jealous of their success with the ladies. Our driver decides they have to die. He picks Quentin up one night, drugs him with complimentary water, and kills him. Maybe the way our driver displays the bodies is his way of humiliating them and showing his superiority over them."

"Or exposing their vanity and lust. The way the killer sliced the victims' bodies is very deliberate. The incisions followed muscle delineation perfectly, and he paid a lot of attention to what was swinging between their legs."

"What if it's another surgeon? One of Quentin's colleagues, and he got a taste for it? What started as professional jealousy ended up with him discovering a new hobby?"

"Gruesome but not beyond the realm of possibility. These are all lines of thought that need following up while—"

"While we wait for another victim?"

"I was going to say while we wait for the toxicology reports on both victims, but yeah, it's an unfortunate fact: more bodies usually equal more clues."

Hamilton made some more notes in his book before he plucked a blank sheet of paper from the ream on his desk. "How are we divvying this up between us and the other guys?"

"We still have Davis and Earl?"

"Yep, and Marks and Williams," Hamilton said. "We'll have them both until the end of the week then we'll have to go it alone, unless another victim comes in. That'll escalate the situation and get the attention of the chief."

Dak raised her eyebrow. "More so than it has already?" The chief's attention was why she was still here and not in Seattle on the next cold case on her list.

"Aw, come on, Farrell. You can't tell me you're not enjoying the change of pace. You've been a lot more animated since the captain press-ganged you into this."

She tossed a paperclip at his head and stood. Was he right? "I'm getting coffee. Do you want one?"

"What about this division of labor? The captain's scheduled a briefing at noon."

She checked her watch. They had a full hour to pull something solid together to appease Burnett. "We'll figure it out in a minute." She yawned and stretched out her shoulders. "I need a caffeine boost."

"Oh, yeah? Late night?" He looked at her expectantly.

"*If* I'd had the kind of late night you're intimating, I wouldn't share the details with you." She threw another paperclip at his head, but he was ready for it this time and deflected it onto his desk.

"But I tell you every—"

"Correction. You *try* to tell me everything, and I always stop you because I'm not interested in your sex life. At all. I was at the gym until late. Nothing for you to get excited about." She offered the tiny piece of personal information because his wounded puppy look got her every time. She needed to work on controlling that. Which reminded her, she needed to call her mom and explain what was happening. She'd been putting the conversation off for days after sending a quick text to say she'd been delayed and wouldn't be home for a while. Then she'd sent multiple calls to voicemail and responded to texts with a quick, "I'll call soon."

It wasn't as if her mom would lay a guilt trip on her, Dak just didn't want to hear the pain in her mom's voice. It was clear her mom missed her in ways she probably wouldn't appreciate unless she had children of her own, and that wasn't about to happen anytime soon or ever, but her mom didn't seem to understand how important Dak's career was to her. It was a promise to her dad that she wanted to continue to honor. That she might be neglecting her surviving family to do so was something she didn't want to really think about, bringing her back to why she was avoiding the inevitable conversation with her mom.

"How long have you been training?" Hamilton asked.

"I first picked up a dumbbell when I was ten, but I got serious when I made the decision to join the FBI." She poured coffee for them both, choosing not to go into more personal details about training with her dad. Hamilton took his mug and added four sugars. "Jesus, Hamilton. Donuts, cigars, a pound of sugar. I can't get my head around all the crap you put in your body."

He flexed his bicep and chuckled. "You should see me drink. In fact, me and some of the other guys in the squad are going drinking on Saturday night. You should come."

Dak had managed to avoid the squad's drinking nights to this point. Sometimes, she'd wanted to go but her self-imposed separation stopped her. She hadn't wanted to get involved or make friendships. Was there something so wrong about keeping things professional? "Sorry, I can't."

Hamilton headed back to his desk. "Surprise."

He said it so quietly that Dak almost didn't catch it, and she willed herself not to respond. "I've got a date, if you must know." She *should* ask for a different partner. She wouldn't acquiesce to any of the others. They were all either her age or older, and none of them bore any resemblance to her little brother like Hamilton did.

"Really?"

She lowered herself into her chair and put her mug on the desk. "You don't have to sound so blown away by the concept that I might date."

"I think I do. You're only ever at work or the gym."

She couldn't argue with that. She didn't have much of a social life, and she didn't have time for one, but everyone needed the comfort of another warm body occasionally. Not that she was about to discuss those needs with her temporary partner. "My neighbor's daughter came home on vacation."

Hamilton bounced up in his chair. "Ah, was that the woman in the coffee shop the other day?"

"Yeah. Now can we get back to the case?" Dak pulled the file containing the surveillance camera details from Arnold's neighborhood.

"Did you know she's a reality TV star?"

He looked so excited that he'd gotten information that she might not have, she didn't have the heart to tell him she already knew. "How do you know that?"

"My uncle drives for the coroner's office, and he took Arnold's body to the Bryan's Funeral Home. He recognized her straight away. Callie Johnson from *Dead Pretty*."

That was something Dak didn't know. CJ had mentioned she was helping out a friend but hadn't said where. "I've never watched it. Have you?" That was a little lie. Up to meeting CJ, she hadn't even heard of it, but she'd been binge-watching before bed every night since.

"God, yeah. I thought I'd seen her before, but I couldn't place her. Probably the make-up and wardrobe—she's kinda glamorous on the show, but she looked like a regular person in the coffee house." He winked and wiggled his eyebrows. "Good catch."

"Thanks." She waved the file. "Surveillance. Anything come up?"

"Nothing that helps. There were too many blind spots around Arnold's house, and some of the cameras were just for show."

That didn't sound right. "A neighborhood like that doesn't have CCTV just for show. Let's get in touch with the security company and have them check the positioning of the cameras. Could be our killer hacked their system and shifted them to create those blind spots."

Hamilton scribbled a note. "I'll get Marks and Williams to follow up. They're the ones who worked the footage. They may have already asked that question. If it turns out the cameras were moved, that's some serious preparation from our killer."

Dak nodded. "That's expected though, isn't it? These weren't crimes of passion, and they weren't committed in the heat of an argument. Our victims were very carefully chosen. The killer made sure he wiped down the crime scene not just so that he didn't leave any clues, but so he could do it again. Taking care of the cameras would be child's play." When she'd seen the first victim, she'd suspected it might be the first of several. It also didn't feel like it was the killer's first murder. In all likelihood, he could've just moved here and started a new spree. That put a time pressure on them over and above the usual. If they got close without catching him, the killer would simply move onto another hunting ground. She rose from her chair and added her thoughts to the notes board. "We need to check across the rest of the country for similar murder victims."

"Because the surgeon's crime scene was so perfect?" Hamilton asked.

"Exactly. We're not seeing the practice runs, and it's unlikely he's this good with his first try unless—"

"Unless he's an exceptional mind."

She nodded. She didn't mind Hamilton finishing her sentences when he got it right. It showed he was learning. She moved to the photos of the surgeon's body. Displayed. Exhibited. "This guy thinks he's an artist. We were talking about his motivation—wrath, jealousy, sexual—but what if his kills aren't driven by the usual things? What if it's all about creating works of art?"

Hamilton tapped his pen on the desk. "Then maybe he'll be at the funeral. You told me that killers often attend vigils and funerals, and that they revisit the scene of the crime to witness the grief they've caused. That'll be even more important if he wants to watch other people's reactions to what he's created, won't it?" He chuckled. "There might be even more people at the funeral because they want to see the work of a celebrity, which could make our job a little harder. But I'll bet Callie Johnson will make Arnold more attractive than he was before he died."

CJ's work on her TV show was quite brilliant, and she definitely deserved her "creative with cadavers" title. Numerous times over the past few nights as Dak had watched *Dead Pretty*, she'd doubted that CJ could do anything with some of the corpses she'd worked on. But her reconstruction of the heads and various body parts of her clients was nothing short of amazing. Beyond that, it seemed to give the relatives and friends a sense of peace they thought they wouldn't get when they saw their loved ones again, in pristine condition. Dak had been hooked, and not just by the beauty of the show's host.

"Okay. Let's get the other guys together in the meeting room and figure out who's doing what before we brief Captain Burnett. I'll start wheeling these boards in there."

Hamilton saluted as he stood. "Yes, boss."

Dak focused on the victim board again. This was someone who believed in what he was doing. Their killer's pride emanated from the photos. The enjoyment was evident too. This was someone who wouldn't stop killing unless someone stopped him. She looked toward the five men gathering in the meeting room. Four veteran detectives and a rookie. And her. She'd solved cold cases with far less resources than Burnett was affording them. But she could maintain a certain distance with cold cases that she couldn't seem to keep a handle on in this live case. She hoped that wouldn't end up biting her on the ass.

Chapter Ten

"I'VE GOT IT." CJ rushed out of the kitchen and opened the door before either of her parents could stand. Dak's outfit of shirt and dark jeans hit the right note of smart casual, and CJ's body responded to the visual stimuli instantly. And the way Dak's arms and chest filled out her shirt then tapered into her waist...mm, delicious. Maybe they could skip the date and go straight to Dak's bedroom. Or sofa. Or kitchen table. All three would be preferable. She didn't have work in the morning.

Dak produced a bunch of flowers from behind her back. "These are for you."

"They're beautiful. I love tulips." She took them and raised them to her nose, inhaling deeply. "They smell divine."

"Good. I had no idea how hard it could be to buy flowers."

CJ tilted her head at Dak's look of relief. "How so?"

"The guy at the flower shop asked a lot of questions about who they were for and what I wanted to say through them. Now I know I have to be really careful about what flowers I give people. Who knew?"

"Not me." CJ held the flowers out and pretended to study them closely. "What *are* you saying with this particular bouquet of flowers, Agent Dak?"

"I hadn't put much thought into exactly what I wanted to say when I walked into the shop. I just thought it'd be nice to show up at your door with some pretty flowers. That's what they do in the movies, right?" Dak shrugged. "I don't really do this kind of thing."

"Buy flowers for women?" That could be both a good and bad thing, but CJ reminded herself that this was just a fling for fun, and she didn't need to like or get to know all of Dak's habits.

"No. I don't get much occasion to. I buy them for my mom, and that's usually to distract her from how long it's been since my last visit. And I've bought them for a few funerals. But I don't think I've ever stood at a woman's door with a bunch of flowers. Anyway, to answer your initial question, the old farmer's almanac which the flower guy showed me says that yellow tulips are supposed to signify the sunshine in your smile." She glanced away briefly, looking a little shy and totally adorable because of it.

"Sunshine?" CJ asked.

"You've got a beautiful smile." Dak's cheeks colored slightly. "And it seemed a little much to go with red tulips since they're a declaration of love."

"I don't think a lot of people are familiar with the 'old farmer's almanac.' I've had way too many red tulips from people who were definitely not declaring undying love." And red tulips on any date—not just the first—would have been more than full-on. That kind of love wasn't on CJ's radar just yet.

"Not undying love. Heliotrope was the thing for that, though they sounded more like a drug than a flower. The guy was eager to know whether my love was undying or transient."

"Or no love at all." CJ lifted the flowers and winked.

"Shall we go before the conversation gets more awkward? I like to save that for after the appetizers."

CJ smiled her newly named sunshine smile. "Wow, you get all the way to the end of the appetizers before it gets weird? I'm still at the bar waiting for the table when it starts getting uncomfortable." She stepped back from the door. "Let me put these in a vase and then we can get going."

When CJ returned, her father was in the doorway deep in conversation with Dak.

"Bye, Dad. Don't wait up." She slipped past him, hooked her arm in Dak's, and pulled her away.

"See you later, Rog," Dak called over her shoulder.

CJ headed toward her Ferrari, but Dak went in the opposite direction so she stopped. "Oh, I thought you might like to ride in my car."

Dak motioned toward the old truck in her driveway. "I didn't want to assume you would be driving."

CJ wondered if Dak had been doing some research and had discovered CJ was quite the party girl. It was a fair enough assumption if Dak looked at her Instagram feed. "I wasn't going to drink tonight. You don't have to be concerned about me drunk-driving."

The brief expression on Dak's face suggested that's exactly what she'd been thinking.

"It wasn't just that. I like driving. And…"

Dead *Pretty*

The way she trailed off hinted there was something she was slightly embarrassed to admit. "Do you get car sick if you're not driving? Or do you just like to be in control?" CJ liked her second conclusion the most.

"I'd like to drive for *you*," Dak said after a brief silence.

CJ wanted Dak to drive her insane with pleasure. The thought of skipping the formalities and going directly next door pushed for her attention once more. "Okay." She dropped her keys into her clutch and allowed Dak to lead her to her truck. Dak opened the passenger door, waited for CJ to get in, and closed it behind her. They locked eyes through the glass and Dak's intense stare made CJ wish she had simply asked to forego the date.

Dak got into the driver's side, fired up the truck, and got them on their way.

"How's your case going, Agent Dak?" CJ asked once they were on the road and heading into the city.

Dak frowned. "Are you going to call me that all night?"

"Maybe. Do you like it? Or would you prefer Agent Farrell?"

"Do you prefer Calista?" Dak glanced sideways and grinned. "How did you find out my last name?"

"I did some detective work of my own—I asked Dad. And no, but you can call me Callie occasionally."

"Did he tell you anything else, Callie?"

CJ shook her head. "I didn't ask him anything else. I want to find out about you on my own, thanks. I don't want my dad's colored opinion." She heard Dak's light disapproval in her sigh. She didn't need to see her eye roll too. "Okay, since we're obviously not going to indulge in small talk, I'll talk about the interesting stuff as long as you promise not to let it influence your decision whether or not to take me to bed tonight."

Dak laughed. "Wow. Is that where you see this going?"

"Don't you?"

"I hadn't anticipated it moving that fast."

CJ pulled the seatbelt away from her chest and sat to the side in her seat so she could look at Dak. "You don't strike me as someone who's slow to move if they see something or someone they want. And if you've never bought flowers for a woman before, you're not a woman who dates. And if you don't date, either you're celibate or you have lots of short-term relationships mostly driven by heat. A woman like you should *not* be celibate, but that's my libido talking. Not to mention we're both here on a temporary basis, so there won't be any misunderstandings about what this is." She looked for a sign of agreement but saw only an amused smile in Dak's expression. "Tell me I'm wrong."

"You're not wrong." Dak adjusted her grip on the steering wheel and placed her hand on CJ's thigh.

The heat of Dak's hand seared through the flimsy, summer-weight material. She waited for more, but Dak said nothing else. "So do you promise not to let our conversation deter you from taking me to bed?"

"That's a tough ask. As you've so astutely observed, I don't date, which means I don't normally get to know much about the women I sleep with. But what if you say you're a right-wing nut and you hope the tangerine tornado gets re-elected? I'm not sure I can unknow that and put it aside just to have amazing sex with you."

CJ sat up a little straighter and pushed out her chest. "You think the sex is going to be amazing?"

Dak stopped at a red light and turned to CJ. "Look at you. Of course the sex is going to be amazing."

Look at you... CJ thought the sex would be wild and passionate, and she hoped there'd be lots of it. "You're saying I'm going to have to relax and hope that nothing I say manages to put you off then?"

Dak nodded. "Seems like you're worried about something specific. What is it?" She held up her hand. "Hold that thought. We're here."

CJ hadn't been taking any notice of her surroundings. She looked out the window just as a valet opened her door.

Dak walked around behind him and took her hand. "Please say you like Mexican, or the sex is off."

CJ suppressed a giggle and the valet looked to be doing the same. "Even if I hated it, I'd eat it just to ensure the sex still happens."

The valet winked at CJ, took the keys from Dak, and left them to move her truck. Dak held out her arm and CJ grasped her bicep, not bothering to resist a sneaky squeeze. Dak's muscle hardened beneath her grip, and CJ let out a low moan. "We might not make it past the aperitifs for a much better reason than our conversation becoming awkward."

"I like the sound of that."

The maître-d greeted them and showed them to a small booth toward the rear of the restaurant, away from the live band, and in a spot quiet enough that they'd have no problems hearing each other. CJ asked Dak to order for both of them once she'd asked for a passion fruit mojito, keeping with the tone of the evening thus far.

"Okay," Dak said when their waiter was out of earshot. "What do you think I'm going to judge you harshly on?"

CJ clasped her hands together and leaned forward. "It's my parents. I've got a complicated relationship with them, and you get a certain look whenever I say something about them—especially when I'm being snarky. What's that about?"

Dak gave a small smile and got a faraway look in her eyes before she seemed to refocus on CJ. "No small talk, and only deep stuff, right?"

CJ nodded, suddenly feeling like Dak might be about to show a vulnerability she wasn't ready for. "For both of us, yes."

"Here goes." Dak sighed deeply. "I had a great relationship with my parents, especially my dad. The truck I drive? We rebuilt it together. New engine, spray job, we did everything ourselves."

"It looks old, but in a good way," CJ said. Dak's story began like the one CJ wished she could have for herself. Her time with her father under the hood of his Shelby was limited, and he spent most of it telling her off for touching things she shouldn't be touching—instead of teaching her how to do things, which was what she wanted him to do. But she didn't miss the use of past tense when Dak described the relationship with her parents, and she prepared herself for a tragic story.

"It's a Chevy 1952 3100 with a V8 engine."

The waiter returned and placed their drinks on the table. CJ sipped her mojito and waited for Dak to continue.

"My mom keeps telling me that I should buy a new truck because of all the traveling I do, but there's no way I'm parting with Betty."

Dak's jaw clenched, and she looked to the ceiling. CJ reached over the table and took Dak's hand.

"It was the last big project we did together," Dak said. "He died when I was eighteen, and for some reason, I can't get past it. I joined the FBI because Dad wanted to after 9/11. He'd already done his share for the country, serving in Vietnam, but he was too old anyway. It wasn't long after that he died."

CJ was beginning to see why Dak had feelings about the way CJ and her parents were. When you've been robbed of something, it's hard to see someone else squander the same thing. "How old was he?"

"Only forty-eight. His organs shut down. He'd gotten hooked on speed, steroids, and pain pills during the war, and he was in a bad place before Mom rescued him and they got married. He stopped using, but the damage had been done."

"So what do you mean that you can't get past it?"

Dak shrugged. "I don't go home anywhere near enough. Mom and my little brother run the family business, an auto repair shop, something I was expected to take over when Dad died. My little brother was only eight."

"That's a big age difference."

"Yeah, he wasn't planned. And they'd had such a hard time getting pregnant with me that they thought they couldn't have any more kids. But home doesn't feel like home without Dad there, and no matter how much I try to logic it out, I don't like going back there."

"So where does the 'people change' thing come from? You've said it a couple of times to me about my parents."

Dak nodded. "My dad said that no one else would've put up with him or given him the time and space to get better, to *be* better, to change. And he turned into the best dad a kid could ever wish for. If Mom hadn't given him that chance, he would've been lost."

CJ took a long sip of her drink. "You think I should give my parents a chance to show me how they've changed because they're still around and won't be around forever?"

"I guess so, but I don't know your story. I shouldn't give advice without knowing everything." Dak thumbed the condensation from her glass. "And I know I'm being a hypocrite because my mom is still alive and I'm not making the most of that either."

CJ shook her head, glad that her parent issues clearly weren't going to be a problem between them. "Maybe we should've stuck to the small talk."

Dak laughed and squeezed CJ's hand. "I'm not a big fan of inane conversation. I'd rather not speak at all."

The waiter brought their starter—a giant platter of nachos loaded with chicken. He returned and set up a small station beside their booth for them to make their own guacamole.

"How spicy do you like it?" Dak asked, her tone lighter again.

"Pretty hot but not so hot that I won't be able to taste the rest of my food." Living in LA had exposed her to genuine Mexican food but her personal trainer strongly *advised* against indulging in it almost as soon as they started filming the first season. Taking a break from TV was great for her taste buds but not so good for her figure. If Paige didn't send news of another station syndicating the show soon, CJ was going to end up back to her regular size. She looked up from watching Dak crush the avocado to see an expectant look on her face. "Before we get to my story, I have one question. Are you in the FBI just because you think it would've made your dad proud or do you actually like what you do? You wouldn't rather be tinkering with cars and trucks for your dad's family business?"

Dak ran her hand through her hair and leaned back in her seat. "I love working the cold cases and solving the puzzles no one else has been able to. That's part of what I enjoy under the hood of a car or truck. All the pieces are there. You've just got to figure out what's not working. It's the same with the old murders. Almost always, everything is there for you to find the killer."

"Almost always? Do you not get your man every time?" CJ loaded a nacho with the fresh guac and popped it into her mouth. She emitted another low moan.

Dak grinned widely. "Nice?"

"Amazing."

"I think the bar's set too low for your use of that word."

"Taste it and tell me I'm wrong. My bar is plenty high, thank you very much."

Dak scooped her own mound of guac on a nacho and ate it. CJ waited for her verdict while munching on another mouthful of possibly the best nachos and guacamole she'd ever tasted.

"You're not wrong."

CJ did a little muted victory dance in her seat. "That's twice tonight. I like this being right business. Back to my question about solving your cases."

"I've solved one hundred percent of my caseload so far. It's too early to say with the one I'm working on now. I haven't been on a live case for over a decade." Dak shook her head. "Christ, I can't believe it's been that long."

"You've been traveling around the country for ten years on your own?"

"No. For the first five years, I had a partner."

Darkness passed across Dak's eyes, and she went silent. CJ's heart ached for the pain in her expression.

"Huh." Dak sipped on her drink. "It's been a while since I thought about that."

CJ didn't press and simply waited to see if Dak might expand. Whatever Dak had been through, she clearly wasn't ready to share it with CJ.

"So, what about you?" Dak asked.

"I don't think my parents should've had children. That's probably the simplest way to put it." CJ had never spoken of her childhood with anyone other than Emily and her LA therapist, and maybe a little with Paige. But Dak had asked for deep stuff, and nothing went deeper than CJ's relationship with her parents. Revealing her whole backstory on a first date wasn't her style, but Dak wasn't her usual first date either. Maybe not sharing her story had been the reason she had never connected with anyone else. She had some time on her hands. Why not see what could happen if she actually opened up to someone who *wanted* to listen rather than someone who was *paid* to listen?

Dak furrowed her brow and looked worried. "Care to expand on that?"

"Don't panic. I'm not talking about abuse." CJ gave a short laugh but stopped abruptly. Her therapist had said she used humor to cover up the pain of her parents' neglect. What she laughed at, others found mortifying. "I'm sorry. My therapist says laughing trivializes my experience and that I shouldn't do it. Hard to break a lifetime habit though, you know?"

Dak nodded. "Mine said that I should allow myself to process my emotions, however difficult they are. Their advice can be hard to follow, can't it?"

CJ raised her eyebrows, surprised that Dak admitted seeing a therapist so freely. She seemed like someone who'd work out their emotions on a punching bag or shooting range, but CJ knew that cops who discharged their weapons had to see a shrink. "Employer-enforced therapy?"

"Kind of." Dak wiggled her finger before taking a drink. "We'll get to that someday. Back to your parents."

CJ sighed. Whatever was behind Dak's therapy story, it didn't look like it would be forthcoming this evening. "If we must." She glanced away from Dak's intense gaze for a moment and tried to concentrate. "They were too busy to have a child, I guess. Both of them had demanding careers—Mom was a chief executive of a blue-chip company and Dad worked for the Army Reserves, training new recruits—and when they had time off, they wanted to be together without a kid tagging along. There weren't any family birthday parties, no parent-teacher nights, no one at my school plays or at my games. After they had me, Dad had the op so he couldn't have any more kids. It's not like they ever said it, but I think I was a mistake. Maybe we would've all been better off if they'd put me up for adoption when I was a baby."

Dak tilted her head slightly. "It must've been tough to grow up with that thought."

CJ shrugged. Dak's words seemed to come with no judgment, which CJ appreciated. She wasn't looking for sympathy either but sharing this had her vulnerabilities rising to the surface of her skin, a discomforting feeling in one way, but it strangely offered solace too. "It was. But I've had a buttload of therapy to help me 'process my emotions,' just like you said. I'd accepted them for who they are and had no expectation of them ever changing." She shook her head, thinking about how much they seemed to have changed since she last saw them. "Then I've come home to a freaky episode of the *Twilight Zone* to find strangely parental parents in their place. At some point I know that I need to talk to them, but I'm not quite ready for that talk yet. I'm still licking my wounds from my show being canceled. I can handle change, as long as it happens slowly and not too much of it at once." She laughed and Dak laughed too. "See? I can use humor in the right places too."

"What's happening with your show?"

"It was canceled, but my agent's trying to get it hosted by another network. She's bad-ass and I trust her, so it should be a matter of time." She locked eyes with Dak, hoping that Paige wouldn't do her job so efficiently that CJ wouldn't get the chance to spend more time with Dak. She'd forgotten how good it felt to talk to someone genuinely interested in her as a human being and not a vague celebrity. She felt like she wanted more of it before she returned to the soul-sucking show town.

"Meanwhile, you have to come to terms with your parents trying to be actual parents."

CJ reached across the table and placed her hand on Dak's. "That's exactly right! Speaking of parents and their jobs. They named you Dak. Is that short for Dakota?"

Dak rolled her eyes. "It would be so much easier if that were the case."

CJ leaned closer, anticipating an interesting tale. "Sounds interesting. Tell me more."

"My mom and dad couldn't agree on a name, and then my meemaw got involved, and she didn't help matters. In the end, they all chose a name, and I don't really like any of them."

CJ pushed her side plate away and tapped the table. "You can't leave it there. If it's not short for Dak, what is it?"

Dak blew out a long breath. "No laughing?"

"No laughing."

"My full name is Daniella Amy Kate Farrell. I use the initials—"

"To make Dak. Clever."

"Exactly. Mom hates it and always calls me Daniella." Dak wrinkled her nose. "And that's okay. But I like Dak."

CJ smiled. "It suits you, Agent Dak Farrell. But talking about names is heavy stuff. I'm not sure we should have discussed the content of our souls on our first date. We should've saved something for another time."

"Meaning there'll be a second date?" Dak gave her a cocky smirk.

"The jury will be out on that until we've had sex. We might not need any more dates. I can just come around to your place and we can have all the sex with none of the awkward dates and deep conversation."

"I'm beginning to think you might just be after my body."

CJ licked her lips and ran her gaze over Dak's upper body, appreciating again the way Dak's shirt pulled taut across her biceps. "And that's such a bad thing? Neither of us are going to be around for long. We're both adults. Why not just enjoy each other with no complications?"

Dak raised her glass. "I can drink to that."

CJ clinked her glass to Dak's. "Let's skip the entrée and go back to your place."

Dak shook her head. "You're going to need your energy."

CJ sighed. *And great things come to those who wait.*

Chapter Eleven

D<small>AK UNLOCKED THE DOOR</small> to her house and pushed it open for CJ to enter first. As she walked past her, CJ caught hold of the buckle on Dak's belt and pulled her in. She pressed Dak against the wall and looked up. The expectancy in her gaze made Dak's knees weak, and she leaned down to meet CJ's lips. Every cell in her body hummed with pleasure. CJ's soft lips, the gentle give of her breasts against Dak's chest, her hands on Dak's waist, all of it heightened the anticipation of what was to come. CJ's honesty about her overwhelming need for them to have sex had led to them both rushing through their entrées and skipping dessert, but they'd still managed to have some serious conversation about their upbringings, careers, and past relationships. They'd talked as if they'd known each other for years, and there were no awkward silences. They'd barely stopped talking to eat, and Dak hadn't wanted the meal to end for that reason alone. She couldn't remember ever having such genuine and open communication with anyone, let alone someone she'd only just met.

But her undeniable physical attraction to CJ battled for supremacy and won out, ending the meal without coffee. Fantastic conversation and the promise of hot sex were a heady combination Dak hadn't expected.

The same valet that greeted them had Dak's truck ready and waiting, like he'd predicted the exact length of time they'd spend in the restaurant. She gave him a twenty for his initiative. His grin and wink made her smile. He was in his early twenties, all raging hormones and no sense. Which was about how Dak had felt all night. It had been a long, long time since she'd been this desperate to have sex.

Dak dragged her fingers along CJ's thighs, pulling her dress up. She pushed away from the wall, cupped CJ's ass, and lifted her up. CJ wrapped her legs around Dak's waist, and her heat warmed Dak's stomach.

"Oops. You might have to wash this shirt now," CJ whispered.

She slipped her hands around the edges of Dak's shirt and yanked it open. Dak heard at least two buttons hit the floor. "Huh. I thought that just happened in the movies."

CJ raked her fingernails across Dak's naked chest, and she let out a deep sigh. The feel of a woman's long nails across her skin always melted her instantly, and tonight was no exception. She turned around and pressed CJ against the wall, kissing her hard and insistent. CJ sucked Dak's tongue into her mouth and Dak followed her lead, deepening and intensifying the kiss.

CJ pulled away and traced a nail along Dak's bottom lip. Dak clenched her thighs. It was like CJ had read her playbook and knew all the right notes to hit.

"Do you have a friend?" CJ asked.

That wasn't in her plan for tonight. Threesomes had never been her thing, and how was that supposed to go? Was she supposed to have a buddy on speed dial or should they already be waiting in the living room in case the need arose? "What?"

She must've looked as panicked as she felt because CJ frowned at her reaction, then laughed out loud and slapped Dak's chest. "Not that kind of friend." She pushed her hips away from Dak and reached down. She placed her hand on Dak's crotch and squeezed. "*This* kind of friend." CJ sank back against Dak's body and caressed her cheek. "Do you understand?" she whispered.

Dak nodded and grinned. "Upstairs." As her arousal increased, her use of language had apparently decreased. One word was all she could manage before sinking into another passionate kiss.

CJ wrapped her hand around the back of Dak's head and pulled on her short hair. "Are you going to make me wait for that like you made me wait to come home?"

Dak shook her head. There could be no more waiting. She wasn't capable of that kind of self-restraint. Part of her wanted to slow down, to savor the moment, to take her time. But the rest of her, the big part that was in control, had no intention of denying them instant gratification.

With CJ still wrapped around her waist, light as a feather compared to the weights Dak squatted at the gym, she took CJ upstairs to her bedroom. She laid CJ on the bed, stood, and flicked the bedside light on. She pulled her strap-on from the drawer and tossed it on the bed.

CJ kicked off her shoes, grabbed one of Dak's pillows, and pulled it beneath her head. "Take off your jeans."

CJ wanted to be in control. Dak couldn't stop the grin on her face. She could roll with that. She unbuckled her belt and unzipped her jeans and shed them both as sexy-slow as she could given that she was beyond eager to be inside CJ.

CJ sat up and slipped her finger in the waistband of Dak's briefs. She put her other hand on Dak's hips and unhurriedly relieved Dak of her underwear. As Dak stepped out of them, CJ's breath blew cold across her pussy and Dak's legs threatened to give way beneath her. CJ stood, spun them both around, and pushed Dak onto the bed.

"Stay exactly like that."

Dak quelled the tiny rise of trepidation that CJ wanted to use her "friend" on Dak. Just like the threesome, that wouldn't be happening either. But once again, her expression must've given away her alarm because CJ's slight smile turned into a wide grin.

Her gaze flicked to the silicone dildo beside Dak's leg. "You wouldn't let me?" She stuck out her bottom lip.

Dak swallowed hard. What she said next could bring a sudden end to the promise of the evening. "I…I couldn't take that size."

CJ raised her eyebrow. "But you think I can?"

Crap. Was she teasing or serious? CJ was far superior at hiding her emotions than Dak could ever be in this situation.

"Relax." CJ laughed. "I'm just messing with you." She gave a wicked grin. "But maybe we can explore smaller options another night." CJ stripped off her dress and underwear, sank to her knees, and pushed Dak's legs further apart. She reached up and pulled Dak's shirt aside to reveal her breasts and stomach. "Perfect," she whispered as she traced her fingers down the center of Dak's body to the small triangle of hair below her stomach.

CJ gently pressed her fingernail on Dak's clit, and she bucked from the bed.

"Sorry." Heat rushed to Dak's cheeks. CJ's touch was electric, and she'd wound Dak up so tight that even the slightest caress had her jolting around like a puppet on CJ's wire.

"Sorry for what?" CJ dipped her finger lower. "Being turned on? I'm taking that as a compliment."

Dak let out a deep sigh. "You definitely should."

CJ trailed her hands from the top of Dak's legs, along her thighs and down her calves to the tops of her feet. Dak involuntarily jumped again.

"Sensitive feet?" CJ asked.

"More like my feet have a direct connection with this." Dak tapped between her legs.

"Interesting."

CJ stroked Dak's feet lightly, making Dak moan quietly. CJ adjusted and dipped her head to trace her tongue along the arch of Dak's foot.

"Fuck."

CJ lifted her head and grinned. "You weren't kidding."

Dak shook her head and CJ returned to her feet, making Dak squirm in pleasure under her tongue. When CJ finally stopped, Dak released a breath she'd been holding long enough to make her slightly dizzy, though that could also have been attributed to the effect CJ was having on her.

"You're looking pretty pleased with yourself," Dak said after CJ had allowed her a few seconds to recover.

CJ moved up the bed and spread Dak's lips gently. "Well, if I can make you moan like that with just your feet, imagine how this is going to feel."

CJ's mouth locked onto Dak's clit, and Dak grabbed handfuls of the comforter. She vaguely felt CJ's hands on her hips, pressing her down onto the bed. But she could barely feel anything else. Everything, every sense, every nerve centered on the sensations between her legs as CJ's tongue licked and flicked her clit. She closed her eyes, dropped her head back onto the pillow, and let the darkness envelop her. All she could feel and see was the light CJ was creating inside her. The rest of her body became almost weightless as the throbbing between her legs intensified. CJ's steady, firm rhythm increased slightly, and Dak clenched her fists hard as CJ's touch took her to the precipice of pleasure. "Oh, God," Dak whispered before she tumbled over the cliff and her body shook and tingled all over with the strength of her orgasm. CJ stayed where she was, as if she was pulling every last ounce of desire from Dak's body. Through the fog of her rapture, Dak heard CJ moan, and she realized CJ was approaching her own orgasm even though her hands were firmly clamped on Dak's hips. She opened her eyes and looked down. CJ's eyes fluttered and she moaned again as she continued to pleasure Dak. A second wave of pleasure rode over Dak just as CJ too cried out, muffled between Dak's legs. CJ lifted her head and rested it on Dak's thigh, a look of pure contentment in her eyes.

"Goddamn, you're good at that," Dak said between short breaths, and

CJ wiggled her eyebrows. "Did you—"

"Come? Yes."

Dak laid her hands on CJ's and checked to see her dildo was still beside her. "But…"

"You're *very* sexy when you come," CJ said simply. She picked up Dak's harness and slipped it over her feet. "Lift your ass."

Dak did as instructed, and CJ expertly secured the harness around her waist in the perfect position.

"Feel good?" CJ asked and flicked the end of the silicone cock with her fingernail.

"Not as good as it's about to feel." Dak began to rise but CJ hopped up onto the bed, pushed her back, and straddled her thighs. Dak let out a short laugh. "Don't tell me—stay exactly like this?"

CJ nodded and lowered her lips to the head of Dak's cock. She ran her tongue around it and took the tip in her mouth.

"Jesus." Dak's breath grew shallow when it seemed like she was actually physically connected to her cock and could really feel CJ's mouth on her, working her up to another orgasm.

CJ released Dak then inched further up the bed to hover over Dak's strap-on. She grasped the shaft and lowered herself slowly onto it, never taking her eyes from Dak. Dak felt the resistance as CJ pushed down fully and took all of Dak inside her. CJ gasped, and the small sound made Dak moan and thrust her hips upward, making CJ cry out.

CJ placed her hand on Dak's chest and opened her eyes. "Let me ride you," she whispered.

Her voice was smooth and husky, so controlled that Dak's arousal somehow went up another notch. She stilled, though she had no idea how she was supposed to resist the desire to thrust herself deeper into CJ. She nodded and grasped CJ's hips as CJ slowly rose from Dak's cock, revealing a couple of inches of it before pushing back down again. The pressure of the cock's base against her own sex provided Dak with more stimulation on top of the cock feeling like it was part of her. CJ rose and fell, rose and fell, her pace slowly increasing. She wrapped her fists around Dak's shirt, bent closer, and kissed her. Dak released CJ's hips and ran her hands through CJ's hair, pulling her in as close as she could get her, wanting to almost meld into one. Dak broke away briefly and gazed into CJ's eyes. Something unspoken passed between them, and Dak's breath caught as she registered CJ's raw beauty and vulnerability. It was like nothing she'd ever experienced before.

CJ pulled back and continued to ride Dak, her thrusts becoming harder and faster. She arched back, and her breasts pushed out. Dak reached up and held them, then lightly pinched her nipples. CJ bucked and moaned in response. Dak continued to massage and pinch, and CJ rode Dak's cock hard, its base banging against Dak's mound, coursing the vibration straight to her pussy. CJ cried out and fell onto Dak.

Dak wrapped her arms around CJ and held her tight as her body trembled, and her rapid breathing slowed. For a second, Dak thought CJ had fallen asleep until she popped up and grinned. The kiss that followed made it clear she was far from done.

She eased from Dak's shaft and got on her hands and knees beside Dak. "We didn't get to dance so how about you show me your rhythm another way?"

Dak bit her lower lip as she took in the sight of CJ in that position and prayed she'd never forget this moment. Yep, Dak could definitely roll with CJ being in charge.

Chapter Twelve

CJ WOKE WHEN THE sun crept through the side window of Dak's bedroom and warmed her face. She was the little spoon and Dak's heavy arm around her waist pinned her in place. She closed her eyes and replayed the movie of last night. She'd been quite the vamp. She hadn't planned it that way, hadn't even known how the sex would go, and had even assumed that she would happily follow wherever Dak may lead.

But it hadn't worked out that way at all. From the moment she wrapped her legs around Dak's waist, CJ had known exactly what she wanted, and she'd been blown away by how flexible Dak had been in giving it to her. CJ certainly didn't need to wonder about Dak's stamina anymore, that was for sure. CJ had become too sore for any more way before Dak had even looked like she might need to take a break. CJ had had plenty of sex, mainly in the past three years, but none of it had ever been quite so sympatico as it had been last night. Maybe that was just an age thing. Dak was bound to have had plenty of lovers with all her traveling. She found her way around CJ's body and located her hotspots, no problem at all.

CJ didn't want the awkward morning after situation though. Morning breath. Morning coffee. Staying for breakfast when really, neither party could wait to be apart so they could process the night before and decide whether or not they might see each other again, whether or not the sex was good enough to warrant a second ride on the merry-go-round, and whether or not the conversation was enough to sustain the time between the rounds of sex. And CJ definitely didn't want to be around to see Dak's expression when she was thinking all the same things, especially if the answer to those questions were negative. Through all of last night, she had somehow been able to read Dak so intuitively it had weirded CJ out a little. CJ had experienced her fair share of letdowns, some gentle, some downright brutal, and she'd been fine with all of them. But something niggled deep inside and told her she wouldn't be quite so blasé if Dak was no longer interested.

She took Dak's wrist and slowly lifted it from her body. Dak murmured but didn't move. CJ slid off the bed and onto the floor before she gently placed Dak's arm on a pillow. She located the clothes and shoes she'd discarded in short order, padded out of Dak's bedroom quietly, and went downstairs. She quickly dressed, slipped out of the back door, and headed home.

After an hour's workout, a quick shower, and having deftly avoided her parents' questions about her date, CJ jumped in her car and drove to Emily's. She texted her on the way, and Emily suggested they go for breakfast.

Emily was already curbside when CJ pulled up outside her house. "Wow." She did a full circle of the Ferrari before coming around to the passenger side to get in. "*This* is a nice ride, my friend, and yet another good reason why I like having you around again." She gestured to her sky-blue Mini Cooper in the driveway. "That's cute and says I'm fun, but this is sexy-sexy and says—"

"Don't finish that sentence. I might not like what you think it says, and I love this car."

"Okay, but it—"

"Nope. Don't do it."

Emily tutted. "Fine." She fastened her seatbelt. "I would've thought you might have gone with classic red or yellow."

CJ pulled away far too fast for the neighborhood, but she couldn't resist, and Emily's squeal of delight rewarded her showiness. "You can't beat black for a car like this. It accentuates the sleek, hard lines. Where are we headed?"

Emily gave her a series of instructions and they arrived at the all-day diner a few minutes later. It was early for a Sunday and wasn't busy, so CJ was able to park directly outside a series of booths behind a wall of floor-to-ceiling windows. Emily got them one of those booths so CJ could keep an eye on her prize possession.

"That's more or less all I have to show for three years in Hollywood," CJ said after the waitress had served them coffee as black as a network exec's soul.

"Still no word from your agent?"

CJ shook her head. "No words I want to hear. 'Enjoy the break,' 'relax,' and 'everything's going to be fine' are about all I get from her."

Dead *Pretty*

She shrugged. "It's only been a week, I guess. Patience isn't my favorite virtue."

Emily sugared her coffee and gave it a quick stir. "Is your distraction at Old Man Bryan's working out?"

"Actually, yes. I thought it might be low-key compared to my TV work, but we got the second serial killer victim, and he was a great challenge."

"Is this guy Salt Lake's first serial killer?"

CJ shrugged. "I have no idea, and I don't want to know. Why would I know something like that?"

"I think it's fascinating. And at least we don't have to fear for our lives."

"What do you mean?" CJ sipped her coffee.

"The paper said that all his victims have been male, similar age, race, and build. Serial killers have a type, like dating but murdering people instead."

CJ wrinkled her nose. "That's not macabre at all."

"Says the woman who works with dead people all day."

The waitress returned and took their order.

"Someone's hungry," Emily said after she'd left.

CJ grinned and shifted in her seat, feeling as well as remembering the memory of last night. "That's what happens when you go on the kind of date I went on last night."

Emily gave CJ's shoulder a light shove. "Do tell."

"Remember at the café, the FBI agent living next door to my parents?"

Emily's eyes sparkled. "The handsome butch one who's exactly your type?"

"Or maybe yours by the way you just reacted."

Emily tilted her head and attempted a coy look. "With a strap-on, I bet she looks androgynous enough to make me forget she's a woman."

"Oh, believe me, she's all woman. You wouldn't forget." Heat rose to CJ's cheeks when the image of Dak on her back with her silicone cock jutting proudly from her harness came to mind. She touched her lips and recalled Dak's sweet, sweet taste.

"You had strap-on sex, didn't you?"

"Shh." The diner didn't have too many early customers, but the ones who were there turned at Emily's words. Most of them glared, but a baby dyke in the opposite corner gave CJ the butch nod and winked.

Robyn Nyx

Emily shoved CJ's elbow, making her coffee spill. "Well?"

"That was *one* part of the evening's activities, yes." CJ wasn't usually one to kiss and tell, but that was more due to a lack of opportunity because she had no close friends in Hollywood than a lack of desire to gossip. Being back home, sharing breakfast with her best friend, made it easy to slip into old patterns. And there was something comforting about having someone to talk to about these things, especially when they had the potential to get complicated and an objective opinion might be vital to not making stupid decisions.

The waitress brought their food over and topped up their coffees.

"Hold that thought. I'm so hungry." CJ dug into her biscuits and gravy and dismissed the voice of her personal trainer in her head. She'd worked out this morning and had three hours plus of vigorous sex. She'd damn well earned this plate of carbs and fat.

When she came up for air and a slurp of coffee to wash it all down, Emily looked at her expectantly, clearly still waiting for the juicy details.

"I want you to tell me *everything*," Emily said. "I have to live vicariously through you until I sort my head out."

CJ clenched her jaw. She hated to see her lovely friend in so much pain. "That asshole really did a number on you, didn't he?"

Emily sighed and nodded. "But let's not talk about him. Talk me through your date."

CJ finished her second cup of coffee and waited for a refill before she regaled Emily with her date with Agent Dak. When she finished, Emily had a knowing, somewhat inquisitive expression.

"What?" CJ asked, not certain she wanted to hear what Emily had to say.

"This could get serious, couldn't it?"

It had only been a few hours since CJ had slipped out of Dak's warm bed and her even warmer embrace. She hadn't had the time to think about whether she could develop serious feelings for Dak. Besides that, it was CJ who had stated they could just have fun sex and skip the deep conversations and dating—though much of their exchange last night had been something else. Something she couldn't define. "It can't get serious. She travels all over the States for work, and if my agent does her job, I'll be heading back to LA soon."

Emily shook her head, her smug expression unchanged. "That doesn't answer my question."

"Do you want pie? I want pie. Cherry pie." CJ waved the waitress over and ordered a piece for each of them after Emily nodded.

The waitress brought their desserts and topped up their coffee again. CJ avoided Emily's intense stare and looked out across the restaurant. Baby Butch nodded again. CJ had never gone for women younger than her, but she smiled back. There was no harm in that, and it'd probably make her day if CJ's youth was anything to go by. Just a small recognition from someone she thought might be like her had kept her going for weeks while she searched for someone to have her first sexual experience with.

Emily tapped her fork on the table. "If Agent Dak didn't have to travel and if you didn't have to leave to go to LA, could it get serious between the two of you?"

"Callie Johnson?"

CJ looked up to the source of the voice and offered her TV smile. She hadn't expected this to happen here, but she'd had enough experience in LA to know how to react. "That's me. How are you?"

The guy looked surprised. "I'm well, thank you for asking. I'm Stuart Jones from the Salt Lake Tribune. Would it be possible to organize a time to interview you about your work on the serial killer's second victim, Wallace Arnold?"

CJ glanced back at Emily, who shook her head and rolled her eyes dramatically.

"I'm working all week until six," CJ said, "but I could do any evening." Regardless of what happened with Dak, she envisaged they wouldn't be able to connect through the week. And for a number of reasons, she wouldn't be able to give Jones that much information about the victim anyway.

"Have a seat," Emily said and shuffled along her bench seat. "She's free now."

"Are you sure?" CJ asked. It wasn't like her friend to allow her to get away with an unanswered question. Though her avoidance of the question was an answer in itself.

"I am." Emily patted the seat beside her. "Sit down, Mr. Stuart Jones of the Salt Lake Tribune, and let's get you some coffee." Emily waved the waitress over and ordered more drinks.

"How did you know where to find me?" CJ asked, suddenly a little disconcerted that she'd been so easily located.

"Your agent, Paige Bailey, let me know." He positioned a recording device on the table between them. "She said she'd email you to let you know to expect me."

Emily slapped her hand on the table and made Jones jump. "Paige Bailey? Isn't that Elodie Fontaine's agent? God, I love her. So, so amazing in *Night Deeds*. Do you know her? Have you met her? She's someone I could turn for, just for a night."

CJ ignored Emily's barrage of questions and focused on her final statement. "I don't suppose that I can be offended that you'd choose Elodie Fontaine over me. She is an Oscar-winning superstar and I'm just a reality TV show pleb." CJ pulled her phone from her bag to see she had two missed calls, several texts, and an email from Paige. She'd forgotten she had the Find my Friend app still active, something Paige had insisted on to "keep my favorite client safe." How she could be Paige's favorite client when, as Emily had just pointed out, she had Elodie Fontaine on her books was beyond believability, but it always made CJ feel good to hear it anyway. She flicked through the missed communications and saw Paige had tried all she could to let her know. It was hard to be annoyed when an interview with a city paper would raise her profile and help Paige's quest to find a new syndicate for her show. Regardless, CJ turned her location setting off and made a note to ask Paige *not* to share her location with the press until she'd okayed it.

"So, Ms. Johnson—"

"Please, call me Callie."

Jones smiled and nodded. "Callie. According to your agent, you've come home to Salt Lake for a break. How did you end up working at the Bryan's Funeral Home?"

CJ gave him the full version, including her apprenticeship with the Bryans and the tragic death of Iris Bryan. She withheld the bit about Iris being like a mother to her. Her actual mom would likely read this article, and there was little to be gained from making her feel bad about her parental failure. They went back and forth about the kind of work she'd expected to do at Bryan's before he got to why he'd come to interview her.

"Did Mrs. Arnold know you were working at that funeral home before she placed her husband's body in your care?"

"I have no idea, I'm afraid." Though she wouldn't have put it past

Bernie to have let that nugget slip if Bryan's had been one of several funeral homes Mrs. Arnold had called, looking for a satisfactory price. He was one of the top three businesses in Utah and his prices matched his reputation so telling Mrs. Arnold that CJ was working there might have provided the push she needed to spend her widower's cash with him.

"That's a question best answered by Mr. Bryan."

"He's my next stop." Jones wrote notes to accompany his recording. "According to the police report, Mr. Arnold suffered over two hundred post-mortem incisions all over his body. How long did it take you to address those wounds?"

She'd never heard it phrased quite like that before, but it was as good a description as any. "A little under two days." It wasn't her place to tell Jones that Mrs. Arnold had wanted all the incisions reversed despite CJ suggesting that she only "addressed" the parts of Mr. Arnold that would be visible in an open casket.

"I want him as perfect in death as he was in life. He'd want that. Damn it, the man was so vain he'd most likely haunt me if I took the shortcut you're suggesting. I don't care how long it takes. I want him perfect again. That bastard doesn't get to send him to the grave looking that way."

And then her strong façade fell away, and she sobbed. CJ held her for several minutes before she managed to compose herself and left CJ to her task. When she returned two days later to view CJ's work, she sobbed again, but this time, they were tears of a different nature. She'd tried to get CJ to accept additional payment just for her, but CJ didn't take it. It was enough for her to see the peace she'd given Mrs. Arnold through her work. That had always been enough.

"Over two hundred cuts?" Emily asked. "That's crazy."

Jones hovered his hand over his machine, perhaps considering whether to hit pause and ask Emily to stay quiet during his interview. He looked across at CJ and she shot him a warning look. He moved his hand to his coffee mug and took a sip. Good decision. If he'd been an ass about it, CJ would've stopped the interview and rescheduled for another day.

"Will Mrs. Arnold will be having an open casket for the funeral on Tuesday?" Jones asked.

CJ didn't answer immediately, unsure if that was something she should reveal. Mrs. Arnold had widely advertised the funeral though, and they were expecting at least one hundred people. They'd know soon enough.

"Yes. It's important for families to remember their loved ones in death as they saw them in life." She smiled inwardly as she recited one of the first things Bernie and Iris had drilled into her. She hoped Iris would be proud. Her eyes welled up and she shuddered.

"CJ? Are you okay?" Emily reached over the table and held her hand.

"Yeah, yeah, I'm fine." CJ took a deep breath and swallowed her grief. *That* was something she needed to deal with. Clearly, not being able to attend Iris's funeral and say a proper goodbye had left a mark. She hadn't been to the grave either, and she'd had free time in the evenings after work. The realization that she'd been avoiding it knocked her off-kilter. Her old coping mechanism resurfaced, and she had the desire to rush from the diner and hide in her room.

That was old Callie behavior, and she wasn't about to succumb to it as an adult. She'd go by the grave after this interview and after she'd dropped Emily home. Iris deserved a real goodbye. CJ owed her that much. She smiled at Jones. Paige wouldn't be impressed that she was pushing for a short interview, but some things were more important. "Do you have any more questions, Stuart? I need to be somewhere else."

Chapter Thirteen

DAK BOLTED UPRIGHT AS the shot thundered past her ear. Her eyes sprang open, and she looked around the room frantically. The partially familiar surroundings slowly came into focus, and she pressed her palm to her chest and told herself to relax. She hadn't had that nightmare for more than three years. The mere mention of her old partner to CJ had been enough to trigger it and undo her attempts to repress the memory.

CJ. The other side of Dak's bed was empty, the covers tossed aside. She held her hand against the mattress: chilled. CJ had been gone for a while. Dak checked the bedside clock to see it was nearly noon. No wonder CJ had gone. Dak didn't remember falling asleep. With CJ wrapped up in her arms, she'd practically fallen unconscious after they finally stopped having sex, and she'd slept like a contented baby. Dak didn't sleep in beyond seven a.m. even on weekends. CJ had exhausted her.

Dak put her hand to her chest again. She was slick with sweat and needed a shower. She swung her legs out of bed and headed for the bathroom. Her stomach ached like she'd done a three-hour core workout. She grabbed the discarded dildo from the bottom of the bed to wash it, remembering that she *had* done a three-hour core workout. She dropped it in the sink, turned on the shower, and got in without waiting for the water to warm.

She rested her head against the tiled wall and closed her eyes. Thoughts of Ben, her dead partner, invaded her mind and demanded attention. The agency-enforced therapy she'd attended taught her to allow those thoughts access, to process them, and then file them away. It sounded easy when it was so clinically phrased. But Ben hadn't died in the agency's therapist's arms after he'd pushed her from the path of a gunman's bullet. Their cold case went white-hot after the suspect they'd tracked down had killed a Federal Agent. And Dak's temper had flared white-hot too. It had taken three cops from the Santa Fe PD to wrestle her from the killer and force her hands from around his throat.

Shower gel squirted from the bottle all over the shower floor. She hadn't realized she'd even picked it up, let alone that she was squeezing the thing. It was June, she reasoned while using her foot to push the slippery substance into the drain. The anniversary of Ben's death was less than a week away. She always gave herself that week to think about him, but this new serial killer case had been filling her mind. Between that and CJ, she'd had no space for Ben. *That* was why she'd had the nightmare. It was his way of getting her attention. He hated being ignored. Hamilton reminded her of Ben too, and she didn't know why she hadn't seen it before. With her temporary partner being a mix of her little brother and her old partner, it was little wonder she was struggling to keep him at a distance.

Dak used what was left of the shower gel to clean up. Wallace Arnold's funeral was the same date as Ben's death. She resolved to make time for her annual ritual at the church and light a candle before or after the funeral. She didn't know if he was still around somewhere or if death was the end of everything. It was more a remembrance ritual than any solid belief that this life was one of many or that there was an afterlife. On reflective moments like this, she was strangely comforted by the thought that there was something after this life.

She got out of the shower, dried off, and brushed her teeth before pulling on some old jeans, a T-shirt, and boots. She'd promised Roger that she'd help him replace all the tubing systems and joints on the Shelby's water coolant system. She hoped CJ might be there so they could spend some more time together. After CJ had explained last night, Dak now understood her complicated relationship with her parents, and she admired how CJ was trying her best to simply let it be after doing so much work on herself in therapy. She'd been so open about that, and it had probably been the perfect opportunity for Dak to expand on her mysterious sentence about having had a partner, but the moment had passed. Dak had become engrossed in CJ's story and, if she were honest, she hadn't wanted to talk about Ben, not yet.

Though after what CJ had said about not needing conversations or dates and just heading straight to sex, maybe they would never get to that difficult conversation. Her doorbell sounded, thankfully pulling her out of her meandering thoughts. She only had a few hours of downtime left, and she didn't want to spend it in the past or with the maybes. Dak jogged down the stairs to see Roger through the glass of her front door. "Hey, Rog. I was just getting ready to come over. I'll be with you after I grab something to eat."

"No need for that. Fran's been making waffles. Can I interest you in some?"

Dak patted Roger on the shoulder. "You can always interest me in waffles." She resisted asking whether CJ would be joining them. She'd said she was spending as little time as possible at the house, hence the vacation job at the funeral home. "Lead the way."

Roger seemed to hesitate and look beyond her as if he was expecting someone else. CJ maybe? Dak grabbed her phone, closed the door behind her, and followed Roger back to his kitchen. She checked for calls or texts, expecting Hamilton but hoping for CJ. Instead, she had a missed call and two texts from her mom. The amazing aroma of freshly baked waffles hit her before she stepped across the threshold. She recalled CJ saying that her mom had been the queen of microwave and takeout meals when CJ was a kid and was now trying to be Martha Stewart. "Hi, Mrs. J."

Mrs. J pulled a tray of waffles from the oven and turned around. "Afternoon, Dak. How are you?"

"I'm good. How's everything with you?"

"Just enjoying a relaxing Sunday. Is Calista not with you?"

"Nope." Dak had been here for countless meals over the past few months, but suddenly she had the feeling that there might be an ulterior motive for Roger's kind invitation. "Thanks for having me over. You've saved me from a bowl of dry granola and black coffee. I forgot milk at the store."

"Did you have a nice time last night?" Roger poured a mug of coffee and handed it to Dak.

And there it was. She smiled at Roger's attempt to inject innocent interest into his question when he was talking to the woman who'd taken his daughter out for a date and didn't bring her home. Had she even been home? "I did. Thanks for asking."

Roger plated waffles for the three of them from a stack of four plates. Yep, they'd thought CJ was still at her place. Maybe they were worried about her.

"Shall we sit at the table?" Roger set the plates down and collected a pan of bacon from the stove.

Dak placed her mug on a coaster and chose a side seat, respectfully leaving the head of the table for Roger. But both he and Mrs. J sat opposite her. The whole thing was shaping up to be a cross between an intervention and a pre-prom night lecture. After the marathon sex session she and CJ indulged in last night, it was a little late for either, and she felt sure CJ should probably be in this seat rather than her.

"Help yourself, Dak," Mrs. J said.

Dak topped her waffle stack with bacon and syrup and dug in, feeling the need to eat as fast as she could and get out of there. But she'd promised to help Roger with the car, so this was just the beginning of the inquisition.

"CJ wasn't still with you?" Roger asked around a mouthful of food.

Dak shook her head. "I didn't wake up until after twelve." God, this was awkward. "She wasn't there. Do you have reason to be worried about her?" It occurred to Dak that she barely knew CJ. There could be all manner of issues she had no knowledge of. She hoped her parents didn't feel the need to censor CJ's sex life. CJ was a grown woman, and if she wanted to sleep with a hundred women on a first date, that was her prerogative.

"We're not worried, as such," said Mrs. J and sighed.

She looked like she was second-guessing herself and what she was about to say. Whatever it was, Dak wanted her to spit it out because this was fast becoming the most awkward scenario she'd ever experienced. And that was saying something considering her occupation.

"We know you haven't spent a lot of time with Calista—sorry, CJ—but has she talked to you about her childhood at all?" Mrs. J picked up a piece of bacon and pushed it around the edge of her plate aimlessly. "Has she told you what awful parents we were?"

Dak almost choked on a chunk of waffle. She hadn't expected that kind of honesty and bet that CJ would like to hear that admission before they said it to a relative stranger. What was she supposed to do with that? CJ hadn't said she was speaking to Dak in confidence, but the confidence was implied. She doubted CJ had anticipated her parents quizzing her date.

When Dak didn't answer, Mrs. J shook her head and dropped the bacon back onto her plate. "Sorry, we shouldn't be asking you a question like that. It's just that this is the first time we've seen Cal—CJ—in over three years, and it was only recently that we acknowledged our mortality. Our time could be up at any moment." She laughed. "Of course, working with death every day, you know that."

"I learned that earlier than most people, yep." Dak said nothing more. Mrs. J needed to talk, and Dak would allow her the space to do so, for now. Mrs. J gave a tight smile. "We made a lot of mistakes as parents, and we thought we had all the time in the world to rectify them, or at least make up for them. But you don't. Not when the people you've let down simply stay away. And we understand why she stays away. Why would she come home to be ignored and neglected? But if she's never home, how can we show her we've changed, and that we want to do better as parents?"

"Is this a practice run?" Dak asked, trying to be as polite as possible but a fierce protectiveness had kicked in from somewhere and she couldn't help herself.

"Dak—"

She ignored Roger's interruption. "Because it's not me you should be telling this to, and I think you know that. CJ is the only one who needs to hear what you have to say. You shouldn't be telling me. I've known your daughter a week, and we've spent less than a full day together—"

"Yes, and we've never seen her so full of life—"

"That's probably nothing to do with me, Mrs. J. The fact is, you don't *know* your daughter anymore." Dak withheld the "if you ever did" part of the sentence. She was still in their house and was trying to remain respectful. She'd like to think CJ had been brighter after spending time with her, but it was far more likely that CJ was a brighter, happier person simply because she'd gotten out of a toxic family environment and had participated in extensive therapy sessions to let it all go.

Roger nodded. "You're right." He took Mrs. J's hand and looked at her. "She's right, Fran. We're being cowards. We can't change things just by acting differently, by how we think Calis—damn it—CJ wants us to be. We need to talk to her. We have to apologize."

Dak's phone rang in her pocket. "I'm sorry, I need to check this. It could be work." She pulled it out, reprimanding herself for hoping it was Hamilton. Nobody should die just to get her out of this uncomfortable situation.

"We've got our next body, Farrell." Hamilton sounded tired already.

Dak excused herself from the table and went out onto the patio. "You're sure?"

"I just got the call, so no, I haven't confirmed it yet. But the unis that found him are pretty sure. Do you want me to pick you up on the way or do you want me to meet you there?"

She didn't hesitate. "I'll meet you there. Text me the location." The brunch with CJ's parents had gotten weird enough. She didn't want to stay for any more of it, even though Mrs. J's waffles were up there in Dak's top three. Roger would have to fix his coolant system alone.

"I'm a half hour away, but you'll probably get there before me. Location sent. See you shortly."

Dak ended the call and re-entered the kitchen. "I'm afraid I have to go. Thank you for the waffles."

"You're welcome, Dak," said Mrs. J, "and thank you for the advice."

"It's a crime scene, Rog, so I won't be back to help with the car. Sorry." Roger waved her away. "Don't worry about that. You need to concentrate on catching this serial killer. I'm glad I'm not ten years younger."

Dak nodded and left, not pointing out that he wasn't in quite the same physical shape as the rest of the victims, and she suspected he hadn't been even ten years ago. She jogged to her house, quickly changed into a more suitable work outfit, and drove to the location Hamilton had sent. It was a fancy neighborhood outside the city that she hadn't had cause to visit before. The houses were huge and a good distance from each other, and all of them had long, tree-lined driveways. She saw a squad car at the entrance to a driveway and showed the patrol her badge. The officer stepped aside and let Dak in.

The guy's mansion stood proud at the end of the driveway, but it was the captain's car she noticed more than the architecture. Of course Burnett would be there for this red ball murder. She didn't recognize the Lexus parked alongside Burnett's car until the assistant chief got out, his phone pressed to his ear.

"Farrell!"

She looked back to the house and saw Burnett at the bottom of the steps at the front entrance. Dak pulled up, left her window down for air, and got out. The heat of the day had passed, but it was still nearly ninety degrees and Betty didn't have A/C.

"Nice truck." Burnett nodded toward Betty. "No wonder it took so long for you to get here."

Dak ignored the dig and made her way up the steps. "Is the body inside?"

Burnett caught hold of Dak's forearm. "We need this case closed,

Farrell. I'm getting way too much heat from the top." He jutted his chin toward the assistant chief, Lansen, as he strode toward them, still engrossed in a phone conversation.

Dak wanted to get inside before he reached them. She didn't have the best reputation for liaising with the people at the top who were mostly interested in managing crime for political reasons.

"I can give you Davis, Earl, Marks, and Williams for another two weeks, and you let me know if you need more help. We can't keep losing these people."

"These people." She knew exactly what that meant: rich, white guys in powerful places. If the latest dead guy was in politics, she'd be surprised if the chief didn't show up too. Dak looked down at Burnett's hand, and he released her before she had to ask him to do so. "We're running down everything we can, captain. It's like we told you at the last briefing, this guy has given us nothing at his first two scenes. Maybe this one will be different."

"How's Hamilton doing?"

She frowned. Seemed like a strange time to ask about the rookie's progress when there was a fresh body inside.

"Burnett, Farrell."

Too late to escape. "Assistant Chief," she said and nodded. She hadn't seen any journalists but with long lens capabilities, they could be in someone else's window taking pictures, so they all had to keep their case face on. Nobody wanted to see photos of themselves in the paper, grinning at the scene of a murder victim. "I need to get inside, captain."

"How's the case going, Farrell?"

Apparently Lansen didn't share her urgency to investigate the scene. She took a calming breath and provided a quick brief of where they were and what avenues they were investigating. So far, they had nothing. The gym and hospital staff checked out, and the surgeon, David Quentin, was at the top of his game: no malpractice suits or even the hint of incompetence. He also appeared to be a faithful husband. They couldn't find any skeletons or scandals associated with Wallace Arnold, unusual for a high-flying financier, but true. She told Lansen they'd be present at the funeral on Tuesday, and he asked her to send the details to his assistant so that he too could attend.

"Sure. I'll get Hamilton to do it after we've looked at the crime scene."

She motioned inside. "Speaking of which, I should get in there."

Lansen nodded. "Of course."

"Captain." Dak caught sight of Hamilton coming up the driveway but opted to go inside. She didn't want to spend another minute with the tall, smarmy Lansen, who she'd pegged as working his way up the ladder with his sights on governor, hell, maybe even president.

The officers inside guided her through to the "screening room," according to the plaque on the outside wall. Forensics were already inside, taking shots around and near the body, but no one had touched him, nor would they until she or Hamilton had given them the okay to do so.

Dak counted thirty seats in the large room that occupied about the same square footage as the ground floor of her temporary house, and the seats faced what should be a giant white screen.

The seats were no longer facing a plain screen, however. Positioned just in front of it was the completely naked body of their third victim, hung as if in flight from an intricately woven rope tree. This time, the wings weren't carved into the victim's flesh. They were fashioned from black rope and somehow fixed into the victim's back. Multiple incisions all over his body, just as with the other two victims.

"Martin Elliott, CEO of Silicone, a huge tech company in the top thirty of the Fortune Global 500. Single. No children. No ex-wives. Avowed bachelor."

Dak turned to Hamilton. "Our killer is going up in the world."

Hamilton waved a copy of *Time* magazine in his gloved hand. "He was the cover for this month's issue. I picked this up on the way through the enormous reception room."

They made their way closer to the body but stopped short of the mini stage, the oatmeal-colored carpet of which appeared to have a blood spill. "That's new." A large glass vessel just like the ones they'd seen at the previous two murders was in its usual position off to the side of the body, but it looked like it had been knocked over before it was corked.

"Tell me they're boot prints." Dak pointed to a series of blood patches leading away from the spillage toward the edge of the stage.

She and Hamilton leaned over them. Each of the large blotches appeared to have been brushed over in an attempt to scuff the imprints.

"Forensics might be able to rebuild an outline from that," Hamilton said.

Dead *Pretty*

Dak tamped down the rush of possibility from their first real clue. "Who's here?"

"Hearn."

"Excellent. She's the best your department has. Get her in here now." Dak slapped Hamilton on the back. "And get the guys in here to take down Elliott's body after Hearn's completed her work."

Hamilton grinned. "This could be a breakthrough, couldn't it?"

"Let's not get ahead of ourselves. The imprints might be too degraded to reconstruct. And a boot print isn't a fingerprint, buddy."

Hamilton's grin grew wider. "Who's your buddy?"

He tore out of the screening room before she could either take it back or punch him for being an ass. She hadn't called anyone her buddy since she'd lost Ben. Things were changing, and maybe that wasn't such a bad thing.

Chapter Fourteen

CJ SANK TO HER knees and placed the bouquet of pink carnations on Iris's grave. After Dak's impromptu lesson about flower meanings, CJ had checked out the Old Farmer's Almanac online, and it hadn't taken her long to decide on her flower choice. "I'll never forget you," she said, reinforcing the message she wanted to convey with the carnations.

Her sobs came unbidden, surprising her with their strength. Her chest heaved and her breathing became labored with the force of them. It took her a few minutes to gather herself and rein the sobbing back to a regular waterfall of tears. She'd never cried like this. It was probably a good thing she hadn't attended the funeral because her parents would've been baffled by her reaction. They had no idea how supportive and wonderful Iris had been during CJ's apprenticeship and beyond, even while she was building her life in LA. CJ owed Iris so much, and though she'd thanked her repeatedly, she never felt that she could ever show her gratitude enough.

"Are you okay, miss? I can bring you a soft cushion to sit on if you're going to be there for a while."

CJ looked up to the source of the softly spoken voice and smiled at the tall guy about her age standing a respectful distance from her. He was dressed in work overalls, leading her to think he was probably one of the grounds people at the cemetery. "That's really kind of you, but I'm okay." She used her sleeve to wipe away the tears on her cheeks.

The guy pulled a pack of tissues from his pocket, stepped forward, and offered them to her. "Are you a relative of Mrs. Bryan's? I don't recall seeing you at the funeral, but you do look familiar."

She waved away the tissues. "I'm ashamed to say that I had to miss the funeral, but I'm not a relative. I did my apprenticeship with the Bryans." There was no way she was doing that minor celebrity thing by adding "You probably recognize me from my show," but it made sense that someone who worked in a graveyard might be inclined to watch it.

"Ah, that's where I know you from, that TV show where you make dead people look like they're alive again."

She shrugged. That wasn't quite the goal, but it was close enough.

"Aren't you working there again? My brother said something about that. Old Man Bryan hadn't managed to replace his lovely wife on account of him being such a grumpy son of a bitch."

CJ clenched her jaw at the disrespectful reference to Bernie, but he had acknowledged Iris as being a wonderful woman in the same sentence, so she let it go. "Yeah. It's not long-term though. I'm just helping him out while I'm on a break from the show."

The guy nodded. "I see." He bowed slightly and backed away. "Well, I'm sorry to have disturbed you. I'll leave you to it."

"Thank you." CJ turned back to Iris's grave. "I'm surprised you didn't strike him with lightning for talking about Bernie like that," she whispered. Iris had always been protective of Bernie and defended her husband's personality to anyone who called him on it. In reality, he was only grumpy to people he didn't like. She laughed. He didn't like many people and preferred the company of his dog.

CJ pulled at some weeds around the tombstone and tossed them aside. "I hope you know how important you were to me, Iris. You were the mom I didn't get at home, and I'll love you forever for being there for me." CJ thought about her parents and what they'd said about being affected by Iris's death. She'd dismissed it, but maybe that was their way of working up to talking about the past. And then there was Dak's philosophy about people changing and making the most of the time you had with the people you loved and who loved you. CJ knew her parents loved her—she hadn't when she was a kid—but their way of showing it was flawed. But who was she to expect that everyone should be perfect at arguably the toughest job in the world? If she was going to move forward and have any kind of relationship with them at all, she had to give them a clean slate. She had to forgive them.

That issue settled in her mind, she decided to call Paige for a progress report.

Paige answered on the second ring. "CJ, my favorite client. How did the interview go? I assume Jones found you."

"About that," CJ said. "Please don't give my location out to people before you've spoken to me."

"I've known Stuart a long time—we went to college together—and I trust him. I wouldn't have given your whereabouts to just anyone. But I hear you, and I promise not to do it again. Time *was* of the essence though, CJ. He had a deadline to meet, and the funeral is on Tuesday. We need to get your name in the national papers to help us secure new syndication."

CJ closed her eyes briefly. Using the victims of a serial killer to further her career didn't sit well, and her stomach grumbled around the delicious cherry pie from the diner. "How are things going with that?"

"Very well indeed. Drum roll, please."

CJ realized Paige was being serious when the line went silent for longer than a pause for breath. She plucked a weed from the ground beside her. "I'm in the middle of a graveyard, Paige. No exciting drum roll, sorry."

"The producer and I have a meeting on Friday with Netflix."

"Netflix?" CJ clamped her other hand over her mouth. "Are you serious?"

"I never joke about my clients' careers, CJ, you know that."

"But Netflix?" She glanced around again, thankful the place was still void of visitors.

"I told you everything would be fine. You sit tight in Salt Lake and keep up the great publicity with the serial killer work. That's just gold, CJ, gold. It must've been fate."

CJ shook her head. She couldn't envisage fate being such a bitch that CJ's career held more value than the lives of the victims. "That's a pretty sick thought, Paige."

"You don't pay me to be politically correct or empathetic, though I'm obviously sorry for the families of the victims. You pay me to keep you on TV and in the lifestyle to which you've become accustomed."

CJ shrugged. She did like the life she'd been living for the past three years, and she loved her Ferrari, but being back home, spending time with Emily, being back at the Bryans', and her relationship with Dak wasn't such a bad alternative. She also loved the big challenges the TV show offered. "Would Netflix be worldwide or just in America?" Coming home with very little in the bank to show for three years of work had been niggling at her since she'd returned. If she was lucky enough to get back onscreen, CJ wanted things to be different. A Ferrari was a wonderful thing, but it wouldn't sustain her forever.

"There are so many possibilities with this development, CJ. If the show was a hit in the rest of the world, we could take you to Europe to record episodes in other countries. The potential is massive."

"Wow, Paige, that's something else." She touched Iris's tombstone. *You opened these doors for me.*

"Like I said to you, a few weeks away would be good for your career. Gold, I said, and I wasn't wrong."

A few weeks at home had sounded like purgatory when Paige had suggested it. She was a week in and coping just fine.

"Is there anything you need?" Paige asked. "Or anyone? I could fly one of your regular friends out to play, if you wanted."

CJ grinned at the thought of the new friend she was already playing with. "I've got that covered, thanks, Paige."

"Ooh, do tell."

"There's an FBI agent on the case, and she happens to be living next to my parents while she's in the city."

"Oh, yes. I've seen the photos. Even in grainy newsprint, she's a handsome one."

CJ nibbled her lip. "You should see her in the flesh."

"And I assume you already have?"

"You know I'm not one to kiss and tell, Paige." Sharing the details with her best friend was different. "But I'm having fun, so you don't need to worry about me."

"Good. And how are things with your parents? Are they testing the limits of your therapy-influenced Zen?"

"They were. That's why I got the job at the funeral home." That, and the cash was nice too. No longer in Hollywood, she was having to buy everything herself. It had taken her three years of hard work and nothing to show after it to begin learning the value of saving for her future. It was one thing to live in the present, entirely another to ignore what was to come. "But we're making peace. They seem to have changed, and they're making a big effort to be good parents."

"Sounds like they might end up being responsible for you getting a big step up in your career. The heat you're getting because of your work on this murder has played a huge part in me getting the Netflix meeting."

CJ didn't want to dwell on that latter part. "Yeah, yeah, I get that."

"The Arnold funeral is on Tuesday, isn't it?"

"Yeah, the family are expecting a big turnout."

"I think you'll get a lot more people than you bargained for. Word on

Dead *Pretty*

the online sites has spread. You'll have a big fan contingent coming your way. You might want to consider switching to a large venue."

"That's not my decision, Paige, but is that true? Are people going to come because of me?" CJ had a feeling Wallace Arnold's family wouldn't appreciate that. She'd have to call Bernie later and let him know. And maybe Dak could do something about it and keep the show's fans behind a police cordon and away from the actual service. CJ had made Wallace perfect again for his family to be at peace. There'd be no peace if hundreds of the show's fans invaded the ceremony just to look at her work. It didn't exactly smack of respect for the dead.

"Of course. *Dead Pretty* is a popular show with a lot of die-hard fans who'll jump at any opportunity to see you, especially in person. You sound a little freaked out by the possibility. Do you have to be at the funeral?"

"Mr. Bryan likes me to be there, yes. Why, what did you have in mind?"

"How about me and Sian fly out? We can handle the press, and we'll organize a separate fan event at the same time as the funeral. That should bring most of the fans to us and away from the service. What do you think?"

"I think you're earning your twelve percent, Agent Paige," CJ said, a rush of relief running through her.

"Agent Paige. That makes me sound very official. I could make that my legal name, so everyone had to address me as Agent Paige." She chuckled. "That's agreed then. We'll get a flight out to you late tonight or early tomorrow morning. Sian will send you the details, along with the location of the fan event. We'll share everything on the official show social networks, but you should share it too, okay?"

CJ nodded. "Yep, absolutely. Thank you."

"No, thank *you*, superstar."

CJ didn't feel like a superstar, but she didn't mind the title. The thought reminded her of Emily. "Can you do me a little favor?"

"Of course, anything."

"My old best friend from high school has a girl crush on Elodie Fontaine. Would you be able to get a signed headshot sent to me, for Emily Woods?"

"Absolutely. I might even be able to bring it with us. Elodie is such a darling."

CJ smiled. She would've liked to have found out exactly how much of a darling Elodie was, but she'd been all loved up with the award-winning journalist Madison Ford for five years and had reined in her playgirl days. Now *there* was a hot lesbian power couple she would've loved a threesome with. "Perfect. Thanks, Agent Paige. I'll see you soon."

She ended the call, thinking of Agent Dak and the incredibly hot sex they'd shared for much of the night. "Sorry, Iris," she said, remembering where she was, though Iris had been understanding and supportive of CJ's sexuality too, encouraging her to explore herself fully. She switched to WhatsApp and sent a message to Dak.

Are you free tonight?

She didn't have to wait long before *typing* appeared beneath Dak's name.

Sorry, I don't think I'll be home until late. We've got another victim.

Christ, that wasn't good. *I need to talk to you about the funeral.* CJ gave a few quick details about the fans gathering and Paige's plan to pull them away from the funeral.

What time will you go to bed?

CJ grinned. *I could be in your bed waiting for you...* She added the devil face emoji for good measure.

So no second date?

I learned enough last night to know we can talk and have sex. Best of both worlds. CJ glanced around the cemetery once again and noticed a few more people had filtered in. She stood up and dusted the grass from her knees and butt. She kissed her fingers and placed the kiss on Iris's tombstone. "Thank you, for *everything.*"

Her phone buzzed a response from Dak.

The back door key is in the garage under the 45lb kettlebell

Jesus, that was nearly half CJ's bodyweight. *If I don't pull my arms off lifting that thing up, I'll see you in bed, stud x*

Can't wait. I'll be with you as soon as I can

CJ slipped her phone back into her clutch and retrieved her car keys. She checked her watch. She had plenty of time to go home and have a serious talk with her mom and dad and get something to eat—probably another gourmet meal her mom had been practicing—before she headed to Dak's place to wait for her. Emily's question popped back up in CJ's mind, but she didn't see the point in spending any time thinking about it. Another victim meant Dak would be around longer, but Paige's news could mean CJ wouldn't still be here in a couple of weeks. However things panned out, she and Dak weren't going to be in the same city for any real length of time so whether or not she could develop serious feelings for Dak was a moot point. She would shove Emily's question to the back of her mind so that she could enjoy Dak in the current moment. After all, death could be around the corner for any of them at any time. Living in the moment was all she had.

Chapter Fifteen

DAK PARKED HAMILTON'S DODGE Charger in the parking lot. It looked out of place among the Porsches, Ferraris, and Aston Martins. "Do rich people have a thing against American cars that I don't know about?"

"Why don't you ask Callie? She drives a Ferrari, doesn't she?"

Dak got out of the car and gave a short laugh. "Funny boy. Her father has a Shelby Mustang. I think she might've bought the Ferrari just to mess with him."

"Ah, Daddy issues. Good luck with that."

"Asshole." She would've punched him, but he wasn't close enough.

"It feels good to be bringing someone in, doesn't it?" Hamilton pulled his badge from his pocket and hooked it onto his belt.

She held the door for him, and they entered the gym where their first real suspect worked. Some digging from the forensics team had shown all three victims used this gym and the same trainer. "I'll let you know in a few hours." Dak was always careful not to get caught up in the excitement of questioning a new suspect. She'd seen how easy it was to get fixated on the wrong person, to the exclusion of more compelling evidence that pointed in a completely different direction. She strode toward reception and smiled at the young man behind the counter, noting his name. "Morning, Ryan. We're looking for Billy Taylor. We were told he was working today."

When they'd gone to pick Taylor up from his home, his elderly neighbor guessed he was working but hadn't been able to tell them much more than that. She'd said she rarely saw him and hadn't spoken to him much since he'd moved in a few months ago. That nugget of information had piqued Dak's interest in him. The neighbor couldn't recall when he'd moved in or whether he'd come from out of town, but it was possible that he'd moved into the area around the same time as the murders had started.

Ryan pointed to Dak's badge on her jacket pocket. "Are you the police?"

She nodded toward Hamilton. "He is. I'm with the FBI."

Ryan looked impressed and edged forward on his chair. "Is this about those guys that were murdered and sliced up?"

Dak sighed. Why were civilians always so fascinated by serial killers? Books, films, TV shows were testament to their appeal. Her brother had even sent her an adult coloring book of "true crime monsters" for her birthday. She'd re-gifted that to Hamilton, and he'd loved it. But it wasn't the obsession that bothered her the most, it was the lack of respect for the victims.

"That's right," Hamilton said. "So, is he working or not?"

He must've sensed her irritation, and his firm tone made it clear they were done talking with Ryan.

"Oh, yeah, sorry. I'll see if he's available."

Ryan used a two-way radio to put out the call, but he had the good sense not to announce why Taylor was being called to reception.

"Don't want to spook the clients," he said and put the radio back in its charging cradle. "Some of the big guys here have already started traveling in pairs to come here, and we've had a few membership cancellations. Management's getting—"

"Management's getting what, Ryan?" The woman who asked the question came from behind Dak and Hamilton and made her way behind the desk with Ryan. "And why are you here?"

"I'm Special Agent Farrell of the FBI, and this is Detective Hamilton of the Salt Lake City police department. We need to talk to Billy Taylor about the recent murders. He was the personal trainer for all three of the victims. We need him to come down to the station to answer some questions," Dak said, keeping her tone even and calm. The woman hadn't asked who they were, and it was clear she'd seen they were cops from the head-to-toe appraisal she'd done of them when she walked in, but it didn't hurt to make her aware she wasn't dealing with just the local police.

Taylor entered the reception from the main floor of the gym. His beaming smile soon faded into an unfriendly glare as he got closer and saw their badges.

"Billy," the woman said. "The FBI want to question you about the serial killings. Is there something you want to tell me about that you didn't put on your resume? 'Likes working out, entering cross-fit competitions, and slaughtering rich white men?'"

Dak hadn't expected that, but it gave her the opportunity to study his reaction. His brow creased almost imperceptibly, but he gave nothing else away in his expression. Ryan guffawed until the woman shot him a look that could wither a rose.

"No, Ms. Lewis, of course not," Billy said, his smile returning for her benefit. He locked eyes with Hamilton. "I have a client in twenty minutes. That's all the time I can offer you."

Dak was never surprised when men ignored her, preferring to address her male colleagues, but it was still a source of irritation, like a tiny splinter that she couldn't get at. "We need you to come down to the station."

He shook his head. "Then it'll have to wait 'til I've finished work."

Hamilton took a half-step forward and Dak caught his arm. Rattling Taylor here would serve no purpose when they could do it at the station in a controlled environment and with the cameras capturing every moment of the interaction. Dak favored a compliant interviewee, one who thought they were in control of the process. "Okay, that's no problem, Billy. We're just glad that you're happy to help with our inquiries. We don't want to inconvenience you." She pulled a card from her pocket with the station's details, handed it to him, and smiled. "What time is your last client?"

He took the card from her. "Four p.m. I can be there by six."

Dak widened her smile and nodded. "That'd be great. We'd really appreciate it."

Taylor studied the card then shoved it into his shorts' pocket. "Okay. I'll see you later," he said and went back into the main gym.

"If that's everything, *I'd* really appreciate if you left the building." Ms. Lewis placed her hands on the desk and leaned forward.

Dak looked at her and nodded. "Of course, Ms. Lewis. We don't want to disrupt your business." During their exchange, eight members had entered the building and given them sidelong glances or outright stares. She had no doubt the gym membership connection with the victims would have spooked staff and clients alike, although not one had made a call to PD to say all three victims were members. Helpful. Dak also didn't want to further antagonize Ms. Lewis lest she advise Taylor to get himself a lawyer before showing up at the station. "Thank you so much for your time, Ms. Lewis."

She turned and Hamilton followed.

"Please tell me that you're going to share the lesson I should learn from that exchange, Yoda." Hamilton pushed opened the door with a little more force than was necessary.

"Aren't I too tall to be Yoda? And yes, we can talk about it on the way over to Mrs. Jones. She wants an update on our progress, and Burnett wants us to do it in person because we're the ones who spoke to her."

"Don't they usually do that by email for convenience?" Hamilton began puffing on an electronic cigarette.

"Not today." Dak wafted her hands through the heavy cloud of white smoke he produced. "Christ, that's worse than the Vatican City chimney after they've chosen a new pope. You know there's very little research on those things. They're probably going to turn out to be worse than actual smoking."

"Give me some credit for my efforts. I'm working my way down to nicotine patches."

"You're doing great, padawan." Dak smiled and got in the car. She couldn't help liking that Hamilton had been cutting down on smoking since she'd repeatedly mentioned her distaste for the foul habit. Having a positive influence on him eased the guilt she felt for not being around to do the same for her actual brother. And maybe if Taylor turned out to be their killer and they could get this case wrapped up, she could spend some real time with Wade, and her mom of course, before she headed to Seattle for her next cold case. Walker had put it on hold while she'd extended Dak's period here, so it could wait for Dak to have a week with her family. Being around CJ and her family and advising her to give them a second chance had caused Dak to reevaluate her own behavior. Even if being home was painful, maybe spending some time with her own family would counteract that heartache. However it might turn out, Dak wasn't comfortable encouraging CJ to do something she wasn't prepared to do herself. If working on these cases taught her only one thing, it was that her time on this hunk of rock could end at any second, and there really *was* no time to waste.

***

Dak stared at the monitor and watched Billy Taylor closely, trying to decide how good a match he was for their killer. His shoe size matched the reconstructed boot print from Elliott's house, and he had the build that would enable him to move the victims around and hoist them into place. He was also the personal trainer for the surgeon, the financial advisor, and the CEO, a pretty massive coincidence if you believed in them. But Dak hadn't spent enough time with him yet to decide if he might be truly capable of the murders and artistry of their serial killer, but she was just about ready to find out.

He'd arrived an hour ago, and they'd placed him in the interview room alone while they "dealt with an emergency." It was a simple device that gave them the opportunity to see how he reacted. For the last ten minutes, she'd been observing him. He'd gotten up and started to pace the room. He began by circling the desk but soon took to putting his back to the wall and carefully placing one foot in front of the other, heel to toe, first along the width, and then the length of the small, rectangular space. He was methodical and calm. Either he was unfazed by being made to wait or he was using a tried and tested coping mechanism. Whichever it was, it spoke to his composure under pressure, and Dak didn't want to wait any longer to interrogate him.

She went back into the squad room to get Hamilton. "Let's take a run at him." She grabbed a bottle of water on the way. When they entered the interview room, Taylor remained standing and glared at them.

"If you say you need me to wait any longer, you can forget it." He tapped his watch. "You've kept me waiting over an hour."

Dak held up her hands. "I know, Billy, and we're really sorry about that. We had to look at some DNA evidence the killer left at the third crime scene."

"Oh." He turned away and walked back to the chair he'd been put in when they arrived.

He'd moved too quickly for Dak to catch any pupil dilation or change in his facial expression. She offered Taylor the bottle of water.

He took it and nodded. "Thanks."

She sat on the other side of the table, positioning herself between Taylor and the door, his escape to freedom. Hamilton sat beside her and placed his pad and pen on the metal table.

"Okay, so what's your name?" she asked.

"You know my name. Don't waste more of my time."

Dak indicated the steno pad Hamilton had in front of him, pen poised. "It's for the record, that's all. Can you tell me your name?"

Taylor looked to the sky and shook his head slowly. "Billy Taylor."

"Is that the full name on your birth certificate?"

He sighed deeply. "William Michael Taylor."

"And what's your date of birth?"

"Nine nine ninety."

"That's easy to remember," Dak said. "Tell me about your friends."

"What do you want to know about my friends for?"

"I'm interested."

"And what about him?" He motioned toward Hamilton.

"Him too. That's right, isn't it?"

"For sure." He tapped his pen on the pad. "I love hearing people's stories. I'm writing a screenplay. It's always good to get ideas for new characters."

Dak kept her expression neutral even though Hamilton's riff took her by surprise. "Is that right? I did *not* know that." See turned back to Taylor. "He's been my partner for nearly a year, and he's never told me about that." She shoved Hamilton. "Why have you never told me about that?"

"Because I thought you'd laugh and tell the rest of the squad, and then *they'd* laugh at me. I'm already the rookie here. If anybody knew about this, they'd never take me seriously."

Dak tilted her head. Hamilton was convincing enough that she could almost believe he was a budding writer. "Your secret's safe with me." She turned her attention back to Taylor. "And you're not going to tell anyone, are you?"

Taylor frowned. "Who am I gonna tell? None of my buddies are p—cops."

She let his near insult roll off her and didn't react. She wanted to maintain this as a conversation…for now. "Excellent. So, what do you and your friends do for fun?"

"I don't have much time for friends right now. I'm working a lot and building my client base."

"Doesn't the gym provide you with enough clients?"

"That's not how it works. I run some classes to get my face known, and I wander around the gym floor, giving members tips on form and suggesting exercises. From that, they approach me to become their personal trainer. They pay the gym. The gym takes a percentage cut. I invoice the gym for all my clients each month."

Dead *Pretty*

"So are you an employee or does that make you self-employed?"

"I run my own business. I have more control that way."

"That, I understand. I wish I could have more control in this job, like picking the easy murders that you can solve in a week. You know, the ones where the murderers make stupid mistakes and may as well have left their business card on the body."

Taylor laughed. "Wouldn't you miss out on the fun part that way?"

"The fun part?"

"Yeah, y'know, the battle between you and the killer, figuring out the clues and what the blood spatter tells you. I watch *NY CSI*. It looks like fun."

"Is it the chase you like?"

"Uh-huh, especially the ones where the murderer is really clever and gives the cops a run for the money. Have you watched *Dexter*, the season with John Lithgow as the serial killer who takes Dexter on and ends up killing his girlfriend? Or was she his wife by then? I don't know, but that was brilliant."

"I don't get much time for TV, but I've seen some of the *Dexter* episodes. Isn't that the guy who thinks his killings are justified?"

"*Thinks?* They are! And the way he kills them—it's like he gets sexual satisfaction from it. That part's creepy, but the rest of it, I love."

"Different people kill for different reasons, don't they? Some do it for sexual gratification—"

"And for revenge," Taylor said, bouncing in his chair a little.

"Others do it just for the fun of it, to test themselves against the police, or like the Artist that's running around Salt Lake. He thinks he's creating exhibitions with his victims."

Taylor shrugged and took a beat. "I've read that's what they think. One man's art is another man's trash."

"What do you think?"

"About what?"

"About killing people, cutting up their bodies, and calling it art?"

Taylor raised it eyebrows. "I'm just a personal trainer. I don't know anything about art." He shifted in his seat and placed his palms on the tabletop. "I've got work early in the morning, and I like to get my beauty sleep. What questions do you really want to ask, Special Agent Farrell?"

From jovial to serious in a heartbeat. This guy wasn't an average personal trainer, but Dak's internal danger radar wasn't blinking off the scale for this guy. He was hiding something, but it wasn't clear whether that was a penchant for killing people in creative ways. "You're right. We don't want to waste your time. Your colleagues at the gym say you're a good personal trainer."

He gave her a smug smile and straightened in his chair. "I'm the most popular trainer there, and I haven't even been there that long."

"No? How long have you worked there?"

"Just over a couple of months."

"Did you work at another gym in the city?"

"No, I moved here from Manhattan. I was a taxi driver there for a while, but I didn't like it much."

"When did you move here?"

"End of April."

A shot of adrenaline coursed through Dak's veins. Taylor's movements matched the start of the killings in Salt Lake. Now they had a city to check for unsolved murders with a similar MO. "So, you're the most popular trainer at your gym—how did you manage that in such a short space of time?"

"Charm and hard work. And I'm the best at what I do."

"But you haven't been doing it for long?"

"I haven't been doing it for long here. I was a competition bodybuilder before I started driving taxis. Now I do CrossFit. I'm working my way up the rankings. Then I can give this up and earn a few million winning the CrossFit challenges."

"You want to be rich?"

"Doesn't everyone?"

Dak shook her head. "Some people hate how the top one percent of rich people have nearly fifty percent of the global wealth. They think it should be shared more widely."

"Isn't that called communism? Screw that. I'm an American, and I want to live the dream."

"All of your clients are living that dream, I guess. They'd have to be to afford the membership fees."

Taylor nodded and laughed lightly. "You're funny for a Fed. But yeah, it's a gym for the rich. I went to Martin's house once. He wanted my help deciding on equipment for a space he was turning into his home gym.

Dead *Pretty*

Goddamn, it was nearly as big as our commercial gym. He really didn't need to waste five thousand dollars on our membership when he could've just had me come over to his house five times a week instead."

There it was. It'd been a while since she'd mentioned DNA evidence at Martin Elliott's house and here was Taylor giving her a reason that his DNA might be present, and he'd slipped it into the conversation nice and naturally. "Do you do home training for any of the gym's clients?"

"No. I've got private clients, but they didn't come from work. Ms. Lewis would fire me if I did that."

"Did you go to the houses of Wallace Arnold or David Quentin and help them set their gyms up?"

Taylor's eyes flickered momentarily. He unscrewed the cap from the water bottle and took a drink, a long drink. Was he trying to figure out whether they had DNA on him at those two crime scenes?

"Yeah, I did, actually. But Wallace didn't really have the room for anything substantial, and David just didn't bother."

Now he'd placed himself at all three scenes legitimately, the presence of his DNA there—even if they had any—wouldn't stand up as evidence to him being the killer. They would have to check the layouts of the victims' respective homes, but it very much sounded like Taylor knew the inside of all three.

"Did you go alone to the houses?"

"Yeah. But I took some pictures so you can check the dates from those, if you need to."

Clever son of a bitch. If he was the killer, he'd thought it through long before he went back to the house to actually murder his victims and secured himself irrefutable evidence that there was good reason for his DNA to be present at each of the crime scenes and that it was there *before* the murders had taken place.

"Would you say that you're friends with your clients?"

Taylor shook his head. "That's like asking you if you're friends with the criminals you arrest. Of course not. They're just a means to an end for me. And Ms. Lewis tells everyone not to get cozy with clients."

Dak didn't bother to challenge Taylor's comparison of his clients to murderers and rapists. "Is that all they are? Don't you see them in any other capacity than the number of dollars you can get from them?"

He narrowed his eyes and tilted his head to the side. "Are you asking about the female clients?"

"Do you want to tell me about them?"

"There are some clients I wouldn't mind having relations with." He winked at her. "You know what I mean, don't you? I reckon you appreciate a fine-looking woman with a body to die for."

She shrugged and smirked but said nothing.

"Some of them make it hard for me to resist. All that money, bodies in perfect condition, husbands who neglect them. I'd be doing them a favor." He leaned back in his chair and spread his legs wider. "But I can't. I've got a plan, and I'm sticking to it."

This guy was good. Unruffled and even brazen enough to establish camaraderie with her. He'd barely acknowledged Hamilton since they'd started the interview, a complete reversal from this morning when they'd gone to the gym to bring him in. The killer's victims were all male and of a similar build to Hamilton. Did Taylor have to ignore Hamilton to avoid distraction, to avoid going off into whatever world he entered that led him to kill?

"Do your clients think you're friends?"

"You mean the guys?" He sneered and shook his head. "Most of them treat me like the hired help, which I suppose I am, but there's ways of treating people, you know? When I'm rich, I won't act like that. There's just no need."

This was his first show of anger, but it wasn't rage, and it didn't indicate a motive toward killing the rich guys. Taylor had ample opportunity, but she couldn't get a handle on what motive he might have. But there was something he wasn't prepared to share with them that had involved him being in their houses. Either that, or he was hedging his bets that they'd found his DNA at the crime scenes. "What about Elliott, or Quentin, or Arnold? Were they rich assholes too?"

He nodded. "Quentin was a dick. He thought he was God's gift to everyone. Hell, he might've even thought he *was* God. But the other two were okay. Elliott was nice enough, but I reckon that was mostly for show. I'm not sure that's who he was under the surface. And Arnold was a man's man. He was about the only one I could see myself going for a few drinks with. He was charming and a real hit with the women. He would've made a great wingman. I bet we could've gotten some serious pussy together."

He maintained eye contact and gave her a grin that made her want to smack him in the mouth, but she smiled back. "I'll bet you could." She couldn't quite decide if he was trying to goad her or make her like him by convincing her they had something in common. Either way, it was time to bring down the hammer. "Where were you on Saturday between the hours of seven p.m. and midnight?"

"At home," he said without hesitation, switching from player to astute murder suspect in a breath.

"Anybody there with you?"

"Nope. I'm between women."

"Any takeout deliveries in that time?"

Taylor shook his head. "I make all my own meals."

"Any phone calls?"

"I don't talk on the phone if I can help it. I prefer messaging."

"Any conversations via messaging?"

"I'd have to check my phone, but I don't think so. I turn my phone off when I finish work so clients don't bother me. I like to keep Saturday nights just for me. I work out, do some meditation, and have an early night."

"Every Saturday?"

"*Every* Saturday."

The laughter and easy smile were gone. He was shutting down fast, and she'd gotten nothing from him that would warrant her arresting him or keeping him in for further questioning. All he'd actually done was gone on record and placed himself at all three victims' houses, thus giving his DNA reason to be present. "So you say you were at home the whole time on the nights of each of these murders, but you've got no one to back you up?" The lack of an alibi didn't look good for him, but with no other physical evidence, their case against him was anorexic.

"That's right. It's not a crime to be alone on a weekend, is it?"

"Nope, you're right. But we'd like to drive you home and take a look inside your house. Would that be okay with you?"

He laughed and shook his head. "No, it would definitely not be okay with me. I've cooperated with you. I came down and answered your questions. If you want to search my house, you're going to have to get a warrant."

Dak doubted any judge in the county would give her a warrant on the evidence they had against him, but Taylor probably wouldn't know that.

They could put a tail on him, and maybe he'd go home and gather any incriminating evidence and try to get rid of it. They'd stop him for a traffic violation and open his trunk to find yards of shibari rope and hopefully whatever souvenirs or trinkets he'd taken from his victims, like most serial killers did.

"You know, that looks bad, like you've got something to hide."

"I don't care how it looks. This is still a free country, and I have the right to deny you access to my property unless you have a warrant."

"Do you have something to hide, Billy?"

"I'm done here. If you're going to arrest me, say so, otherwise, let me go."

Dak leaned back in her chair and gestured to the door. "You're free to go."

He nodded and looked smug as he rose from his seat. "That's what I thought. Let me know if you've got any more questions for me, and I'll get myself a lawyer."

Hamilton stood. "I'll show you out," he said, opened the door, and left with their one and only suspect.

She caught the resignation and disappointment in his voice. He'd obviously pinned his hopes on Taylor being their guy and on him cracking at their first try. Dak was under no such illusions. A killer as organized and sophisticated as the Artist wouldn't just confess, especially when they had no real evidence. Dak had just used this initial interview to get a feel for Taylor, and she'd done that. He wasn't just what he said he was, she felt sure of that, but that didn't make him their killer. He'd given them something to work on, and if there turned out to be unsolved crimes in Manhattan, then maybe her radar might blink a little faster. They'd put a tail on him and see how he behaved over the next few days. But she wasn't convinced he was the guy they were looking for. Maybe they'd have better luck at the funeral tomorrow.

Chapter Sixteen

"THANKS FOR TAKING THE time to have dinner with us tonight, honey." Her mom laid a plate of home-made biscuits on the dining room table then headed back to the kitchen.

CJ leaned over the plate and inhaled deeply. They smelled as good as if God himself had made them.

"She's been perfecting that recipe for months," her father said, reaching over and taking one from the top of the pile. "They melt in your mouth. So moist. I could eat that whole plateful and still want more."

Judging from his burgeoning gut, he *had* been eating the platefuls her mom had been making over those months. Her mom returned with a golden turkey big enough to feed the whole street and put it on the table in front of her father. "Jeez, Mom, this is like Thanksgiving five months early. What's the occasion?"

Her mom squeezed her shoulder as she passed her before taking her seat on the opposite side of the table. "We've got some stuff to give thanks for, and we don't want to wait until November."

The penny dropped. This was another case of her parents making every moment count since their not-so-close brush with the Grim Reaper. That was okay. She'd wanted to have a serious talk with them, and it hadn't panned out yesterday after Emily called and invited her out for dinner. CJ recognized that she was avoiding her parents even though it was her idea to talk to them. But tomorrow was a big day with the funeral and the event Paige had organized. She wanted her head in the game, and the need for this conversation was taking up too much space in there. All the what ifs and what will they says were driving her to distraction.

"Roger, will you carve the turkey?"

The three of them made small talk while her dad served them all, and they piled the feast of food on their plates. But it felt like they were treading water, trying not to drown in the depth of the conversation waiting to be had. CJ took the plunge. "What do you want to give thanks for then,

Mom?"

Her mom had just loaded a forkful of turkey and green bean casserole, but she rested it on her plate. "Lots of things." She sighed and looked at CJ seriously. "But our main one is you."

Heat flushed CJ's face. She hadn't envisaged her mom saying anything quite that soppy. CJ blinked. They weren't tears that prickled the back of her eyes, damn it. They'd only just started to talk. What the hell? Her mom and dad held hands across the table, something she'd never seen them do. During her therapy, after CJ had revealed the lack of affection shown in her house as a kid, she'd soon been coaxed to realize that her lack of intimate connection beyond sex was a direct result. She suddenly thought of Saturday night with Dak. She'd been kidding herself that she'd left before Dak woke simply to avoid morning breath and the awkward dance of shall we or shall we not do this again? Admitting that she'd never been truly intimate with anyone was the first step to growth, but she hadn't taken any other steps since that realization. Maybe Dak was the prompt she needed to continue on that path.

"CJ, we were awful parents."

CJ blinked. "I'm sorry, what was that?" she asked her father because he surely hadn't just said what she thought she'd heard.

"We've been terrible parents," her mom said.

Nope, she'd heard it right. She couldn't bring herself to disagree though. And she knew she shouldn't. Her therapist had drilled it into her that honesty was the only policy if you wanted to develop real relationships. "You did your best."

"It wasn't anywhere near good enough," her father said. "I was never here. I was always at the base training other people's kids, and I had no time for you when I was at home." He pressed his lips together and laid his cutlery down. "No time and no patience."

"And I was too busy with my career to take the time to even try to be a good mom to you."

Her mom picked up her glass and took a sip of wine, perhaps for courage. CJ did the same, though she didn't really want it. Her hunger and thirst had both deserted her.

"You had to make your own way and grow up way too soon so you could look after yourself." Her mom's knuckles whitened as she gripped the stem of her glass. "And you didn't have a real mom until Iris Bryan took you under her wing."

CJ tensed her legs beneath the table. She had no idea her mom knew about her relationship with Iris.

"I'm sorry that you didn't get to say goodbye to her properly."

"How did you know about Iris?" CJ had thought she'd been careful not to reveal how close she was with her mentor. Even though her mom was never really there for her, she'd never wanted to make her feel bad that she'd gotten her young adult needs met from another mother.

"It was easy to see, honey. The way you talked about her when you came home every day after working with her—your eyes would light up." She shook her head. "I ignored it at the time. I didn't want to see it, and it gave me an excuse to stay focused on my job and fool myself that it was okay that someone else was looking after you properly. I'll never forgive myself for that. And I want to say sorry. It's such an insignificant, small word considering what it's supposed to achieve, but it's all I have, all we have to give you. There are no excuses that absolve us from neglecting you. And we don't want any. We know what we did was wrong, and we're truly, truly sorry for that."

Her mom reached across the table for CJ's hand, and CJ reached across to meet her in the middle.

Her mom entwined their fingers and looked into CJ's eyes. "I hope that one day you might forgive us, but we know that we don't deserve it."

CJ swallowed hard. Silence engulfed the room, and it stretched on while she considered her mom's words.

"And I'm sorry, CJ."

Her dad held out his hand, and CJ took it so the three of them were joined in a way they never had been before. Just hearing him call her by her preferred name was progress, but to hear him say a word she'd never heard issued through his lips, that was a miracle.

"I'm sorry for all those times you tried to spend time with me, and I shooed you away or treated you like an inconvenience. And I'm sorry that it's taken this long for us to realize it, and that someone dying was the trigger for us to see that we haven't done right by you, our only daughter, and our greatest achievement."

If she'd had wine in her mouth, CJ would've spluttered it all over the table. An apology was earth-shattering enough, but this pure outpouring of emotion was blowing her mind. No amount of therapy could ever have prepared her for this huge rollback of three decades of her life, of feeling alone and unloved. "I don't know what to say."

"You don't have to say anything, CJ." Her mom squeezed her hand. "We want you to know that we'd like the opportunity to try to be the parents you deserve, but we don't expect you to be open to such a huge change, just like that."

Her father nodded. "And we know that we can't make up for the mistakes of the past, but we'd like to make the best of whatever future we have together, whatever future you *let* us have together." He released her hand and stood. "And in that spirit, I also want to apologize for not believing in your artistic talent when you were young and not supporting you to follow your dream of going to art school and becoming a sculptor."

CJ was torn between mirth at her father's apparent preparation for an even bigger speech than he'd just made and floods of tears for the speech he'd just made. She'd anticipated this conversation getting deep, but she'd been completely ignorant that it might have the power to affect her like this.

Her mom stood up too, and CJ frowned. Talking through their issues had been expected. She'd idly hoped for an apology, but she had no idea what this was about to become. "You're kind of freaking me out. What's happening?"

Her father laughed gently. "Sorry, CJ. We don't want to do that. We want to show you something."

He headed for the door and waved for her to follow him. Saying and showing her that they were sorry was a huge enough step in one sitting. What giant cherry were they going to put on top of that? Overcome with a truckload of unexpected emotion, CJ wasn't sure her legs would support her if she tried to stand. Her mom looked like she was waiting for CJ to go so that she could bring up the rear to keep CJ from turning back. She might need her mom to help her stay upright. What she wanted to do was stay seated and process everything that had just been said, run it over and over in her mind and absorb the enormity of their confession.

"I'd like to share this meal with you, if you don't mind. You've gone to so much trouble, Mom, and honestly, just sitting with you both, having a family meal… It'd mean so much to me." She stopped, a rising ball of something, joy or relief maybe, pushed her to the brink of tears. She hadn't cried since Jonny Mills had pushed her onto her ass in the school playground and she'd run home for sympathy, only to find an empty house. It had almost always been an empty house. And she could count on one hand the number of meals they'd had together here as a family. There were always too many of her parents' friends taking up space at this table on special occasions, so CJ had been forced to eat in the kitchen or on the sofa. It bothered her early on, but she made the best of it, convincing herself that she was happier sitting alone and not having to put up with boring adult conversation.

Her father came back to the table, and both he and her mom retook their seats. "Of course. Of course we should eat. Sorry, we're a little excited to see your reaction, that's all."

As intrigued as CJ was, she really did want to enjoy the amazing feast her mom had put together. "This way, I get to think about what the surprise could be." She smiled genuinely and thought of Dak again. If it hadn't been for her, CJ might not have agreed to this meal at all. After the first few days of being back home, she'd even considered going to stay with Emily instead but the draw of Dak being next door and being able to catch glimpses of her every morning on her way to work had played a part in her decision to stay. Dak's regular refrain that people change had seeped into CJ's consciousness and that, along with what she'd learned from extensive therapy sessions, had allowed her to open her heart to the possibility of a different kind of future with her parents.

"Do you want to tell us about work? You've been working on the victim of that serial killer, haven't you?" Her mom visibly shuddered. "I read he had over two hundred knife wounds. Was that right, or was it just the paper's exaggerating?"

CJ shook her head, not in answer to the question but in mild disbelief at her mom's interest in her work, something she'd never shown before. "It's true. It took nearly two days to re-sculpt him."

"Is that what it's called or is that your word for it?" her father asked before he scooped sweet potato casserole onto a biscuit and took a massive bite.

She shrugged. "I don't know, Dad. It's just how I've always seen it."

He waved his half-eaten biscuit her way. "Because of your talent in clay sculpture?"

Talent? He'd never used that word to describe her first love. Waste of time and effort, he'd often said, but never talent. "I guess." She buttered her own biscuit and took a bit. "Oh, wow, these are amazing. Best biscuits ever. Have you been taking classes to learn all this stuff?"

Her mom's cheeks flushed. "You're just humoring me. I don't think they're anything special. Are they, Roger?"

Her dad had just popped the last chunk of his biscuit into his mouth and was happily chewing on it. When he'd finished, he kissed his fingers. "Bellisimo, my sweet. CJ's right. They are absolute perfection."

"So, have you been taking classes?"

"Nope. I've been teaching myself using cookbooks. I follow the recipe, to begin with, and then I play around with it. Your father's been a very willing guinea pig," she gestured toward his belly, "as you can see."

Then she giggled. An honest to goodness giggle. The kind of unreserved giggle that doesn't care what someone thinks of it. CJ laughed hard enough to almost make her cry.

"This?" Her father rubbed his belly. "I'm cultivating this so I can audition for the mall's Santa Claus this year."

The free laughter bounced off the walls and filled the room with a lightness that CJ was struggling to comprehend but willing to try. The past couldn't be forgotten, and it wouldn't melt away in the warmth of this new family atmosphere, but the future could be a study in opposites.

"Seriously, Mom, everything you've cooked or baked since I got home has been top quality. You're really good at it. You could open your own restaurant."

Her mom smiled. "Oh no, this is just for you and your father. I'm done with the rat race. I want to spend as much time with my family as God is willing to give me."

CJ liked the sound of that. The dreams she'd had as a child of family gatherings for holidays didn't seem so far-fetched anymore. If she was willing to let the past go and look only to the present, it seemed she could have the family time she'd always wanted.

Her mom returned to questions about CJ's work, and they worked their way through their giant plates of food accompanied by easy-flowing conversation. The minutes ticked by, and CJ learned more about her parents over the course of one dinner than she had in a decade.

When her father ate his last mouthful, he looked at her mom and wiggled his eyebrows. His clear impatience was childlike and endearing in a way she hadn't ever associated her father.

He looked across to CJ. "Can I interest you in a little walk to the den before dessert?"

"What's for dessert?" CJ asked.

"Pumpkin cheesecake," her mom said.

CJ leaned back in her chair and cradled her own, slightly bloated stomach. She hadn't eaten so much food in forever. There was no way she could face a piece of cheesecake without trying to shake some of the food into her legs. "A long walk to the den via a three-block detour sounds appealing."

Her dad led the way—directly to the den on the second floor of the house, unfortunately for her digestion— and stood at the door.

"I'll bet you've been wondering what's been going on in here," her dad said.

CJ shook her head. "Not really. You never let me in the den when I was a kid, and I eventually lost interest in the mystery of what was behind this door." That interest had taken quite a long time to wane. As a child and even a teenager, she'd longed to be invited beyond the solid oak door into the room where he would entertain his friends, retreat to after dinner, and spend any other spare time in there that he could muster. Her father looked repentant, and a pang of guilt sat leaden in her full-to-the-brim tummy. "I'm teasing. Of course I've been wondering what's been going on in there." She hadn't known anything was going on, here or anywhere else in the house. She'd been too busy with Dak, and Emily, and work, but his excitement was rather contagious, so she played along.

"I said earlier that I was sorry I didn't support your wish to go to art school, and again, we know what's behind this door won't make up for that." He grinned at her mom. "But we are hoping that this might encourage you to spend a little more time here when you're not recording your show."

He flung the door open with a dramatic "Ta dah!" and gestured for CJ to venture inside after he'd switched the light on.

"Oh. My. God." The floor-to-ceiling windows that made up two of the walls afforded the space so much light that it was practically as good as being outside. She'd often looked up at them from the yard and wished she knew what was behind them. Whatever it had been was all gone. On one of the remaining walls were rows upon rows of chisels and hammers, cutting saws and diamond grinding wheels, polishing tools and hand files.

A countertop ran along the length of the wall with a stationary grinding machine on it. A drill and various sizes of angle and straight grinders sat in their boxes, unopened and pristine. Wedgers and shims, pitchers and cleavers, rifflers and rasps adorned the other wall. Not one, but three sculpting tables were placed around the room and on each was their own block of stone, marble, and rock.

She walked slowly around the den—the studio—and ran her hands along the virgin tools, the sensation of steel, wood, and plastic beneath her fingers making them tingle with the desire to create. In turn, she went to each of the blocks and held her hands to the materials, immediately beginning to see the finished sculpture hiding within, patiently waiting for her to set it free.

Finally, she turned to her parents waiting in the doorway. She held out her arms and her mom rushed forward and embraced her. Her dad followed behind and enveloped them both in a strong bear hug. CJ allowed her tears to fall unchecked. She'd dreamed of one day having a studio like this, but it wasn't a dream she ever thought would become a reality. She'd pushed any thought of being this kind of artist away into the deepest recesses of her wish pit. Her father had convinced her it would be a waste of time and money to pursue, and she'd believed him.

But now, it seemed, he believed in *her*. And that somehow opened up all kinds of new possibilities.

"This is so wonderful," she said. A tiny part of her wanted to gripe a little. But the *why now* of her question had already been answered. They wanted to make amends. They wanted to be good parents. And this was better late than never, wasn't it? She hugged them harder, and a sense of deep appreciation for life wrapped her in a warm cocoon. The all-pervading feeling of being alone in this world, of being self-sufficient and self-reliant from such an early age, could that all begin to slip away this easily? If she let it, it could.

"We love you, CJ," whispered her mom.

CJ buried her head into her father's chest and sobbed. "I love you too."

Simple words. Words that she'd never said to anyone before. But time could give as much as it could take away. And it was giving them all the chance for something better, to be someone better than they'd been before. And CJ vowed to take that chance.

Chapter Seventeen

DAK TRIED TO KEEP the smile from her face when she saw the rear of CJ's distinctive, and unmissable, black Ferrari in the back parking lot of the funeral home. She and Hamilton were doing their part of a final perimeter check before the funeral director drove Arnold's body to the church. The captain had authorized a five-hundred-yard boundary around the church and the same around the cemetery, thanks to the information CJ had shared before they'd toppled into bed the night before for yet another run of hot, sweaty sex that left them both panting.

The police had fenced off the route between the two locations like they would for a parade, and squad cars were positioned at key points along the way. The whole operation was costing the police department a chunk of change, and CJ's name had been accompanied by an impressive array of curse words. Hamilton gave her an apologetic look every time CJ was mentioned, and Dak had stayed quiet about her current connection with the TV celebrity. She didn't like that her personal life was lightly entangled with her case, and it was something she'd need to think about.

No one outside the family or not local to the area would be allowed within the safe area so that the family and friends of Wallace Arnold could say their final goodbyes in relative peace. The captain had suggested family and friends only should be allowed in the area, but Dak had pointed out their killer was unlikely to be in that group. She and the rest of the team wanted the opportunity to observe who attended from the local area. She'd said the killer was unlikely to be able to resist the funeral, particularly with the additional furor of press frenzy. Their only suspect, Billy, was unlikely to be there, unless he wanted to taunt them. But somehow, she figured he wanted to stay outside their field of view.

The service was an hour away, so Dak had time to see CJ briefly before she left for the fan event. "I'm going inside to check the surveillance is set up."

Hamilton grinned and raised his eyebrows. "Say hi to your celebrity for me and tell her I'm looking forward to meeting her."

"You're an—"

"Asshole, I know." Hamilton winked and slapped her on the back. "But I'm your asshole, buddy."

He'd taken her one-time use of "buddy" to heart, it seemed. Dak let him walk away without retort and headed toward the entrance. A convertible yellow Mustang pulled out of the parking lot and tore down the street, too fast for her to catch the license plate. She opened the door and pressed the bell at reception. It took a minute before CJ came from a side door and greeted her with a smile worth getting up in the morning for.

"Who was that in the Mustang?"

"Someone named Dani. She said she was in the neighborhood and just wanted to drop by and say thank you for my work with the dead. She said it was very important, and a lot of people appreciated it."

"Weird."

"Not really," CJ said. "What I do can bring a lot peace to a family."

"I get that." Dak yawned.

"Are we keeping you up, Agent Dak?"

Dak looked around before answering. "*You're* keeping me up. I've had three coffees and two donuts and it's not even eleven o'clock."

CJ narrowed her eyes. "Is that a complaint?"

"It's a statement of fact, that's all." Dak let her gaze wander over CJ's body. "You're looking very glamorous."

"You won't recognize me after Sian's had me in the chair for an hour."

Dak jutted her chin, taken back by the instant pang of jealousy. "Is Sian someone I need to worry about? I'm the only one who should be having you in a chair for any amount of time, let alone an hour."

CJ tilted her head and smirked. "Is that right? Did we agree to an exclusivity contract?"

"We didn't, but I don't share anything, especially not my..." What was CJ to her after two dates and a bundle of hot sex?

"My what?"

Dak looked away, unable to hold CJ's intense and amused gaze. "Is everything set at the Regency? Your agent has organized enough security, hasn't she? There are some crazy fans out there." She stopped herself from continuing. She had a whole plethora of horror stories, kidnappings, and murders associated with starstruck fans she wasn't about to share that might raise CJ's anxiety. She seemed relaxed enough. Dak guessed she was used to this kind of thing after three years, and Dak didn't need to coddle her. CJ wasn't hers *to* coddle.

"This is small fry for Paige. She handles movie stars and real celebrities, remember? Are you ready on your end?"

That was a good question. "I hope so. Everything's in place, and for the most part, this is a good PD. Your involvement has increased the audience for the funeral exponentially, but the killer might see that as a good thing— more interest equals more people to see his art."

CJ frowned. "His art?"

"That's how he thinks about it. They're not his victims, they're his collaborative partners. If you saw the way he exhibits the bodies, you'd understand." The PR department released lots of details to the press, including the shibari rope tree, but not enough for the public to truly understand how the victims were arranged. "You don't want to see it, though, trust me." Dak couldn't unsee this or any of the crime scenes and photographs she'd seen. She often wished she could at least wipe her brain of them once the cases were solved, but her mind held onto everything as if it thought they might be of use on some other case.

CJ shivered. "His incisions were very precise. It wouldn't surprise me if the killer was in the medical profession or had at least trained to be. It took me a long time to undo all of his 'art.'"

Of course, CJ had been in closer contact with Arnold's body than she had. CJ was probably more used to blood and gore than Dak was. She checked her watch and realized she had to get to the church. "Are you coming over tonight?"

CJ stepped in closer and tucked her finger inside Dak's belt. "I thought you were tired and needed some sleep?"

"No, that's not quite accurate. I'm happy to caffeinate and sugar myself up to fuel our late-night trysts."

CJ released her and stepped back, shaking her head. "What are you doing to me, Agent Dak? It's bad when I can't control myself at work."

"Are you coming over?" Dak repeated, already praying CJ didn't have plans with her agent and their entourage. Their sensual workouts had made it so she slept like the dead and no nightmares intruded. She could get used to that.

"I'm having dinner with Paige and Sian, but I'll be home by eleven.

I'm leaving for the interview site in a minute. I just wanted to make sure everything here was okay first."

Dak wasn't expecting to be home much sooner than that. It could even be later if they got any leads from the people attending the funeral service. "You still have the back door key?"

CJ shook her head. "I put it back in the garage, but I put it in a drawer because I nearly injured myself moving that ridiculously heavy kettlebell. What do you even do with that thing?"

"Watch me work out one night and I'll show you. It builds my stamina that you're so enamored with."

"Farrell. We need to get to the church on time," Hamilton said through her earpiece.

"That's something I never thought I'd hear from a man," Dak said. Mr. Bryan came out of a nearby door and was studying Dak closely. "Good luck with your adoring fans." Dak exited the building and walked straight into Hamilton waiting for her on the front steps.

"We should all go for dinner on a double date," Hamilton said as they jogged down the steps and headed toward his car.

Dak shook her head but said nothing.

"I'm your buddy now. That's the kind of thing buddies do together." Hamilton shoved her shoulder and deftly evaded the right hook she lazily threw at him.

She got into the driver's side and was pulling away before Hamilton had managed to shut his door.

"Can you at least get me a signed photograph?"

"How do I know you're not going to put it on the ceiling above your bed?" Dak asked.

"Because it wouldn't stick on the mirrors."

"Christ. That's way too much detail."

Hamilton chuckled. "Just kidding… it'd stick, no problem."

She punched his shoulder, hard, and he yelped.

"Remind me never to get into a fight with you."

They drove to the church discussing the case and its lack of leads. She guided him on the types of body language they would be watching for in the crowd, and he listened attentively. The captain had authorized a rush on the reconstruction of the boot prints. Forensics was sure it was a Dickies work boot, size thirteen. Part of the tread on the left boot was

Dead *Pretty*

compressed in a way not consistent with regular wear, causing them to posit that the guy could be a construction worker. Their killer had to be six foot plus: good to compare to their suspects when they eventually had any. And the boots were widely available online and in workwear stores, and they were the choice of protective footwear for lots of blue-collar workers. The leads they'd pulled from the local providers of shibari rope had taken them to a handful of people into bondage, and no one was purchasing in the quantities needed for the killer's elaborate trees and harnesses. Searching providers across the country was going to take a lot more time, and Davis and Earl had taken on that duty. Marks and Williams were looking for victims with similar wounds from other PDs but had nothing so far. Dak and Hamilton had to follow up on the new avenues from Elliott, their third victim, and the chief was raining all hell down on everyone from above. It was enough for Dak to wish she'd gotten out of Salt Lake before the second victim was found.

"It's been just over a week between victims this time, but there was a month between the first and second one." Hamilton flicked through his notes and chewed on the end of his pen. "Is our killer getting bolder or more desperate?"

Dak sighed. "That's a good question. I'm not convinced our first victim was the killer's first victim. It was too neat, too practiced. He's positioned the bodies in different poses each time, but they all have wings. The last wings were embedded into Elliott's skin rather than carved, which indicates a progression. He's getting bolder in that respect. But maybe the media frenzy over Callie Johnson's involvement has prompted another victim so soon. Maybe he wants to get as much publicity as he can while interest is high. The spilled blood indicates he was in a hurry or that he was overexcited when he was working on the body. And while he tried to get rid of the boot print, he obviously didn't have the time to bleach it."

"He could've been disturbed. Do you think he wasn't expecting the maid, and he had to make a quick exit?"

"It's possible. Let's take another run at her after the funeral. Maybe she can remember hearing or seeing something that could help us. We should tell the PR department to reveal we have the boot print reconstruction and release details of its size. That should spook him and put him off killing again so soon, at least until he's calmed down."

Hamilton nodded. "Genius."

Dak shook her head. "It's conjecture, that's all. Working through all the possibilities and following them through to their conclusions. You've got a good head for this stuff too. You're doing great." She didn't need to glance sideways to know his smile was so big that he'd look like a lottery winner. They showed their badges to get past the checkpoint and she pulled into the church parking lot. Dak spotted the captain, assistant chief, and the chief of police. "I'm going to need a minute inside. Can you head him off and tell him what we've just discussed?"

Hamilton frowned slightly but didn't question her request. "Sure thing."

They got out of the car, and Hamilton strode toward the trio in their official white uniforms while she ducked into the church. She looked at the giant cross and its crucified Jesus at the altar, and memories of her mom taking Dak and her little brother to church came to mind. She decided to call her mom again that night before she got home. She hadn't been inside a church for a year, only ever visiting to light a candle for Ben.

She approached the steel tray with five rows of candle holders, pulled five dollars from her wallet, and deposited it in the donations tin. She plucked a long candle from the box on the bottom shelf, lit it from one of the already burning candles, and placed it in a vacant holder. She closed her eyes. "I miss you, buddy," she whispered.

After a minute of remembrance, she turned to see Hamilton waiting a few paces behind her. She hadn't heard him enter or approach.

"The chief wants to speak to you," he said quietly.

It was clear from his tone of voice and the look on his face that he'd been there a while and had heard what she'd said. "It's the anniversary of my old partner's death." She felt the need to explain herself for some reason. "I light a candle for him every year."

He nodded slowly. He got it. She didn't need to say any more. The events surrounding Ben's death were a matter of public record, and if Hamilton wanted to know more, he could easily look it up. Or he could wait for her to tell him. She hoped he'd just leave it alone for now.

"Okay."

She walked past him and took a deep breath of fresh air into her lungs. She needed her mind clear today. Every sense and instinct needed to be on high alert. She scanned the line of people slowly filing through police security. A few tall males stood out but none of them looked anything other than forlorn. She guessed from the way they filled their suits that they were probably from Arnold's gym. The funeral procession of cars came into her sight line, and the uniformed officers moved the barriers to allow them access. *Perfect timing.* She caught Burnett's eye and motioned to the cars entering the parking lot. She couldn't speak to the chief now, she had to do her job.

Hamilton joined her, unusually silent.

"You know what you're looking for," Dak said. They'd spoken about it extensively over the past few days.

"Yes, boss."

She squeezed his shoulder. "Let's catch us a killer."

Chapter Eighteen

Emily grabbed her arm after she left the stage. "You were fantastic, Ceej."

CJ did a happy dance and pulled Emily into a hug. "I didn't know you were coming. I would've gotten you a seat on the first row." CJ had been blown away by the large audience for the interview and Q&A. Being on that stage, answering all those questions, had her jonesing to be back in front of the camera. She wasn't sure whether that was a good thing anymore or not. But it might lead to Netflix picking up her show and if that happened, CJ was determined not to blow her earnings on flash living.

"Your agent called me. I got to watch the whole thing behind all the monitors. You were amazing. I'm so proud of you."

CJ pulled away. "Paige called you? How—" But then she remembered giving Paige Emily's full name. Sian would've done the rest.

"She's invited me to come to dinner with you all this evening. Would that be okay with you?"

"Of course. I'd love that."

Emily took CJ in her arms and squeezed hard enough that CJ squeaked. "Goodness, you're so skinny, I could almost break you. I think you need more of those brownie bites."

"You know the camera adds ten pounds, and I might be going back in front of it again soon."

Emily grabbed CJ's arms and bounced up and down. "That's so exciting. Tell me everything."

"Callie Johnson, that was spectacular." Paige slipped past Emily and kissed CJ's cheek. "You had the crowd eating out of your hands. Netflix will be begging to make the show after that performance."

"NETFLIX!"

Emily's exclamation made even Paige jump a little.

"You must be Emily. Sorry I didn't have time to say hello before the event." Paige took Emily's hand in hers. "Did you enjoy it?"

Emily nodded. "It was amazing. How did you get James Corden on such short notice?"

Paige winked. "He owes me a few favors. A lot of people do." She placed her arm over CJ's shoulder. "Shall we go to dinner? Sian booked a table at Log Haven. We have the whole patio to ourselves."

"That sounds perfect, Paige. Thank you." CJ embraced her briefly, thankful she had such a caring agent. "I'll take Emily in my car."

"This day is rapidly shaping up to be one of the best days of my life. Watching my best friend headline and smash a huge public event, dinner at the most exclusive restaurant in Salt Lake, and a long ride in my favorite sports car. I don't think it could get any better unless Brad Carlton showed up as my dinner date."

Paige handed CJ the envelope she'd been carrying and nodded.

"We can't get you Brad, but Paige did manage to get you this." CJ passed the envelope to Emily.

"Oh, wow! That's amazing." Emily hugged them both. "God, I've missed you, Callie Johnson."

CJ smiled. She hadn't realized how much she'd missed having her best friend close by for the past three years. "I've missed you too."

"Your car's here." Sian waved from the far side of the stage corridor.

"Okay. CJ, you spend thirty minutes signing autographs and chatting to fans, then we'll head off to the restaurant. We have a lot to celebrate and a lot to talk about." Paige gave CJ another kiss on the cheek and did the same to Emily. "Let's go."

The time on the floor with the show's fans flew past in a blur. CJ had done Clexacon twice, so she was prepared for the craziness of it all. As she signed and chatted, joked and posed for photos, she knew she would've missed this if Paige hadn't been able to sell *Dead Pretty* to Netflix. Though she was aware she probably shouldn't, CJ allowed herself to jump ahead since Paige seemed convinced Friday's meeting was just a formality. It was what she wanted. She loved this life, but maybe now that she and her parents were on a path toward a better relationship, she could spend some off-season time at home and make sure she saw Emily more often, including inviting her to LA to stay. And Dak? That was more complicated. CJ couldn't get a handle on how Dak felt about whatever was building between them. They'd both made it clear it was just for fun and *mind-blowing* sex, but Dak had shown a jealous side earlier at the funeral home indicating that there might be more developing than either of them had anticipated.

CJ posed for her final photograph and pushed thoughts of Dak aside. Maybe they'd talk tonight, but for now, she was going to spend some quality time with her best friend at a fancy restaurant.

She hooked her arm into Emily's and led the way to the private parking lot section that was reserved for VIP guests—another thing Paige had arranged. As she approached her car, she spotted a white envelope beneath her windshield wipers. Some fans were dedicated enough to find a way past security. If she had a less distinctive car, maybe it wouldn't be quite that easy for them to deposit love notes and whatever else they wanted to get to her but couldn't face giving to her in person. The most amusing one was a big sister and little sister silicone dildo pairing hiding beneath a fruit basket she found on a blanket on the Ferrari's hood.

"Secret admirer?" Emily asked.

CJ took the note and deposited it in her clutch to read later. It'd give her something to do while she waited for Dak. "They are devoted."

Emily climbed into the passenger side. "You've got a lot of superfans?"

CJ started the engine and left the parking lot. "Don't be silly, I was joking. Although…" and she told Emily about the fruit basket and its hidden bonus gifts.

Emily laughed. "That's so funny. Have you had any marriage proposals?"

"One or two, but mostly it's just people with a consuming interest in death."

"Y'know, I don't think you've ever told me how you got a TV show."

CJ sighed. It was another reminder of how she and Emily had grown apart before CJ had even left for Hollywood. "I worked on a woman who'd had a really bad accident on her bike in New York. Her husband only knew it was her because of the outfit she was wearing and her wedding ring. He was desperate to have an open casket, so the funeral home called in a favor with Iris, and she sent me over there. The husband turned out to be a TV producer, and he came up with the idea for the show a few months after the funeral and gave me a call. He pitched it to Fox. We recorded a pilot and audiences liked it."

Emily sighed deeply. "Your life makes me feel like I've wasted mine. And now things have collapsed with Jason…" She sniffed and pulled a tissue from her shoulder bag. "We had such big plans, and I'm nowhere near achieving any of mine. I can't even keep a guy so that I can have a family."

CJ took Emily's hand and squeezed it gently. "You're still young. You've got plenty of time to work on your dreams. I just got lucky with the TV show. And it wasn't like I'd always wanted to be a mortician. I wanted to be a sculptor, remember? But Dad said I'd never make money being an artist." She could still remember the arguments over her desire to go to art school. Her father had been strangely convinced that she'd want to go into the military just because he'd spent his life training the National Guard. It was a leap by any standards, but when they'd had such a tenuous connection, barely spending any time together, it made no sense at all. "Reconstructing dead people probably wasn't an obvious choice, but it made sense to me. I love what I do, but it wasn't my dream, Em."

Em opened the window and took a deep breath of fresh air. "Being part of your world today made me see how closed down my own is." She turned in her seat toward CJ. "I've loved having you back in my life this past week or so, and I don't want to go back to reality when you head home to LA for your show."

CJ contemplated Emily's use of the word "home." Home still felt like here, where she'd come from, where she was raised. She rented an apartment in LA and hadn't bought a house, let alone a home. If home was where the heart is, where was her heart? Did it have to be anywhere? She found herself thinking of Dak again and slapped the steering wheel. "What do you want to do about it?" CJ asked.

"What do you mean?"

CJ glanced sideways. "You don't want to go back to your old reality, so what are you going to do about it? How are you going to change it?" She squeezed Emily's hand again and released her. "You're in control of your reality. What do you want to do with the rest of your life?" They'd talked over the past week about Emily's job and how unfulfilled she was, but CJ had put it down to regular ennui. Few people had the luxury of loving their jobs and most people complained about them with no intention of ever doing anything about it. She'd taken Emily's grumbles in that spirit, but she would be happy to help if Emily really wanted to make a change.

"I want to get out of Salt Lake and start fresh," Emily said after a few moments of quiet contemplation.

Dead *Pretty*

"Okay, that's a start. Doing what?"

"I want to do what Sian does for Paige, and then I want to be a Paige."

CJ nodded. That sounded achievable, and Emily had the people skills for that kind of career. "Perfect. Let's talk to Paige over dinner about how you can make that happen."

"Just like that?"

"Just like that." CJ smiled, and Emily grinned widely before she sat back in her seat. CJ gunned the Ferrari up to sixty-five as they hit the I-80. Emily had a plan for her future, and that was great, but the road ahead for CJ seemed far less tangible than it had ever been before. She resolved to focus on her career, just as she had for the past decade. Everything else would fall into place…hopefully.

***

CJ pulled into her parents' drive and waited to see if the car behind her stopped too. The bright headlights made it impossible to see the car they belonged to, but it didn't seem to slow down and continued along the street. She'd been followed a few times from the studio, and it had only ever been excitable fans wanting a photo with her or for her to sign a show T-shirt or even just to follow the car itself. She'd only spotted the car behind her after she'd dropped Emily home, and there was every chance it wasn't following her at all. There were plenty of cars on the road, and it wasn't like she'd engineered a long and winding route home to lose them.

She got out of the car, popped in to see her parents briefly—a strange but warm experience of checking in with them—and went to Dak's house. Once inside, she poured herself a glass of chilled water and flopped onto the sofa to wait. She opened her clutch and checked her phone.

I'll be home around 11

The living room clock said ten-fifty. She was grateful she wouldn't have to wait long. Bernie didn't need her in tomorrow, and he wanted her fresh for Thursday when the next victim of the serial killer came in because the family wanted a quick funeral once the police released the body. The long day had drained her of energy, but she still wanted to have some time with Dak before she slept. She repeated the thought in her head, a little weirded out by the fact that she wanted more intimate time with Dak. Was it a red flag given that they had no future? She couldn't deny that she'd miss her when the inevitable separation came around.

She went to close her bag and saw the envelope she'd found on her car at the hotel. She pulled it out and read it. Pinpricks of fear ran down her back.

"Shit." She read it again.

You're an artist. You should understand what I'm doing. Stop interfering with my art. You wouldn't paint a smile on the Mona Lisa. Go back to Hollywood and you won't get hurt.

The front door slammed shut and she jumped up from the sofa, her heart racing. "Dak?" she called out.

Dak came into the living room and smiled. "Were you expecting someone else?"

CJ rushed into Dak's arms. She calmed herself and rolled her eyes. It was just a note. Since when did she get so spooked?

"Are you okay? Did something happen at your event?"

She pulled away and shook her head. "No, it went great. How was the funeral? Not swamped by the show's fans?"

"No, thankfully not. Just a lot of local people there to pay their respects, but I think they were hoping to catch a glimpse of you too." Dak put her hands on CJ's shoulders and looked at her seriously. "What's wrong?"

CJ offered the note to Dak. "This was on my car."

Dak took it and read it. "Jesus, CJ, when did you get this? Why didn't you call me?"

"I've literally only just opened it. It was on my windshield when I went to my car after the event. I put it in my clutch and went to dinner with Emily, Paige, and Sian. I'd forgotten it was there."

"It was put there while you were at the hotel?"

"I think so. I would've seen it if it had been there when I got in my car at home or at work."

"No one else has touched it?"

CJ shook her head. "I took it from the windshield and dropped it into my bag. Why?"

Dak pulled a latex glove from her trouser pocket and used it to hold the edge of the paper. She went into the kitchen and CJ followed. Dak opened a drawer and pulled out a large Ziplock bag.

"Could you open this for me, please?"

CJ did as asked, and Dak carefully placed the open note inside before she took the bag, laid it on the table, and sealed it. She pulled her phone from her pocket, hit a speed dial number, and waited.

"Hamilton. Yeah, I know it's late. Just shut up and listen. We've got a note from the killer... No, not like BTK. He sent something to CJ, warning her to stop fixing his work... I need to meet you at the Regent now. They're bound to have CCTV coverage... Yeah... No, don't call Burnett until we've got something solid."

CJ listened in something of a daze as Dak continued her conversation, sounding almost excited. When she ended the call, she pulled CJ into a tight embrace. CJ waited for Dak to say something, but she remained silent as if the embrace would do all the talking for her. Whatever Dak wanted to say, CJ had no idea.

"I'm not leaving," CJ said into Dak's chest.

"I don't want you to, but it might be a good idea to go back to LA for a while." Dak released CJ and stepped back, the sadness in her eyes unmissable.

"I can't go anywhere. Bernie has Elliott booked in for Thursday."

"Elliott as in the third victim?"

"Yep. The family wants an open casket."

"I don't think that's a good idea. You're on the killer's radar because you've reversed his work once. If you do it again—"

"So what? I should let him win and stop me from giving the family some peace?"

"I can talk to the family and explain the note." Dak reached out but CJ took a step back. "They'll understand. They won't insist on an open casket if they know it's going to put you in more danger."

"What if he sends you a note because you start getting close to finding him? Will you stop your investigation because it's too dangerous?"

"The risk is part of my job. That's different."

CJ didn't appreciate the condescension in Dak's tone. "No. No, it isn't. I'm helping the families say goodbye to their loved ones so they can remember them the way they were in life. I won't stop doing that because I get one threatening note." CJ turned, went back into the living room, and grabbed her bag. "You're going back to work so I'm going home."

"Wait." Dak caught hold of CJ's arm. "I'm worried about you," she said softly.

CJ caressed Dak's cheek, and her anger settled. "I'll be fine. He only kills men," CJ said, though that was founded more in hope than in certainty. Dak wrapped her hand around CJ's neck and pulled her closer. "I'll call for a patrol car. They'll be at the end of your driveway if anything happens."

CJ kissed her, hoping to convey the calmness that was rapidly slipping away. "I'm sure I'll be fine." The car with the bright headlights popped into CJ's head. She didn't want to make a big deal about it. There was no way of knowing for sure that the car had even been following her, and she had no details or a license plate to give Dak so there really was no point in troubling her with it. "I'll be safe at home. Dad has a gun. I'll tell him what's going on."

Dak touched her forehead to CJ's. "I don't want anything to happen to you," she said, her voice cracking slightly.

CJ stood on her tiptoes and kissed Dak's nose lightly. "Nothing's going to happen to me. Keep me posted." She gave Dak one last kiss and turned to leave but Dak pulled her back into her arms.

"We'll get this guy, I promise."

CJ rested her head against Dak's chest. "I know you will." She hoped that saying the words would make them true.

Chapter Nineteen

DAK YAWNED SO WIDE she thought her jaw might break. She'd spent all night going through the CCTV footage from the various cameras on the exterior of the Regent. Of course, they didn't have cameras on the VIP area because privacy was "extremely important to our clients." But they did have six other cameras covering the rest of the underground parking structure and the outer areas of the hotel. Hamilton yawned. He'd insisted on staying with her and working through the videos by her side, and they'd finally spotted their guy.

Now they were back at the station looking at a series of full color, high resolution stills taken from the footage: six foot three, maybe a hundred and eighty pounds, black sweatshirt, blue jeans, and tan work boots. Sunglasses hid his eyes, and the hoody he wore, along with the way he dipped his head, hid pretty much everything else, giving them no facial features at all. He'd entered the VIP parking structure at 2:36 p.m. and exited at 2:38 p.m. He got onto a trials bike with no plate, and Marks and Williams lost him after trawling through the traffic cams less than a mile away.

It wasn't much. But they had their first image of the killer.

"I need some sleep," Hamilton said and stretched in his chair.

It was past eight, meaning they'd both been up for twenty-four hours straight. Dak rubbed her eyes. She couldn't deny she was exhausted too, and while copious amounts of coffee had kept the sandman at bay, not to allow herself some rest now would be counter-productive, making it likely she'd miss something important, and they had a follow-up interview with Elliott's cleaner scheduled later in the day. "Okay, let's take a break. When are we speaking to Mrs. Shackman?"

"We said we'd be at her house at two after she finishes work for the day."

"Be back here by one. I want to spend some time looking at how he's arranged the bodies and see if we can find anything in art that he might be copying. Maybe he's not as much of an artist as we're giving him credit for, and he's being derivative." Hamilton stood and groaned, flexing his back. He put his hand on Dak's shoulder. "We'll get this guy." She'd stupidly said the exact same words to CJ *and* added a promise. What the hell was she thinking? Her mom always told her not to make promises she had no right to make, and this was one of those promises she was nowhere near being able to come through on. So far, they had nothing but a picture of a guy who could be any tall guy in the city and a boot print from a make of footwear available all across the country. "I hope you're right."

Hamilton looked puzzled. "You haven't failed yet. I don't think you're about to start."

She appreciated his faith in her, but he was talking about cold cases. This was different. Lives were on the line here. CJ's life had been threatened. Their killer could already be stalking his next victim and planning his next exhibition. They had no pattern to follow, and she needed a pattern. She hoped the blood spillage at his last victim's scene might be enough to get him to take a step back. The press had released the print, specifically the left boot with the strange indentation across the sole. If the killer panicked, he might try to get rid of the boots, and if they showed up somewhere, they could be a trove of DNA treasure. Thrift shops had been asked to contact the police if anyone donated tan work boots. Davis and Earl had lost a coin toss on that duty and hadn't stopped complaining about it. Dumpster-trawling and a tour of the local thrift shops wasn't high on any detective's wish list.

"I'll see you at one, Hamilton," she said when she noticed he was still standing there.

"Sure thing, boss."

Dak waited until he'd gone before she looked at her phone. She'd had a couple of messages from CJ, one at midnight and one at seven a.m., both confirming she was okay. Apparently her dad had slept downstairs in his La-Z-Boy chair with his Sig Sauer P226 across his chest. His military training, and the presence of the squad car at their address all night, had eased Dak's worries but she wanted to be there herself. *She* wanted to protect CJ from the guy the media had dubbed "The Artist."

She thumbed a message to CJ. *When are you going to work?* When she didn't get an instant response, Dak stood and stretched and made similar noises to Hamilton. God, she'd gotten stiff in her chair. She took a last look at her phone before slipping it into her pocket and heading out to her truck.

She was just out of the main city when her phone vibrated. She waited until she was at a stop sign before getting it out of her jeans.

I have the day off. Why?

Dak hit call and waited for CJ to answer.

"Hey, handsome."

"Hey, babe." Dak's response came so naturally, and she didn't think to censor it.

"I didn't hear your truck come home. Were you out all night?"

Dak smiled at the thought of CJ listening out for her return. "Yeah. We were at the Regent most of the night then we headed back to the station."

"Any luck with the CCTV?"

"We've got photos of the guy leaving the note on your car, but they're not clear enough for face recognition."

"You must be exhausted."

"I am. I'm headed back to the house for a few hours now. Any chance you can join me?"

Hearing CJ chuckle made Dak smile.

"I thought you said you were exhausted."

"I am." Dak wasn't calling for CJ to come over and have sex. She just wanted to hold her and fall asleep with her in her arms, knowing that she'd be safe there, that maybe they'd both be safe together. The longer the silence stretched on, the more Dak wished she hadn't called. She was making a fool of herself, thinking that someone like CJ would just want to lie in her arms. That was relationship territory, and CJ had made it clear she wasn't in that market.

"I'll go over now and start warming the bed," CJ said after what seemed like five minutes but was more like five seconds.

Dak didn't comment that it was nearly ninety degrees outside, so the bedroom would need the A/C turned on rather than the bed warmed. She liked the idea of CJ getting into her bed and being there when she got home. It was a vision she could see herself getting comfortable with quite easily. "I'll be with you as soon as I can."

"Okay."

"Okay." Dak ended the call before she said anything else. Any conversations they had about where this might be going had to be face-to-face so Dak could look into CJ's eyes. That was something she could get used to seeing the moment she woke every day. If she stopped to analyze what was happening, she could see that there were a lot of pieces slotting into place the more time she spent with, and away from, CJ. The dull ache in her stomach and tug of melancholy at the back of her mind when they were apart were signs enough, but the way her heart raced and her mood lifted when they were together told Dak she was in unfamiliar territory.

And what was she supposed to do with all these feelings anyway? Before this case, she'd barely involved herself in friendships, let alone a relationship with a woman. She and CJ lived such different lives. Dak moved from city to city, following the work, and CJ would inevitably head back to Hollywood. There was almost certainly no future for them, but Dak found herself unwilling to make any moves to stop any of it. She didn't want to deny herself this, no matter how short-lived it ended up being.

She pulled into her driveway and checked in with the unis in the patrol car. Mrs. J had been taking good care of them. One had maple syrup on her tie. "Good breakfast?" Dak asked.

"The best waffles I've ever tasted, and this coffee," the officer raised her mug, "is out of this world. This isn't a great situation for Ms. Johnson, but it's been damned good for a babysitting job."

Dak rapped her knuckles on the top of the squad car. "Stay alert for me, guys. I'm just grabbing a couple of hours' sleep."

The officer smiled and winked. "Sleep. Sure."

Dak nodded and walked away. The officers had either seen CJ go into her house or Mrs. J had told them that was where she was going. She pulled out her phone and set an alarm for three hours before going in the front door and racing upstairs.

CJ threw back the covers and patted the mattress. "Get in here, handsome."

She was relieved that CJ wasn't naked but being stripped down to white lace briefs and a matching camisole didn't improve the outlook for Dak's self-control. Maybe she wasn't so tired that she couldn't manage a little something.

"No," CJ said. "You need some sleep."

Damn, CJ could read her too easily. "Spoilsport. How could I ever be too tired to make love to you?" The words were out before she could stop them. They weren't the three words she'd never said to anyone but family and never in the way she might say them to a lover, but the L word was still in there.

"Is that what we've been doing?"

CJ gave the smile that Dak had come to recognize as playful and mischievous. Dak stripped down to her shorts and jumped into bed. She pulled CJ into her arms and kissed her. "What if it is?"

CJ traced her nail along Dak's lips and even through the haze of exhaustion, her body responded instantly.

"Then we'll have to have a serious talk some time. I really like being with you, and I don't want it to stop." CJ kissed her lightly. "But right now, it's nap time. Huddle up."

Dak turned onto her side and laid her arm across the bed. CJ rolled over, pushed her butt into Dak's crotch, and snuggled in. Dak draped her other arm over CJ's waist and pulled her in tighter. She traced circles on Dak's forearm, and her slow, gentle rhythm began to soothe Dak to sleep. She kissed CJ's neck. "Thank you for napping with me."

CJ sighed and squeezed Dak's hand. "Thank you for asking."

Dak had other questions to ask, but they could wait. Whatever this was, right now, she just wanted to enjoy it. And with CJ wrapped tightly in her arms, she was already drifting into the welcoming depths of sleep.

***

"How'd you manage to look so fresh after just a couple of hours?" Hamilton rubbed his eyes and yawned. "I think I feel worse."

"The young people of today have no stamina." Dak logged onto her email. She'd had the sleep of queens. Three hours of solid Zs, and she hadn't moved an inch with CJ in her arms. When her phone alarm woke her, she felt refreshed and ready to roll. Being sent off to work with a kiss and a promise to be careful was even better.

"I'll second that," Williams said as he passed through the office and dropped into his chair.

An email from a Sergeant Cooper at Chicago PD with the subject "The Artist" caught her eye. After she'd read it, she waved Hamilton over to see it.

"You were right. Quentin wasn't our guy's first murder," Hamilton said.

Williams leaned forward. "Do you have something?"

"An email from Chicago." Dak pointed to her screen. "They had four murders over a period of four months, and they bear a striking resemblance to our killer's M.O." She pushed away from her desk and approached their case boards. "Four guys, all in great shape, and each of them with over two hundred post-mortem incisions to their bodies and wings carved into their backs." She tapped the close-up photograph of the shibari tree in the Elliott murder. "None of these though."

"Were the bodies still hung on the wall?" Williams asked.

"No." Dak studied the photos of each of their victims, paying particular note to how they were suspended. She wondered if Burnett would fund an art specialist to view the photos and see if they matched anything from the past. "They were all placed on the floor, but the floor had been cleared like a canvas. I'm printing the photos to add to the wall."

Hamilton straightened up from reading Dak's screen and joined her at the boards. "Is our killer improving or experimenting?"

She stepped back to get a different perspective. "We need to see what they've got." She dropped back into her chair and began typing. "I'll ask them to FedEx everything they have over to us." Her fingers stilled as she processed the information Sergeant Cooper had given in the email. "We have a new problem."

"Aside from some crazed killer tearing around the city slicing up rich white guys?" Williams laughed without humor. "What's that?"

"Chicago has four victims starting with one in mid-December and they've had nothing since April," Dak said. "Our first victim was mid-May, and we had our third victim over the weekend." When Hamilton nodded, she waited for him to finish her train of thought.

Hamilton tapped the empty space on the second board alongside Elliott's photo and details. "We may only have one more victim before he moves out of state and onto another hunting ground."

"Then he'll be someone else's problem, and our CR goes back to normal."

Dak didn't know Williams well enough to know if he was more concerned with the PD's murder clearance rate than he was in actually solving the case. He was only a few years from retirement. Maybe he'd grown too detached from his work and was just waiting out the clock until he got his pension. His partner, Marks, was a similar age, but she couldn't imagine him saying that, even in jest.

"That's not funny." Hamilton turned on Williams. "Don't you *want* to solve this case?"

Williams grunted. "Quit being such a tight ass, rookie. You're not gonna survive this shit show if you don't have a sense of humor."

"Leave it," Dak mouthed to Hamilton. Joking or not, Williams' work on the case so far had been impeccable, and they needed all the experience the PD could offer if they were going to catch this guy before he moved on after victim number four. "It's been nearly a week since we found Elliott, and he was as close to an impulse kill as we're going to get. We have to hope that his slip-up with the blood jar has spooked him enough to slow down to his regular schedule." She finished the email to Sergeant Cooper and stood. "Come on, Hamilton, you're driving. We've got the interview with Elliott's maid in a half hour."

They headed down to the basement, and she could practically feel Hamilton's frustration vibrating off him.

"Williams can be hard to take." Hamilton unlocked the car and bounced into the driver's seat. "I better not get partnered with him when you leave."

"Why would you? He's worked with Marks for years, hasn't he?" Dak knew the basics of the squad she liaised with while she worked on the Rat Bucket case, but the ins and outs of it didn't interest her. Her interest in Hamilton's career was the exception.

"Before the second victim came in, Burnett said he was thinking about splitting them and putting me with Williams so I could 'benefit from his years of experience.'" Hamilton started the engine and drove out of the parking lot. "I'm worried that if I end up with him, my career will stall because he's just waiting out the clock."

Hamilton's concerns mirrored her own. "His work on this case has been thorough. Maybe all his bluster is for show. I think he takes his job seriously, but he uses humor to shield himself from the horrors of the occupation." Dak began to regret giving Hamilton the keys when he swerved wide to avoid a dog straining on its leash. "You seem a little distracted. Do you want to pull over and let me drive? If I'm going to die, I'd really like it to be during some act of heroism in the line of duty."

Hamilton chuckled and his shoulders seemed to drop and relax a little. "Huh, you want to go out in a blaze of glory? I didn't expect that."

"I don't want to go out in any way just yet, but I definitely don't want to die because of my partner's bad driving."

Hamilton pulled over. "Okay, you drive. You always drive. I don't know why you gave me the keys."

"Nor do I, and now I know *why* I always drive." She got out and swapped seats. "When we get back, we'll take another look at the gym membership and staff. It can't be a coincidence that all three victims went to the same gym, and the guy on CCTV looked pretty well built."

Hamilton tsked. "You're not worried about stepping on toes? Marks and Williams spent four days running through the gym."

"Maybe they missed something. Fresh eyes can go a long way. And I want to speak to the staff at the funeral home and the cemetery. Maybe they saw something at Arnold's funeral that we missed." Dak tried to keep her tone light, but she was beginning to feel the pressure. There had to be something they were missing. Nobody could leave three crime scenes completely void of any clues. With only one victim left before the serial killer skipped town, the clock was running out on their investigation. Not only that, but he'd threatened CJ, and that had made this case personal. She only hoped that wouldn't prove to be detrimental to her ability to find him before it was too late.

Chapter Twenty

CJ SPRINKLED SOME MORE chili powder into the sauce and gave it another stir. "Can I taste it now?"

Her mom laughed lightly. "Don't be in such a hurry, honey." She pulled out the tray of meatballs from the oven and placed them on a trivet.

"I've never seen anyone oven bake meatballs before. What's that about?"

"And how many people have you watched making meatballs, CJ?"

Her mom had a point. That was a club of zero. "So, what's it about?"

Her mom huffed and moved each meatball individually from the tray onto a plate covered with a paper towel. "They're less fatty, and it's easier to cook them more evenly." Her mom hung over CJ's shoulder and inhaled deeply. "That smells good. You're doing a great job."

How CJ had wanted to hear those words as a child. Since their big family talk and her parents' apology a few days ago, home had been exactly that. A different place to the one she'd grown up in, it was full of laughter and joy. She didn't dwell on the fact that Iris, her pseudo-mom had died in order to transform her real mom into the parent CJ had always wanted. She was just enjoying being looked after and feeling wanted, rather than the inconvenience she'd always felt that she was as a kid. She didn't think about how long the changes might last or if they'd last at all. She simply resolved to accept life as it was in the moment and gave her parents the clean slate they'd asked for.

"I think it's ready for the taste test," her mom said. "Go ahead."

CJ lifted the spoon, scooped the sauce with her finger, blew on it, and popped it into her mouth. "Wow. That tastes a-maz-ing."

Her mom, the queen of carryout and frozen meals, had been neglecting a God-given talent.

"Time for the meatballs." Her mom gestured to them. "Drop them in the sauce but do it carefully so the sauce doesn't splash and burn you."

CJ took the plate and placed the meatballs into the sauce one by one until the sauce was covered by the little brown balls.

"Now fold them in slowly so you don't smush them up."

CJ completed the task and smiled. "Do you think Dak will like them?"

"I think she'll love them." Her mom put her hand on CJ's shoulder and squeezed gently. "All you have to do now is keep the sauce simmering and make the spaghetti fresh when Dak gets home."

"I hope I don't mess it up." CJ turned the heat to low and placed the wooden spoon on the chrome spoon rest.

Her mom turned CJ around to face her. "Are you talking about the meal or something else?"

CJ wrinkled her nose before she walked around to a bar stool and sat. "Something else."

Her mom poured them both a glass of wine and sat beside her. "What's going on?"

CJ sighed, a little overwhelmed with both the Dak situation and with having a relationship conversation with her mom. "We're just supposed to be having fun."

"And aren't you?" her mom asked softly.

CJ blew out a breath. "Yeah."

"Then what's the problem?" Her mom clinked her glass to CJ's and sipped her wine.

That was a good question. What *was* the problem? She wouldn't be exaggerating if she told her mom that they'd had the best sex of her life. But she was never going to say that, not to her mom, even the new and improved version. "We cuddled."

Her mom laughed and sputtered her wine all over the breakfast bar. When she'd recovered and mopped up her spillage, she smiled. "Since when has cuddling been perceived as a problem in a relationship? Have things changed that much since my generation?"

"Mom! You're not that old."

She lightly tapped CJ's hand. "I wasn't saying I was old, thank you very much. But still, cuddling is a problem, why? Isn't that part of the fun?"

CJ shook her head. "Cuddles are serious." Just like Emily had asked her a few days ago, *This could get serious, couldn't it?*

"Join the dots for me, honey. Serious can't be fun?"

CJ sipped her wine and contemplated her mom's question. She'd never been serious with anyone before, so she had no comparison for what was going on between her and Dak. But the depth of connection that seemed to be developing between them was…it was something intangible. She'd never fallen asleep in anyone's arms before either, preferring to retreat to the other side of the bed, leave, or ask the other person to leave. But Dak cuddling her? Not to mention the comment about making love. And falling asleep within seconds even though she wasn't tired, the peace she felt with Dak's arms wrapped around her so tightly. That was beyond her experience.

"Are you in love with Dad?"

Her mom coughed into her wine glass again but with no spillage this time. "You've got to stop doing that to me." She dabbed the corner of her mouth. "Yes, we're in love. I fell in love with your father more or less instantly. There was lust first, but of course, you won't want to hear about that. Children rarely want to even think that their parents might have *those* sort of feelings."

CJ widened her eyes and took another, much longer, drink of wine. "Correct. Move on, please."

"You ask because you want to know what love feels like?"

That was exactly why. "You're quite good at this, Mom. I wished we'd started doing this earlier."

Her mom's expression turned serious. She placed her glass on the counter and pulled CJ's hands into hers. "If I could change one thing in my life, it would be that. I wish I'd known how to be a good mom to you."

CJ slipped her hands from her mom's grasp and pulled her into a long embrace. "Hey, you weren't so bad. I turned out okay." She released her and leaned back in her chair. "And this is great. I love talking to you."

Her mom wiped her eyes and tapped the table. "Enough of me. This conversation is about you. You're wondering about the love thing?"

"Yeah."

"You don't think you've been in love before?"

CJ shook her head. "I've had a few relationships, but I've never found myself wondering if it was love."

"How do you feel when you're around Dak?"

CJ grinned widely, unable to stop herself. "She makes me happy. Like, ecstatic euphoric happy. And we have a lot of fun, laughing and teasing each other." And the sex is out of this world, but again, boundaries. "I think about her all the time when I'm not with her, and I can't wait to be with her from the very second we part. It's crazy, Mom. It's like I'm missing something when we're not together, which is even more crazy because we hardly know each other at all. And yet, it somehow feels like it could be something special." She shrugged. "Does any of that make sense?"

"It makes no sense, and it makes perfect sense."

Her mom smiled one of those infuriating knowing smiles, and CJ threw up her arms. "Mom! That doesn't help at all. *You're* not making any sense."

"Ah, sweetheart. I can't tell you what you feel." Her mom pressed her palm to CJ's chest. "You'll feel it, and when the time is right, you'll say it to yourself and then perhaps you'll say it out loud. But there's no rush. And being in love shouldn't be seen as a problem. It's a blessing."

CJ put her head in her hands. "I think it's a problem when I'm going back to LA and Dak will go back to her job traveling all over the country."

Her mom peeled CJ's hands from her face and held them in hers again. "If it's meant to be, love always finds a way. *You'll* find a way."

"Thank you, Mom." CJ's phone buzzed. "Dak's on her way home," she said after checking the message.

"Then we'd best get this stuff over there."

Her mom released CJ's hands and got to work. CJ watched as she turned off the stove and gave the sauce one last stir. Warmth enveloped her heart, and she was overcome with gratitude for this moment right now and for having the courage and openness to give her parents a second chance, to give herself a second chance. "I love you, Mom."

Her mom dropped the spoon into the pan, making the sauce splash all over the stove top. She rushed back around the breakfast bar and drew CJ into a hug that almost stopped her breathing.

"I love you, CJ. So much."

Her mom let her go and returned to the stove. CJ heard her sniffle but didn't draw attention to it. She could have a good cry when CJ went over to Dak's. She pulled Dak's house key from her pocket and gave it to her mom. "Would you get the doors for me?"

"Of course."

CJ gathered everything else she needed, then gripped the pan with its handles and headed out. Her mom led the way and unlocked Dak's back door.

Dead *Pretty*

"Have a lovely evening, CJ."

"Thanks, Mom."

CJ closed and locked the door. The squad car had been at the bottom of their driveway all day, and it had given CJ a certain sense of safety, but it didn't hurt to keep the doors secure. She hadn't admitted it to anyone but the note had affected her. She wasn't about to show it, least of all to Dak. And that wasn't because she didn't want to appear weak or vulnerable, it was because she didn't want to give Dak anything else to worry about. She had a serial killer to catch, and she needed one hundred percent of her focus on that. CJ was sure Dak didn't need the distraction of a paranoid lover. It was most likely an empty threat anyway. It wasn't like anyone saw his handiwork once his victim was in the casket, and the wider public didn't see it at all.

She pushed the thoughts away and concentrated on getting dinner ready. It wasn't long before Dak arrived.

She stood at the kitchen doorway and whistled. "That's a sight I could get used to."

CJ did her best to strut across the kitchen like a sexy fifties' housewife. She got on her tiptoes and greeted Dak with a passionate kiss. "Is that right?" she asked when they came up for air. "You expect me to give up my TV career and follow you around the country while you solve decades' old murders?" She ran her fingernail across Dak's bottom lip, the way she'd quickly learned drove Dak crazy. "That sounds a little backward to me."

Dak put her hands on CJ's hips, lifted her up, and lowered her to sit on the table. "You're making assumptions. Maybe I envisaged me coming home from a shift with the LAPD and you were on one of your rare non-shooting days, making me my favorite dish of," Dak sniffed the air, "spaghetti and meatballs." She ran her fingers through CJ's hair and pulled her in for a deeper kiss. "And maybe it's my only night off from cooking for *you* every day."

"Is it really your favorite dish?" CJ asked, beginning to unbutton Dak's shirt.

"Not yet, but it has a strong chance of getting up there, especially if you're the dessert it always comes with."

CJ pulled back and looked into Dak's eyes. Beyond the plain-to-see desire, CJ searched for something else, something that matched how she felt.

Dak gently caressed her cheek. "What are you looking for, babe?"

"I'll tell you if I find it."

Dak smiled. "Or you could just ask me."

CJ bit her lip and shook her head slightly. They'd been sleeping together less than a week. Surely it was too early for any kind of heavy conversation. And what would she ask Dak anyway when CJ wasn't sure what was going on in her own head, in her own heart? But there was more behind Dak's lustful expression. CJ thought she could see and feel it, unless it was just what she wanted to see. "How was your afternoon?"

Dak chuckled. "Or you could just say you don't want to talk about it and change the subject?" She kissed CJ's nose and untangled herself. "Did you make this?" She pulled out the wooden spoon, gave it a quick blow, and tasted the sauce. "That could definitely become my favorite meal."

CJ hopped from the table and wrapped her arms around Dak's waist. "I made it under the strict supervision of the new Dominique Crenn. Who knew my mom was a fancy chef?"

Dak turned to face CJ. "Do you really want to know about my day at work? It doesn't seem like that might be in keeping with the casual fun you were looking for."

CJ shrugged. "Neither was spooning, but that happened."

Dak frowned. "Regrets?"

CJ shook her head. "I don't believe in them." She laughed and placed her hand on Dak's bare chest. "That's total BS. Everyone has regrets, but no, falling asleep in your arms after *not* having sex isn't one of mine. So, yes, I do want to hear about your day, particularly since I have a vested interest in you catching the guy before he gets to me." If she made light of the situation, maybe it wouldn't seem so scary. Dak's jaw clenched, indicating she wasn't prepared to joke about it.

"I don't suppose you've had second thoughts about working your magic on the third victim, have you?"

CJ raised her eyebrow and gave Dak her most serious glare, though it was incredibly touching that Dak was so protective of her. "Have you had second thoughts about not abandoning this case and going back to your regular work?"

Dak rolled her eyes. "You're very stubborn."

CJ stroked Dak's soft skin and sighed. "And you're very sexy."

"I can't talk about work if you're going to keep doing that." Dak caught CJ's wrist. "And your culinary masterpiece will definitely burn."

CJ pulled away, reached around Dak, and turned off the stove. She was torn between wanting Dak to take her upstairs and hearing all about any developments on the case. Her desire to be safe trumped the rest of her desires. "Stop woman-handling me then, and I'll serve our dinner."

Dak grinned. "I'll pour the wine."

They moved around the kitchen in a silent dance as Dak got drinks and CJ plated their food.

"Are you hungry?" CJ hovered over Dak's plate with a third scoop of meatballs.

"Starving. I haven't eaten anything substantial since breakfast."

CJ took the chair that Dak held out for her before she joined her. CJ smiled at the small gesture and quietly enjoyed it. "So, good or bad day at work?" She wound a forkful of spaghetti and popped it into her mouth, suddenly aware of the blissful domestic scene she was a central part of. It was simultaneously a tiny bit scary and completely comfortable.

"A little of both. It looks like our killer has been active in at least one other city before coming here."

"And is that the good or the bad part?"

Dak chewed on a meatball before answering. "It's bad that there are four more victims, but it's good because it gives us more data and hopefully, more clues."

CJ took a sip of wine, only briefly thinking about how her personal trainer probably wouldn't approve of her consuming her second glass of wine of the day along with a red meat and pasta dish. "Four victims killed and displayed in the same way?"

"Very similarly but arranged on the ground instead of hung up. And no shibari trees."

"Do you think he's going to stop at four and then move on again?" Relief washed over her, which she immediately felt guilty for. She hadn't wanted this killer's attention, but now that she'd got it, she wasn't doing anything other than inviting more by agreeing to tend to his third victim. She couldn't have it all ways.

"I can't predict a pattern with only one other set of victims."

CJ saw the hesitation in Dak's expression. "You're expecting more to be discovered, aren't you?"

Dak nodded. "I'll know more when we get the evidence boxes from Chicago PD tomorrow."

They were silent for a few moments while they ate. Dak put her fork down and placed her hand over CJ's.

"I'll protect you, CJ. I wouldn't ever let anything happen to you."

CJ smiled. She wanted to believe that with every fiber of her being, but she accepted it might well be something beyond Dak's control. She couldn't be here, babysitting her all day and night. She had a killer to catch, and all her focus should be on that. CJ found herself wondering if she should pull back from whatever was happening between them. Wasn't she an unnecessary distraction?

"No, you're not." Dak squeezed her hand gently.

"Did I say that out loud?" Christ, what else had Dak heard? She pushed away her wine with her free hand. Maybe she needed to lay off that for the rest of the night.

"I do need to concentrate on catching this guy, but that doesn't mean we can't carry on doing...this."

So, Dak was unsure about them too. Perhaps they could talk about it after all.

"I don't want to put the brakes on whatever is happening between us," Dak said. "I won't stop my life when..."

"When what?" If Dak laid out her cards, maybe CJ would find it easier to do the same.

"When we're having so much fun being in the moment. My regular job is all about the past, what's gone before, and I analyze it to the nth degree. But this, what's going on between us, is spontaneous and freeing. Honestly, I've never had it happen before, and I like the way it feels. And I want to see where it leads if that's okay with you. Maybe it'll work out, maybe it won't. But maybe means possibly, right?"

CJ's heart melted at Dak's willingness to be so open, especially since CJ wasn't feeling courageous enough to match it. And CJ needed to figure out exactly what it was she did feel before talking to Dak about it. For all she knew, she could just be caught up in the idea of something serious. Returning home to lick her wounds and connecting with her parents had already been emotionally taxing. She needed to process all of that and not get carried away with her feelings or pseudo-feelings for Dak.

"*Is* that okay with you?"

Dead *Pretty*

CJ sighed deeply. She wanted, more than anything right now, to explore their relationship. She hadn't been in love before. She was sure of that even if she wasn't sure how love actually felt. She nodded. "It's more than okay."

What was the worst that could happen anyway? Dak could break her heart. But wasn't that what hearts were for?

Chapter Twenty-One

"I won't stop my life when it feels like it might finally be starting," was what she'd wanted to say. But that seemed too strong, too heavy to say to CJ when she'd been very clear about what she was looking for. And CJ was right. Dak did need to concentrate on catching this serial killer, especially if he had plans to move on after four victims.

Last night, instead of heading straight to bed after dinner, they'd settled on the couch with their wine, and they'd talked. They'd talked about high school, about dreams, about foods they thought were disgusting. They'd laughed and teased each other. And when they'd gone to bed, Dak had taken her time, tracing every inch of CJ's body, memorizing it. They'd fallen asleep wrapped around each other, and when she'd woken with CJ in her arms, it had been just about perfect.

She opened the first of three boxes that had arrived this morning from Sergeant Cooper. *Focus.*

"Farrell. My office. Now." Burnett left his office door open and flicked his blinds closed.

She didn't appreciate his barked instruction, but she was still too nicely chilled from her evening with CJ to care. Shit was probably just rolling his way from the chief, and he had to pass it onto the squad via her.

Hamilton's eyes widened. "What have you done, golden goose?"

"Nothing, as far as I know." Dak punched his shoulder as she walked past his desk. "It's probably about you. He's checking in to see if I want to swap partners."

"Why are you so mean?"

Dak winked. "You bring out the worst in me, buddy." She caught his satisfied smile. It was almost cute that he was so easy to please. "Captain?"

"Close the door."

She clenched her jaw and pushed the door closed with more force than was necessary. Maybe she wasn't as chilled as she thought she was.

"Apparently I don't need to waste money on overtime for a patrol outside your girlfriend's house at night."

"Excuse me?" She eased into one of the comfortable chairs by the window rather than one of the office chairs in front of his desk. If he wanted to play power games, she'd be happy to. She'd gotten a little rusty over the past couple of weeks, having settled into a relaxed partner jive with Hamilton, but she'd had years of captains and chiefs all over the country acting high and mighty, throwing their weight around and trying to intimidate her. It never worked.

"It's come to my attention that you and the TV star are intimately involved."

So the officers in the squad car couldn't keep their mouths shut. Dak doubted that they'd snitched directly to the captain. Juicy gossip like this had a habit of making its way up the chain of command. She could've said that she and CJ were just friends when she spoke to them yesterday. Christ, word traveled fast in this PD.

"And then there's this."

Burnett tossed a magazine across the office, and it landed on the table in front of her. She didn't recognize the name of the publication, but she did recognize the face and body on the front page: Wallace Arnold. The sub-headline promised more "stunning pictures" inside. Dak flicked the paper open to see color photos of Arnold's body before and after CJ had worked on him.

"How do you suppose they got hold of those?" Burnett asked. "I hear your girlfriend's show got canceled. Is this her sick way of drumming up attention to get herself a new contract?"

Dak didn't know her that well, but she was sure that CJ wouldn't pull a stunt like that. CJ spoke highly of the owner of the home too, so she didn't think he was responsible for this either. He was getting enough free publicity just from CJ working on the victims. He didn't need to do something this low. Still, she didn't know that for certain and would have to ask them both. "First of all, who I'm sleeping with is none of your bus—"

"It damn well is when they're part of a murder case you're investigating."

Burnett smacked his hand on his desk. The central vein in his forehead bulged, almost comically. Dak closed the magazine and placed it back on the table. "I'm almost certain that Ms. Johnson isn't responsible for this leak, but we've got the funeral home on our list to visit today to interview staff, so I'll be sure to ask her. And I'll find out who else had access to Mr. Arnold's body while he was at the funeral home."

"I want you on this case, Farrell, but this complicates things. If you lose perspective, I'll have no choice but to kick you off it and you'll have to go back to your field office and chase your next cold corpse case."

He'd been happy enough when her work on the Rat Bucket case caught the most prolific serial killer in Beehive state history. His apparent disdain for her work was new and no doubt borne from receiving a shitstorm from the chief or the assistant chief. And he seemed to have forgotten that she'd never asked to be involved in this case. All that said, now that CJ's life had been threatened, there was no way she could leave them to it and head off to Seattle, via a quick visit to her mom. She tried to ignore the part of her that knew he was partly right. When she'd gotten involved with CJ, Dak had no idea she'd end up working on the victims and get caught up in the case. By then though, it was too late, and Dak hadn't wanted to entertain giving CJ up. Dak just had to play ball and let Burnett play the big dog. "I can guarantee I won't lose perspective, captain."

He tilted his head slightly and seemed to relax a little. "I've got the brass breathing down my neck on this one, Farrell. We haven't had anything like this in our city since the twenty-year-old case you just closed. And that's why I wanted you to stay on and help us solve it." He got up from his chair, came around his desk, and looked through the window into the squad room. "Hamilton's going to be a great homicide detective, and you mentoring him is playing a big part in that." He turned back and stared at her. "Look me in the eye and tell me this isn't going to be a problem."

She stared into his eyes. "It's not going to be a problem." Her phone buzzed in her pocket. "Do you mind if I check this?" She'd already retrieved it and seen it was a text from CJ. "It's from Ms. Johnson. She's working on Elliott's body today, and I asked her to contact me if she found anything unusual."

"Sure."

The slow and labored way he returned to his desk and dropped into his chair reinforced Dak's long-held notion that she never wanted that kind of promotion. He looked five years older than he had two weeks ago, before the second victim was found. No, a desk job wasn't for her, especially one with so much external and political pressure. She liked working alone. Well, she'd adjusted to it after Ben's death, and it had been working just fine until she was landed with Hamilton.

I've got another letter from the killer. What do you want me to do with it? X

"Shit." Dak jumped up from her chair. "CJ—Ms. Johnson has received another note from the killer."

Burnett waved her out of the office. "Go. Handle it. Catch this motherfucker."

"Yes, captain." She picked up the magazine, left the office, and whacked Hamilton's shoulder. "Come on, rookie. We've got another note from the killer. We're headed to the funeral home." She called CJ while he grabbed his jacket. "Are you okay?"

CJ laughed gently. "Of course I am. It's just a piece of paper. Our clerk got it from the mailbox and is the only one who's touched it aside from me."

Dak heard the nerves in CJ's voice. She didn't sound quite like herself. Whatever the note said, it had more impact than the first one. Dak had been impressed with CJ's reaction to that note and had hoped she wouldn't have to test her courage with a second one. Its arrival was inevitable once CJ had agreed to work on Elliott. "That's great. I'm coming over with Hamilton now. We should be there in less than half an hour. Don't let anyone else touch it."

"I won't. Hurry."

Hearing CJ's fear was like the killer had reached into Dak's chest, wrapped his cold fingers around her heart, and squeezed. She followed Hamilton down to their car silently. She'd guaranteed she wouldn't lose her perspective on this case, but now she wasn't so sure. She reasoned that CJ's life being under threat would only serve to sharpen her resolve…as long as she could see past the choking dread that she might not be able to find the killer before he made good on his threat to harm CJ.

"What did the captain want?" Hamilton asked once they were on the road.

"He'd been told about my relationship with CJ."

He snapped his head around so fast, Dak thought his neck might break. "I didn't say anything to anyone about that. You believe me, right?"

Dak allowed a smile to form and didn't have the spite in her to mess with him. "I do."

"I'd never snitch on a partner, especially not you."

Dead *Pretty*

"Relax. I said I believe you, and I do. He was more concerned about the photos in some nasty gossip magazine that's printed photographs of Arnold before and after CJ had worked on him. It was clear the pictures were taken at the funeral home, and Burnett thinks CJ leaked them to get her show back on the air."

Hamilton tilted his head and looked serious. "And did she?"

Dak shrugged. "I really don't think so. She's not *that* kind of celebrity. But I'll have to ask her just to eliminate her from suspicion."

Hamilton whistled. "Rather you than me. She's got that fiery woman thing going on. She looks like a pussy cat but there's a mean mountain lion inside just waiting to pounce."

Dak had exactly the same thought. "That's a great idea. You can ask her."

"Hey, that's not what I meant at all."

Dak took one hand from the steering wheel and patted his shoulder. "Divide and conquer, buddy. I'll talk to the clerk, and you ask CJ if she's leaked disturbing photographs to a gossip magazine for money and or to boost her career."

Hamilton squirmed in his seat. "I'd take a bullet for you, Farrell, but I don't think I can take on your femme fatale."

Dak's mood turned at the mention of taking a bullet. Ben had done that and not lived to joke about it. "Forget it. I wouldn't make you do that."

"I will, if you really need me to."

He sounded panicked and had obviously picked up on her cool tone, but he'd misjudged the reason. Now seemed as good a time as any to tell him about it. She turned the radio down and glanced at him. "My last partner took a bullet for me, Hamilton. He didn't survive."

"Ah, shit, Farrell, I'm sorry. I didn't know. I'm an ass."

She shook her head. "No need to apologize. I'm not telling you to make you feel bad, I'm telling you so that you understand some of the crap I carry around. That's all." She'd never told anyone about Ben before this case, and now she'd shared her story with her new partner *and* her new… Her new what? Girlfriend? Whatever, that wasn't something that should be on her mind right now.

"Is that why you usually work alone?" he asked quietly.

Dak nodded. "I'm a cliché, I know. But he'd be too hard to replace." And she didn't want someone else's death on her conscience again. One was more than enough. She was thankful when Hamilton said nothing else, and they rode the rest of the way in silence.

CJ greeted them at the main door and ushered them into a side office. "There it is."

Dak pulled on a pair of latex gloves and opened the note.

I thought you were a real artist, but you're not. It seems like you're the kind of fraud who would fix both arms on the Venus de Milo. You were warned. You've given me no choice.

Dak glanced at CJ and saw her hands shaking. Dak folded the note back up and dropped it and the envelope into the evidence bag Hamilton held open for her. "No one else at the funeral home has touched this apart from you and your clerk?"

CJ nodded. "That's right."

"We got your prints after the first note, but we're going to need your clerk to come down to the station and give theirs. What's their name?"

"Donald Burns. He's in the office at the end of the corridor if you want to talk to him?"

"We will. We want to talk to all the staff that work here, about the murders and the magazine." Dak studied CJ for her immediate response and saw nothing to raise her suspicions, thankfully.

"Magazine? What about a magazine?"

Hamilton blew out a noisy breath beside her, and Dak glared at him before she pulled the offending publication from her jacket pocket and placed it on the table. "This one."

CJ drew it close to her and gasped. "What the hell? How did they get those pictures?"

It was exactly the response Dak was hoping for. CJ was on TV but she wasn't an actor, and she couldn't fake that reaction or fool Dak. "That's what our captain wants to know." Dak leaned over the desk and flicked through to the four-page feature. She tapped the photographs. "It's clear they were taken here. You can see the home's branded white jackets hanging on the wall. They've been taken by someone who had access to your preparation area while Arnold's body was here."

CJ looked at Dak and narrowed her eyes. "You don't think—"

Dak raised her hand. "No, I don't. But my captain does, and I want to disabuse him of that notion by giving him the person who did."

"I can't believe anyone here would do this."

Dead *Pretty*

Dak grimaced. "Yeah, but someone has. Can you give me a list of names of the people who could have gone down there?"

CJ shook her head slowly. "That area's locked when there's no mortician present, so the person who did this has to have keys. That's a small list. Are you ready?"

Dak indicated to Hamilton to note down the names, and CJ gave him the details of four people.

"That's a small outfit. Are any of those people here now?" Dak asked.

"All of them, and yeah, Bernie has always resisted the big companies who wanted to take the business and make it a faceless franchise." CJ gestured to the filing cabinet behind the desk. "All the personnel records are in here, and Bernie has given permission for you to go through all of it. Is there anything else you need? I have to get started on Mr. Elliott."

Dak looked over CJ's shoulder and through the office window. She spotted a guy in their height range loading a hand truck of flower boxes into the back of a panel van. "Who's that?"

CJ turned around and followed Dak's gaze. "Terry Mitchum. He's the groundskeeper at the cemetery. He's just collecting some flowers from an order error."

Mitchum wasn't on the list of people CJ had just given them, but his size and build matched someone capable of hoisting dead men in the air and suspending them from fanciful rope trees. "Do you know anything about him?"

"Only that he's very nice. I met him when I went there to say goodbye to Iris, and he comes by every day to see Beth, our clerk. He brings her flowers *every* day."

Dak ignored the unsubtle hint for now but filed it away for later use. "Iris is the woman who gave you an apprenticeship here and was like a mom to you?"

CJ arched her eyebrows. "I'm impressed."

Dak smiled. She would've remembered everything CJ had told her on their first date anyway, but she was bound to remember something that important. She turned to Hamilton. "Make a start on that list and see if you can shake anything loose. I'm going to have a chat with that guy."

Hamilton frowned. "You don't want to do it together? What if he runs or turns violent?"

"Pah." CJ laughed. "Terry? Beth says he's a gentle giant."

"Let's hope so." Dak nodded toward the door to get Hamilton moving. "I don't want to spook him going in heavy with two of us. You'll hear me if I need you." She waited until he'd left before turning her attention back to CJ. "You're not going to be here alone at any point today, are you?"

CJ looked like she was suppressing a grin. "You make a very good protector."

Dak tapped the badge hanging from the top pocket of her jacket. "It's a pre-requisite for the job. Answer the question, please." Dak still heard the niggle of anxiety beneath CJ's teasing.

"No, I won't be alone. Bernie always insists on locking up with Beth." CJ stepped closer to Dak and ran her finger along the lapel of her jacket. "But I love this side of you."

An old man and a clerk. It wasn't exactly heavy security. Dak gently brushed CJ's touch away and moved to the office door. She wanted to catch Terry the gentle giant before he left. "Weren't you the one telling me I needed to keep my focus on catching this killer? I can't do that if you're going to put the moves on me when I'm at work."

CJ giggled. "Then I'll wait to 'put the moves' on you until you get home."

Home. There was that word again. Where was her home if not with her mom and brother? Wherever she laid her badge? She pushed those thoughts away and headed outside. "Hey. Terry, is it?"

Mitchum looked up and held her gaze. "Morning, officer. Yep, I'm Terry. Guilty as charged."

His easy laugh matched his relaxed general demeanor. He wasn't squirrelly or nervous at her approach.

"I'm Special Agent Farrell with the FBI. Do you mind if I ask you a couple of questions?" Dak mirrored his smile and stepped off the curb to join him on the road so she didn't stand taller than him, though he didn't seem the type who might intimidate easily.

"Oh, I'm sorry to call you officer. Fire away, Special Agent Farrell." He loaded the last box and the trolley onto his van, closed the doors, and leaned casually against them.

She glanced at his boots but couldn't tell if they were Dickies or not. "I assume you've heard about the serial killer active in the city?"

He nodded. "Yes, ma'am. I read they're calling him 'the Artist.'"

Nothing. He didn't break eye contact. No body movement or shifting on his feet. He was completely comfortable.

"That's an unfortunate moniker and not really deserved. I think people might just celebrate when he's dead rather than celebrating his work after he's dead." Dak smiled, and Mitchum laughed.

"Ha, that's funny. No one'll be buying his work for millions of dollars either."

"I hope not. Anyway, we're looking to scrub off guys who match the killer's height and build—"

"Ah, I get it." He turned and faced the van before kicking up each of his legs in turn to show her the soles of his shoes. "I read you had some boot prints at one of the crime scenes, huh?" He faced her again. "I'm a size thirteen. I don't know if that takes me out of the picture or not."

Dak nodded. "Thanks, that's helpful." She wasn't about to tell him the size of the print they'd found and have him tell the press. Burnett's heart would probably explode if they had another leak on the case. She'd said to Hamilton that she hadn't wanted to spook this guy, but if he was any more laid back, he'd be in a coma. She decided to go in harder. "Maybe you could tell me where you were on the nights of the three murders between five and eight p.m. They were the fifteenth of May and the fifteenth and twenty-second of June." She held no expectation that he'd know his whereabouts. She simply wanted to study his reaction.

"Between five and eight?" He tucked both hands in his pockets and leaned back against his van. "That might be easy then. I spend a lot of nights visiting my mom in her nursing home. I'm there Mondays, Tuesdays, Wednesdays, Thursdays, and Saturdays." He shrugged and pulled out his phone. "I don't know what days those dates fall on, but I can check."

Dak took out her notepad and jotted down Mitchum's visiting evenings. "That's okay. I can check those later. Could you tell me the name of your mom's nursing home so I can corroborate your alibi and stop bothering you?" She kept her tone light and non-threatening, but he seemed completely unfazed by her questions.

"Sure thing. It's the Willows Residence on Kennedy Boulevard."

She saw the sadness flicker behind his eyes.

He sighed deeply. "It's one of the top homes in the country for people with dementia. It's why I moved here in April. I want her to have the best care for however long...y'know." His voice faltered.

"I'm so sorry. Alzheimer's is such a cruel disease." Dak noted the name and quelled the rush of excitement at Mitchum's dates matching with the end of the Chicago murders and preceding the ones in Salt Lake. The press knew nothing about Chicago yet or how they might be related. Hell, she hadn't sorted through the evidence boxes and come to that conclusion yet, but coincidences were very rarely unexplainable. He'd given up that information without prompt though. If this was their guy, could he be that cool or was he just that arrogant?

"She still recognizes me and that's what I'm hanging onto." He smiled but his chin quivered slightly. "I don't know how I'll cope if that day ever comes."

"I can't imagine how hard it must be." She swallowed the sudden bubble of sorrow as her own dad's demise jumped into her mind. "That's so wonderful of you to relocate your own life so your mom can get the best care."

He put his phone back in his jeans and shrugged. "I wouldn't have a life if my mom hadn't given me one. I figure this is the least I can do."

His commitment and loyalty to his family put her to shame. But this wasn't about her. "Where did you live before?"

"Cedar Rapids, Iowa. It's where I grew up."

She nodded, and the rush of adrenaline slowed...a little. Cedar Rapids was four hours from Chicago. That'd be a hell of a commute. And that didn't discount him as a suspect, not until his alibi checked out. "Was it a sudden decision to move your mom?" Four victims in Chicago, and three victims here already. If he was the killer and he'd been forced to relocate, maybe four wasn't his magic number and he wasn't about to move on.

"No. She'd been on their waiting list for over a year. We moved here as soon as a place became available."

Hamilton came into her periphery in the doorway of the funeral home and waved for her attention. "Looks like I'm needed elsewhere. Thanks for your time, Mr. Mitchum. Do you have a card, or can I get your home address in case I have any follow up questions?"

"Or my alibi doesn't check out?" His easy laugh returned. "I don't have a card, but I can write my details in your little book."

Dak turned the page over to give him a blank sheet and offered it to him along with her pen. He duly obliged then handed them back to her. Dak clicked her pen and slipped it into her inside pocket, along with her leather notebook. She'd get forensics to lift his prints from the pen, but again, he'd given them freely. Or stupidly. And their killer was far from stupid. "That's great. Thanks again."

"Don't mention it, Agent Farrell." He put two fingers to his temple and saluted her before walking alongside his van and getting in.

She watched him drive away, smooth and unhurried, then headed back up the walkway to Hamilton. She stopped, pulled out her notebook, and studied his handwriting. Neat, block capitals that gave nothing away, just like he'd done with the rest of the impromptu interview. They'd visit the nursing home and check his alibi. She wanted a read on him from the staff there, and a quick look in at his mom, if they'd allow it.

Mitchum had been more than accommodating with her questions and hadn't been defensive or nervous at all. She'd talk to Beth too, to see if he was as great a catch as CJ had made him out to be. Flowers every day. Who had the time for that? He was probably taking them from someone's mausoleum. But that wasn't the kind of crime she was interested in. She had a pen in her pocket with at least a partial print, and some leads to follow up. The personal trainer remained their prime suspect, but Dak still wasn't convinced. He had opportunity and he knew all three victims, but she couldn't identify a motive. A lot of homicide detectives didn't care for motive. As long as the evidence nailed their guy to the cross, that's all they needed. But Dak always wanted more. The why of it, understanding what was natural and what had been carelessly nurtured was what got her out of bed every morning.

She put her book back in her pocket and went to see what Hamilton had called her away for. The personal trainer and the cemetery grounds keeper—she couldn't see a motive for either of them. Two weeks into the investigation and that's all she had. Dak couldn't help thinking they were clutching at straws with both of them.

Was this killer beyond her abilities, or did she just need more time? The problem with more time was inevitably there'd be more victims. And more victims would mean more work for CJ. That intensified the killer's attention on her. He'd made a mistake with Elliott, rushed it, not done his due diligence with Elliott's schedule, and left the scene in a hurry. It was likely CJ's presence that had prompted him to kill when he wasn't properly prepared. Her high-profile work with his victims might lead to his downfall, but Dak couldn't shake the dread that CJ might also fall with him.

Chapter Twenty-Two

CJ RAN HER HANDS over the uneven alabaster block and a warm glow filled her heart. In the last light streaming through the windows from the setting sun, hues of orange, red, and purple danced on its surface. She'd thought about drawing something first, but she was impatient to start. She wanted to see if her ability to create without planning was still there, or if it had deserted her after such lengthy neglect. Sculpting dead people into their former selves was different. There was no freedom to express herself, and there were photographs of exactly how the person had looked prior to their usually untimely death. In LA, she'd been asked to "fix" the occasional movie star who'd died from old age. Their loved ones invariably wanted the clock turned back a decade or so, and that afforded a little more room for artistry. But here, older people were far less vain, and her skills weren't required for the deaths from natural causes. Even the victims of the Artist were mostly about filling and blending.

She'd worked on Elliott for a total of nineteen hours after Bernie had completed the initial embalming process, and she was exhausted. But the draw of working in this studio for the first time had been too hard to deny, and Dak still wasn't home from work. Last night, she hadn't gotten back until nearly midnight, and her latest text predicted the same for tonight. With Dak getting to work at seven a.m., CJ wasn't the only one too tired for anything other than a quick tumble and an all-night snuggle when they fell into bed.

CJ picked up her hammer and chisel and began, not yet sure what the alabaster might reveal but also knowing that Dak might well be her current muse. CJ hadn't sculpted anything since college when she'd been part of a club. That had been the closest she could get to art school after her father had forbidden her from applying. Almost a decade later, and the same father had built her a studio and equipped it with the finest tools. Would she still be able to coax the stone into something special, or would her first effort in eight years be a complete disaster? She grinned. She didn't care, and it didn't matter. She was just ecstatic to have these tools in her hands and a lump of rock in front of her, ready for her to do her worst.

Her phone pinged the arrival of a message. "Siri, read message."

"Meeting went—"

Her phone ringing interrupted Siri's robotic tone. "Siri, answer phone."

"CJ, it's Paige. Is it a good time?"

CJ placed her tools on the tray beside her stool and pushed away on the stool. It wheeled her to the desk where her phone sat in a special phone-sized leather armchair of its own. Apparently, her father had become quite quirky as well as super supportive. She suppressed the army of anxious butterflies in her stomach as it dawned on her why Paige would be calling. CJ had almost forgotten that the Netflix meeting had been today. Well, she'd tried to forget it, especially as she'd figured the one p.m. meeting—two, her time—could only have lasted a couple of hours and that Paige was likely trying to find the words to let CJ down gently after getting her hopes up at the fan event.

"Yeah, of course." CJ swapped seats into the phone's matching adult leather armchair. "I was just about to start hammering at a chunk of rock."

"You've taken up your sculpting again?"

CJ loved that no matter how minuscule the detail and how long ago she'd told her, Paige remembered every little thing she'd ever told her. CJ supposed it was why she attracted all the big stars *and* kept them. "I am, and you won't believe where I'm doing it."

"I really have no idea. Tell me."

"Dad turned his den into a studio for me."

"What?" Paige shouted so loud that the sound distorted slightly. "He did what?"

"You wouldn't believe it." CJ propped her feet on the oak desk and looked out the window. The sun was bidding farewell in a halo of burnt sienna-edged cloud, and it cast a romantic blush over the lawn and trees in their backyard. *She* couldn't believe it. With this view, there was little wonder her father had spent so many hours locked away in here. "They've completely changed, and they're trying to be better parents. They're interested in my work, they want to support my art, and Mom's become the world's best cook."

"That's wonderful, CJ. I'm really happy for you." She coughed a little. "What I've got to tell you won't matter too much."

Dead *Pretty*

Shit. The deal had gone down the toilet and Netflix wanted nothing to do with her. Maybe it was for the best. With super sexy Agent Dak living next door, the new and improved 2.0 version of her parents, her friendship with Emily revived, *and* her job back at Bernie's, she'd somehow built a whole new life for herself in less than two weeks of being home.

"CJ? Are you still there?"

"Sorry, yes, of course. Netflix took a hard pass on the show?"

Paige laughed. "What? No! They love you, and they were even more desperate to get the show after all the coverage you've been getting on that serial killer case in Utah."

"Oh, really?" CJ bounced in the chair. "Because it's been so long since the meeting, I thought that you were trying to decide how to let me down gently."

"No way. I've only just come out of the meeting. It took so long because they've got huge plans for the show, and we had to talk terms on the various elements they want you to commit to. We need to have a long, long conversation so I can take you through everything they want from you. I have another studio meeting with Elodie tomorrow, so Sian's going to organize flights for us to come to you on Sunday. Does that work for you?"

CJ hadn't made any other plans than dinner with her parents and a little time with Dak if she could get away from the station for a few hours. "Of course." She paused. This turned everything upside down, but it was upside down in a good way, wasn't it? "How soon will it be before we start shooting again?"

"That won't be for a little while," Paige said. "They don't want to rush it. They want the relaunch to be absolutely perfect. There's so much planning to be done, CJ, you won't believe it. But I'll tell you all about it on Sunday. Sian will email you with the details of our flight and hotel. And also, can you get Emily to come with you? Sian's been looking into her background and work history, and everything's looking very promising. I want to talk to her about joining me."

CJ grinned and slapped the arm of her chair. "Yes! That's great news."

"But not as great as your Netflix news, superstar."

Emily would probably disagree, but Paige was right from CJ's point of view. "Thanks again, Paige. You really are the best agent. I lucked out persuading you to take me on."

"Let's just say that we're both lucky. I've got another call coming in, CJ. Sian will be in touch. See you on Sunday."

"Perfect."

CJ sat in the darkening dusk of the evening, the vibrant screen display of her phone the only illumination. She remained there for a while, trying to process everything Paige had just told her. The deal sounded huge, and CJ was excited to learn more details over the weekend. But then there was Dak and her parents. Things were going so well here, though Dak would be moving on as soon as she solved the Artist case. Would she have to sacrifice that new happiness to go back to Hollywood, to being alone? Although, it looked like Emily would be relocating if she and Paige could agree on terms.

She leaned forward, grabbed her phone, and called Emily. Talking about her new fantastic opportunity would mean CJ didn't have to think too hard about her own.

"Hey, babe, what's up? Have you heard anything about the Netflix meeting?"

CJ put her phone on speaker and placed it back in its comfy cradle. "I have. Do you want to come out and celebrate with me?"

Barely a nanosecond had passed before the effusion began.

"Oh my God, it's good news, isn't it? You've got a huge deal. That's bad news for me, isn't it? You're leaving us, aren't you? I love having you back home, and now you're going again. When are you going? It's not soon, is it?"

"Whoa, slow down." CJ laughed at her friend's stream of questions. "Do you want to go for a quick drink? I'll have you home before the Ferrari turns into a pumpkin."

"Yes, yes. Of course, yes. What are you wearing?"

CJ looked down but could barely see what she was dressed in. She turned on the desk light and glanced across to the untouched alabaster. It would wait. "Scruffy clothes right now, but I'll throw on a pair of jeans and a T-shirt. Just casual. We'll go to Corky's and shoot some pool."

"What about your police escort? Will they come with you? Is at least one of them a hot guy?"

CJ hadn't considered that, but she wasn't about to let the killer ruin their night. "They can come if they want, but I'm not staying in with the news I've just had."

"What news is that?" Dak asked.

CJ hadn't heard the door open. She jumped up and held her hand out to Dak. "One second." She picked up her phone. "Em. I'll pick you up in thirty minutes. Ciao, babe." She ended the call and tossed her phone onto the desk before running across the studio and jumping into Dak's arms.

Dak lifted her off her feet, held her tight, and kissed her hard. "That's a very nice welcome. What's your news?"

"Paige called to let me know that Netflix wants the show, and that they've got some big plans for it and me. She's flying up here on Sunday to walk me through their proposal." She wrapped her hand around Dak's neck and pulled her into another kiss. "*And* Paige wants to talk to Emily about offering her a job."

Dak guided CJ back to the floor and released her. CJ didn't miss Dak's jaw clench and unclench a couple of times. Bad day at work or something else?

"That is good news," Dak said and released CJ from her embrace. She wandered over to the window by the desk. "This is a great room. That's a beautiful view."

"Is something wrong? Have you had another victim?" CJ asked.

"No, we haven't." Dak turned back to face her. "I've sent the patrol home. Can Emily come here for you to celebrate?"

CJ frowned. "Absolutely not. I want to go out for a few drinks with my best friend to toast some of the best news either of us has had in a long time."

Dak raised her eyebrows. "That's not very responsible, CJ."

CJ scoffed. What the hell was this? "What have I got to be responsible for?"

"Your safety, and your friend's. You've had two death threats from a serial killer, CJ. You can't gallivant around the city like nothing's happening."

"Gallivant?" She laughed but Dak's expression remained serious. "If I want to 'gallivant around the city' dancing and drinking, I will." She took a few steps toward Dak but sensed the distance between them was currently more metaphorical than physical. "I'm not going to allow some psycho with a knife to stop me from living."

"No one's asking you to stop living, CJ. There's no need to be so melodramatic. But the squad car has gone, and I can't get them back to escort you on a girls' night out with your bestie."

Dak's tone had hardened in a way CJ hadn't heard before. She didn't care to hear more of it. She turned and headed for the door. "Me and my melodramatic self are going to pick Emily up. See yourself out." CJ exited the studio and stormed to her room. She got changed in record time and chose tighter jeans, a sexier and tighter T-shirt, and heels two inches higher than all of the ones she'd originally thought she might throw on. She went downstairs, quickly let her parents know she was going out—and no, she didn't want to invite Emily over instead—and went out the front door. Dak stood by her truck, which was blocking CJ's Ferrari in the driveway.

CJ took a deep breath. "If I reverse *this* car into your old truck, the insurance bill is going to be astronomical."

Dak held up her hands. "Relax. I'm not trying to stop you going anywhere. I'll just follow you…if that's okay?"

Dak's uncertainty was sweet, especially following what CJ would probably class as their first fight—though it was more of a disagreement, really. She wasn't about to start allowing anyone to clip her wings. Still, she wasn't happy with how Dak had spoken to her so there was no way CJ was about to ask her to join them. "We'll be fine. I don't need a police escort."

Dak gave a small smile. "Lucky I'm not the police then." Dak opened her truck door. "I'll hang back. You won't even know I'm there."

CJ huffed. Dak was a brick shed of a woman, nearly six feet tall, and commanded the attention of any room she entered—like she could be *anywhere* without everyone knowing she was there. And she'd changed into CJ's favorite outfit of shirt and jeans. How was she supposed to keep her eyes off her and concentrate on anything? Because she was angry with her, that's how. Dak could make it up to her when they got back. "I'm going to sit with my back to you the whole time."

Dak's smile turned into a grin. "Lucky for me, I like that view of you."

No doubt she was going to enjoy all the bending over the pool table action then. CJ arched her eyebrow. "More than my face?"

"No, of course—You're teasing me." Dak got into her truck, started the engine, and reversed out of the driveway.

She opened her window and rested her forearm on the edge of the door. "Don't go faster than forty-five, or I'll pull you over and give you a ticket."

Dead *Pretty*

"You're not the police. You can't give me a ticket." CJ gestured toward Dak's truck. "And you wouldn't be able to catch me to give me a ticket anyway." She kept a straight face, got in her car, and closed the door before she laughed. It was hard to stay mad at Dak when she was so damn cute. She reversed and pulled alongside Dak's truck. "In case you don't keep up, I'm going to Corky's after I've collected Em." She sped off without a backward glance.

If she hadn't promised to meet Emily, CJ would have taken the scenic route, hit the highway, and broken the speed limit. What was the point in having a Ferrari 488 Spider that went from zero to sixty in three seconds if she couldn't have a little fun with a Federal Agent in pursuit? She resolved to do that on the way back after dropping Emily home.

Emily was already waiting curbside when CJ pulled up.

"I will never get tired of seeing you pull up in this car," Emily said and climbed in. "Do you ever have the top up in LA?"

"Funny you should ask that…"

"Funny why?"

CJ smiled and headed to the bar. "I'll tell you when you win your first game of pool."

"Ha." She gave CJ's shoulder a light shove. "You're only saying that because you always used to beat me at pool, but I've been practicing and I'm going to whup your ass." She pulled a roll of dollars from her purse. "And I say, we should make it interesting."

"If you wanted to hustle me, you probably shouldn't have told me that you've been practicing." CJ glanced in the rear-view mirror, strangely comforted by the sight of Dak's truck hanging back a hundred yards.

Emily must've seen her because she turned around to look back. "You've checked your mirror like, ten times since you picked me up. Is someone following you?"

CJ shook her head. "Oh my God, you're as bad as Dak. No one can be bothered to follow me."

Emily snorted. "Are you serious? Your work has garnered you some rather undesirable attention from a certain serial killer. I think it's healthy to be hyper-aware of your surroundings right now. If the police are concerned enough to put a patrol car outside your house when you're home, maybe you should be taking it a little more seriously."

CJ sighed and rolled her eyes, fully aware that Emily wouldn't see.

"I think they're only doing that as a favor to Dak. And if you must know, it's Agent Dak who's following us." She parked in a large space directly outside the bar and got out before Emily could respond.

Emily whistled as she came around the car. "Way to rock casual. *Very* nice. Almost makes me regret not being attracted to women."

"Not bad for a five-minute quick change, huh?" CJ nodded to the doorperson, who opened the door for them.

"If you can do that in five minutes, maybe I could be attracted to you if you had thirty minutes."

"Y'know, it *wasn't* awkward that you told me that you knew about my unrequited love for you in college, but now you're making it weird." CJ ordered drinks and claimed a vacant pool table.

Emily pulled a bill from her pocket and carefully smoothed it out on the edge of the pool table. "Show me your money."

"You were serious?" CJ pulled her wallet from her clutch and laid out a twenty on top. "I'm sorry, that's all I've got."

"You've only got twenties?"

"No, *that* twenty is all I've got."

"Oh, I see. Because you're a celebrity, you don't have to carry money and everyone else buys you everything you need."

CJ swatted Emily's backside. "You're lucky I even have that. Who carries cash anymore? No one wants to touch anyone else's germ-riddled money."

Emily tapped the pair of bills. "I do, and I'm going to take all of this from you. And then I'm going to take it home and frame it and hang it on my living room wall."

CJ laughed and shook her head, then thanked the waitress who brought their drinks and placed them on a table close by. Beyond her, Dak walked in, looked around, and then settled on a bar stool in the far corner with her back to the wall and a full view of the entire space. CJ quashed her rising grin and though she made eye contact with Dak, she didn't smile. She did half wish that she could approach Dak as if she were a stranger, pick her up, and take her home. Maybe she wasn't as tired as she thought.

Emily nudged her. "If you're going to be distracted with hot-stuff over there for the next couple of hours, this is going to be like taking candy from a baby."

"Will you go easy on me if I tell you what's happening on Sunday?"

Dead *Pretty*

Emily picked up their drinks but didn't give CJ hers. "I will, but first I need to tell you that *that* over there," Emily pointed in Dak's direction with her right hand with her left hand held up doing a deliberately terrible job of hiding her pointing, "is incredibly sweet and super romantic. Agree or disagree?"

CJ scrunched up her nose. It a no-brainer question. "Agree."

Emily handed her drink over. "You may partake."

CJ grinned, once again thinking how much she enjoyed Emily's company and how she'd missed her in LA. It made her happy to think that she wouldn't be without her again when Emily moved to LA to work for Paige. She clinked her bottle to Emily's and took a sip of the non-alcoholic beer she was learning to tolerate.

"And second—"

"There's a second thing?"

"Yes, and a third. Stop interrupting. Second, I asked you almost a week ago if this," again with the exaggerated pointing, "could get serious, and you didn't give me a straight answer." She placed her hand over the mouth of CJ's bottle. "No more drinking for you until you tell me. Is it serious or not?"

It was another no-brainer question. CJ just wasn't sure if she was ready to say it out loud. She was only just getting used to the idea in her own head. She was thirty-one and hadn't had a serious relationship since she'd started dating. Therapy had made her realize she had intimacy issues rooted in her childhood, and now Dak was challenging her heart and mind to break those issues down and let her in—she hadn't asked CJ to do any of it, and she was completely ignorant of the war going on in CJ's heart and mind, but she was the catalyst, nonetheless. She hadn't planned on her fling with Dak to be anything other than casual sex, and she had no idea what Dak thought about their relationship, though her protectiveness spoke to some depth of feeling on her part. Serious didn't have a time limit, but it didn't mean forever either.

She blew out a long, dramatic breath. "We snuggle—of course it's serious."

Emily pulled her hand from CJ's drink and did a little dance on the spot. "You may partake."

Another clink and another sip. "What's the third, and final, thing? I want to shoot some pool and stick my ass in Agent Dak's direction."

Emily clasped her hand over her mouth and giggled. "Third, and yes, final thing. I'm going to miss you so, so bad when you go back to LA for what has to be your super Netflix deal because you said we were celebrating not commiserating." She stuck out her bottom lip and placed her hand over CJ's bottle neck again. "You'll miss me too. Agree or disagree?"

"You're on a roll with easy questions tonight. I would agree—of course—*but* that was the thing I wanted to tell you about Sunday."

Emily didn't remove her hand this time. "I don't know if I can allow you a drink if there's a but after your answer."

"Trust me. You can." CJ pulled her bottle from under Emily's hand and threw back a quick slug.

"Okay, you know I trust you. I'll play along. What's happening on Sunday?"

"Paige and Sian are flying up to talk about my huge Netflix deal, yes—"

"Yes! I knew it. You were never going to be off air long."

CJ took Emily's bottle and put both their drinks back on the table. She took Emily's hands. "But Paige is also coming to talk to you…about offering you a job with her agency in LA."

"No?"

"Yes!" CJ pulled Emily into an embrace and hugged her tightly. "You see why there was a but after my answer? I won't have to miss you because if you want that job, you're coming to LA too."

They separated after perhaps the longest hug in the history of hugs.

Emily shook her head and didn't stop. "This is happening, isn't it? It's not a joke. You're taking me to LA."

"Technically, you're taking yourself. You impressed her. Your job history has blown her away. This is all you, Em. A new chapter in your life, away from this place."

"This is going to take some time to sink in." Emily gestured to the pool table. "You break?"

CJ nodded and glanced at Dak. "Sure." She bent over the table, her ass directly in Dak's eyeline, and took her sweet time to line up the shot. If Dak was going to sit there and watch them play pool for two hours, CJ was going to give her a show. When they finally did get home, CJ wanted Dak so fired up, they wouldn't make it up to the bedroom before they ripped each other's clothes off and enjoyed the fiery lust that came with the first flushes of… yeah, the first flushes of love.

Chapter Twenty-Three

"THE CHICAGO VICTIMS PUT our personal trainer out of the running." Dak couldn't decide how to feel about that. On the one hand, her instincts had been correct when she'd thought it wasn't him, but on the other, solving the case seemed farther away than ever.

"Yep. He moved from New York, just like he said, and the dates of the Chicago victims don't match with any of his travel so it's not like he could've just dropped into the Windy City for a quick murder and then headed back to the Big Apple."

Dak frowned. "What's with the all the nicknames? You sound like a tourist."

"What's wrong with that? Not all of us have been lucky enough to travel all over the country with their work." Hamilton leaned back in his chair. "I've never been out of this state."

"What's stopping you from using a vacation to see something interesting? What's your poison? Ski holiday? Grand Canyon? Gambling in Vegas?"

"Yes, yes, and yes—but I haven't had a vacation for three years. I've been too busy working my ass off, trying to get assigned to homicide."

"And is it all you hoped and wished for, Cinderella?"

"Well, it's pretty bad that my cherry-popping murder case is a serial killer. But then, it's pretty damn good that my cherry-popping murder case is a serial killer." He jutted his chin toward Dak. "And I've got you as my partner—temporary, I know, before you jump down my throat—to guide the way. So, yeah, it is all I hoped and wished for, Fairy Godmother."

"You call me Fairy Godmother again, and anything the ugly sisters did to you will have been like tickle time compared to what I'll do to you."

"Promises, promises."

Dak picked up a Salt Lake PD stress ball and threw it at his head. "You should be thankful I can't reach my staple gun."

Hamilton unsuccessfully dodged her effort and grinned. "Anyway, you never liked Taylor for the killer, did you?"

"Nope, but it was obvious he was hiding something. Steroids make sense, and they'd give him cause to be at all our victims' houses, which was why he was eager to point that out to us."

"A couple of the gym's staff indicated that he was encouraging members to try 'roids, and they weren't comfortable with it but didn't have the courage to challenge him. It wouldn't surprise me if his boss knew all about what he was doing. She seemed mighty protective of him when we went to pick him up."

Dak wrinkled her nose, not convinced. "Maybe. But I don't know what she'd get out of it."

"A cut from his profits?"

"It's not beyond the realm of possibility, I suppose. Narcotics will take everything we've got on him and figure it out, won't they? Hell, they might even come after you."

"No way, Farrell. This is all natural." Hamilton stood and flexed a variety of poses before retaking his seat.

"Yeah, yeah."

Hamilton gestured to Dak. "I could say the same about you."

Dak looked down at her arm as she flexed it. "This is a youth spent lugging tires and engine parts around for my dad." The thought filled her with nostalgic pride, but a short stab of grief got her attention too. "But back to the Chicago victims. They were all members of the same gym, just like our victims. That points to someone on their staff or a member. Let's have Marks and Williams get in touch with the Chicago gym for a list of staff and members who left between the middle of April and the end of May then cross check it against everyone who joined the gym in the same time span."

"Do we want them going straight there or calling first?"

"Let's call first. We need the manager to cooperate without us having to get a search warrant. Anything that slows us down right now is a very bad thing."

"Are you expecting another victim tonight?"

Dak shook her head. "After the mistakes he made with Elliott, I think our killer will go back to his previous schedule." She checked her watch. "We'll know in less than ten hours."

"Unless the body isn't discovered for a few days like with Arnold."

"Aren't you supposed to be the half-full glass guy around here?"
Hamilton shrugged. "You're rubbing off on me."

"Asshole." She was sure he wasn't supposed to pick up her more
negative traits, but she didn't see it so much as pessimism but realism. "Did
Davis and Earl get anything from the guy running the shibari course?"

"Travis? Nope. He's only been running it for six months, and he gave
up his list of course attendees over that whole time. Davis and Earl are
working backwards from the most recent courses, but so far, they've
got nothing but people trying to spice up their sex life with a little fancy
bondage." Hamilton took a big gulp of his coffee then spat it back into his
mug. He stood and retrieved Dak's mug from her desk. "Fresh cup?"

"That'd be great." Dak took the short break to fire off a text to CJ.
After watching her play pool for two hours last night, the sex they'd had
when they got back to Dak's place had been something else. But after
they'd fallen next to each other, completely exhausted, CJ had looked
at her with such a tender expression. It was the kind of look that said a
hundred silent words, but Dak hadn't dared to risk interpreting it. She
had a feeling her own expression held a similar longing. There was no
ignoring the fact that she was falling in love with CJ, and it seemed like
CJ might even reciprocate. But Dak also felt CJ might be holding back.
Their lives were so very different, and Salt Lake was a temporary stop for
them both. What kind of future could they have together between Dak's
constant traveling and CJ's TV schedule? What Dak was feeling though
urged her to seriously consider finding out. CJ had effortlessly broken
down Dak's longtime avoidance of relationships. Dak had no idea how
she'd done it, and she'd been completely powerless to stop it.

Thinking about you x
So lame.

Hamilton returned with two steaming cups. "I was thinking of joining
myself, but I think the whole killer vibe has ruined it for me."

"What are you talking about?"

"The bondage classes. The website makes it look very sexy. No basic
slip knots for these guys—and they've got arty photos of a hot woman all
bound up in black rope. Mm."

"How many times do I have to tell you I'm not interested in your sordid
little sex life? And emphasis on little."

"Infinite times, boss. I have a short-term memory problem."

She shook her head and looked for something else on her desk she could throw at him without doing any serious damage. She came up empty and decided to breeze past it. "Sergeant Cooper said their mortician didn't receive death threats."

"All of the Chicago funerals were closed caskets, weren't they?" Dak flicked through the Chicago files on Cole, the final victim. "Yeah, but that detail was never revealed to the press or public so the killer wouldn't know whether or not someone had messed with his art."

Hamilton tapped the photo thoughtfully. "Unless he works at the funeral home. Were all four victims buried by the same company?"

"Let's check." She handed two of the victims' files to Hamilton and began to flick through the other two. "Diaz Home for Cole."

Hamilton closed one of the folders. "Vernon's Funeral Home for Grayson."

They came up with the same home as Grayson for the third victim and another place for the second victim.

"Someone working at the morgue?" Dak slammed a file closed when a second option dawned on her. "A cop?"

"Christ, I hope not." Hamilton tidied the folders and passed them back to Dak.

"But it's a possibility, isn't it? Even if we don't like the thought of it, we've got to investigate it so that we can discount it." She pulled the keyboard closer and began to compose an email to Sergeant Cooper. "We'll ask for a list of cops who've left the force or transferred in our time period and check it against—"

"You're doing what now?"

Williams stepped up to Dak's desk and stood way too close with his crotch in her eyeline. She pushed back from the desk and leaned back in her chair. "The killer didn't threaten any of the morticians in Chicago because he somehow knew they didn't do any real cosmetic work on them. By the looks of it, they weren't even embalmed. The media and Joe Public didn't know that, so our killer had to be one of the last people to see the body. Three different morticians worked on the individual victims, so it can't be someone who worked at the funeral homes. We were thinking it might be someone who talked to the mortician, like someone from the morgue or the station."

"And you're checking out cops for our killer?"

Dak heard the accusatory tone laced with contempt, and she took a breath. No cop liked the thought of a dirty cop, especially in their own precinct. But they liked the cop *investigating* a dirty cop even less. "We're working the leads so we can discount anyone working at the station."

"*This* station?"

"Yeah. We'll look to see if anyone transferred from Chicago to Salt Lake in our date window." She shrugged. "It's a long shot, and in all likelihood, it'll be a short or even non-existent list. The faster we cross-reference, the faster we can discount any cops as potential suspects." She knew what he was thinking—he wasn't exactly hiding it—but she'd never solved a case by not exhausting all possible avenues, and as unsavory a thought as it was to consider that an officer of the law might be their killer, a murderer hiding behind the badge wasn't new. "Same goes for anyone transferring into the morgue. Like it or not, you can't get away from the fact that our killer moved here from Chicago."

He wrinkled his nose but left his challenge at that. "Just take it easy, Farrell."

She didn't need him telling her how to do her job, but she nodded out of respect. In her peripheral vision, she also saw Hamilton clenching his jaw and looking for an opportunity to intervene. She needed to close this conversation fast and get Williams out of her face. "You got it."

Williams tapped her desk as if to reiterate his point then left.

Dak wheeled her chair back to her desk and looked at Hamilton. "Any other thoughts?"

"Could the threats to CJ be personal because she's a celebrity?"

It seemed highly unlikely, but she wasn't prepared to shoot any theory down since neither of their suspects were looking like their killer. "You're thinking that the killer genuinely didn't know what happened to his victims before burial in Chicago? And it's only because CJ's work on our victims has been publicized that she's received the death threat?"

"Could be." Hamilton opened the Quentin file. "But the mortician didn't do anything to this guy, so your theory still holds."

"If we follow your thought process, we should ask CJ if she had any other death threats before she came home. I think our killer's been too busy with his own work to worry about CJ before she started working on his victims, but it's best to discount it fully rather than leaving it out there. CJ's agent is flying in tomorrow, and she might have more info about other threats. I'll let CJ know we want ten minutes with the agent."

"That'd be great."

Dak could see the pride in Hamilton's smile, and the hopes that he'd offered something that might be of use in the investigation. Across the office, Williams was deep in conversation with Marks, probably catching him up on the possibility of the killer being a cop. Dak's gut told her the lead was thin. Cops knew the system and usually knew how to cheat it. A cop wouldn't be stupid enough to move to a new city and begin his killing spree immediately, especially when their tableaus were so unique. This guy wasn't just going around shooting people, a ten-cent crime that could be attributed to anyone with the same caliber gun. This killer was making a loud statement with each of his victims and wanted his work to be seen, even celebrated.

He was arrogant though. He seemed convinced that he could shift cities and that the local police wouldn't connect the dots to another city and another streak of murders. That was probably why he'd stopped at four in Chicago and moved on before the police got anywhere near him. In that sense, he was clever. But the mistake with the blood vase and the hurry with which he'd committed his third murder in Salt Lake indicated he'd been unsettled. CJ must have been the cause of that, and now he'd branched out into death threats. CJ's work was forcing the killer into an area he probably had no experience of, *and* he was targeting a woman, something that had been entirely off his radar since his victim profile was very specific and thus far limited entirely to males. There was no evidence that might change, which made Dak think that he was playing out a key event in his life where he'd failed to act—the homogeneity of his victim pool indicated the original focus of his anger was of similar build and status. He was all powerful over them whereas he'd been completely powerless in his past. If she could figure out the motivation, she might be able to match it to the history of a suspect—if they could find one any with any true promise. Terry Mitchum unsettled Dak, but if his alibis panned out at the nursing home, they were really back to square one.

"But for now, we've got the graveyard guy to follow up on today, don't we?"

"Yeah, but didn't you say that all the dates line up with his visits to see his mom in a nursing home?"

That was a sticking point. "Conveniently, yes, they do."

Dead *Pretty*

"Sounds like there's a but coming."

"I don't know. A gut feeling, I suppose. He seemed dedicated to his mom and her care. He even said he'd moved out here to place her in one of the best facilities in the country. That's commitment." She remembered his emotional reaction when he talked about his mom. It had seemed the most genuine part of the conversation. Throughout the rest of it, he'd just been way too relaxed. Even the most pious person exhibited nerves when talking to a cop, let alone a Federal Agent. His emotional control had been particularly noteworthy. "But maybe he's lying. Maybe we check the register at the nursing home, and he missed visiting on those days. And the second victim wasn't found for a while, so the time of death isn't definitive."

Hamilton narrowed his eyes and tilted his head like a confused pup. "Sounds like you really want it to be this guy."

She gave a short laugh. "Not at all. Getting tunnel vision is a trap I've always tried to avoid. Otherwise, you can miss clues and open doorways, and when you go back, realizing you've messed up, those clues are gone, and those doors are shut."

Hamilton scribbled in his notebook. "Have you ever thought of writing a manual, like a how-to homicide?"

"Homicide isn't a verb. And no. I don't profess to be any kind of knowledge font for other people. I'm still gathering experience. Every homicide is as unique as a snowflake, and you can learn something new from each of them."

He tapped his pen to his nose before going back to his little book. "See, there you go again. Maybe it's something you could do when you retire." He began to spell out "snowflake."

"Can it. I don't want to even think about retiring yet." She replayed parts of the conversation with Mitchum in her head. She *did* have a feeling, but she followed her gut best when it was backed up with physical evidence, and they had nothing tying him to any of the scenes. He had the same build and height as the guy in the CCTV from around CJ's fan event, but whoever the murderer was, he'd been intelligent enough to keep any part of his face from being caught on camera. She looked up at the clock and tapped her mug. "Better put these in to-go cups. It's time to visit the nursing home."

Forty-five minutes later, Dak pulled into the parking lot of the Willows

Residence on Kennedy Boulevard.

"How is CJ handling the death threats?" Hamilton asked as they approached the main entrance.

Dak shook her head. "She doesn't seem to be taking them all that seriously. I sent the patrol away when I got home last night only to find that she was about to go out for a few drinks with a friend with no one watching her." There had been perks to watching CJ from a distance, especially when she was taking her shots on the pool table, but Dak had been on edge the whole time. There was no way to tell how the killer might strike if he was going to try to make good on his death threat, and that uncertainty was dangerous. He'd clearly stalked his previous victims, and maybe he was already doing his homework on CJ. There'd been no signs of a tail when Dak had followed CJ, but if the killer was good at his prep, then he wouldn't make it easy to spot him. "I admire her belief in her work, and when I asked her to consider going back to LA, she said she wasn't going to let this guy stop her."

"The patrol might've scared him off," Hamilton said. "If he wants to continue making his 'art,' maybe he's decided to let CJ's work on his last two victims pass. It could be that he's already moved on to another city."

"Maybe." The professional side of Dak didn't want that to be true. If he'd moved on, the trail would go cold, and there'd be no way to know where he might set up next. And now that he was on the FBI's radar, his pattern might change completely, and he might only risk two murders before moving on again. But if he *had* moved on, CJ would be safe, and the non-professional side of Dak would be very happy about that. Dak's conflicting analysis indicated Burnett might've been more right than she cared to admit. Maybe her perspective was off, and her focus had been pulled away from the end game by getting involved with CJ.

At the main reception, Hamilton introduced them, and after signing in, they were shown to the manager's office.

"Thanks for making some time to see us, Mr. Newton." Dak shook his hand and sat in one of the two chairs in front of his desk. Hamilton sat beside her.

"Always happy to help the FBI, Agent Farrell." He nodded toward her partner. "And the local police, Detective Hamilton. And to that end, before we begin, I'm afraid I'm not in the position to allow you access to Mrs. Mitchum. Her son, Terry, is very protective and any visitors must have his permission to see her." He leaned over his desk as if they were sharing a secret. "And since I've not received a phone call from Terry, I can only assume that he doesn't know you're here."

Newton clearly liked to peddle in gossip, but Dak wasn't about to indulge him. "Mr. Mitchum is cooperating in our inquiries, and he's fully aware that we'd be here to confirm his alibis."

He arched his eyebrows and smiled gleefully. "So, he *is* a suspect in the serial killer case? I need to know that it's safe to allow him in this building, Agent Farrell. I have a responsibility to the vulnerable people in my care." He tapped on his desk three times. "The buck stops here if anything untoward happens in this home. I have to have all the information so I can protect my residents and my staff."

More like he wanted all the information to share with his drinking buddies. What happened to innocent until proven guilty? She gave a tight smile. "Mr. Mitchum isn't under suspicion. We're simply working through all the people who have been close to the victims, either when they were alive or after they were murdered, in order to discount them from our investigation. We'd like to take a look at your signing-in sheets for the months of May and June, please."

"When is Terry saying he's here?"

Newton wasn't to be deterred from his information-mining, apparently, but they needed his cooperation, so she'd have to humor him and answer his questions. "Every evening Mondays through Thursdays and Saturdays."

Newton nodded and wagged his finger. "He's a dedicated son, for sure. And all of the murders took place on those nights?"

Dak wasn't about to tell him anything about the case that wasn't already widely known, but the PR department had released the approximate times of death for all three victims. There was still room for interpretation on Arnold due to them missing the first stage of rigor mortis, but they hadn't made that known. The release of the boot print had already hurt their investigation, and Burnett would carpet them if they were responsible for another leak, intentional or not. "That's right."

"Mm." Newton used his intercom to ask his secretary to bring in the sheets Dak had requested.

"To your knowledge, has Mr. Mitchum visited his mom consistently since she moved here?"

He rolled his eyes as if she'd just accused him of eating a half-eaten

Robyn Nyx

hotdog discarded in a trash can.

"I don't have the time to keep up with the comings and goings of all our visitors, Agent Farrell. We have twenty-five residents, many of whom have multiple visitors per day."

Dak nodded, sensing she had to play to his ego before they lost his "always happy to help the FBI" attitude. "And it's an exclusive group of people in here, isn't it? Mr. Mitchum said that his mom had been on a waiting list to come here for some time?"

"Mm." He nodded and sat up in his chair, puffing out his chest. "That's correct. We're one of the three top specialist dementia homes in the country. That's quite an achievement when you consider how many there are across this great expanse of land we call the U.S. of A."

His preening was nauseating. Dak glanced at Hamilton, and she could tell from his blank expression, he was as impressed with Newton as she was.

"When I took over this reclamation project of a residential home five years ago, it was in a terrible state."

Dak smiled and let Newton ramble on until his secretary knocked and entered, carrying two folders of signing-in sheets.

"Here are the months you asked for, Mr. Newton."

She placed the folders on the desk and cast a sidelong look at Hamilton. Clearly liking what she saw, she offered him a seductive smile. Hamilton flushed and didn't hold her gaze, and Dak controlled a laugh. For all his big man talk, he obviously wasn't as smooth with the ladies as he made out to be. The secretary left, and Newton pushed the folders toward Dak.

"Go ahead. I can't let them out of the building, so you'll have to check your dates here, I'm afraid."

Hamilton retrieved the folders, kept one, and handed the other to Dak. She quickly flicked through to the dates that were seared into her brain and saw Mitchum's name. She looked across to Hamilton, and he nodded.

"He was here according to this," Hamilton said. He flicked through subsequent pages. "The signatures are the same on every day that he claims to be visiting."

Dak closed the folder she had and replaced it on Newton's desk. "How far back do you keep your CCTV hard drives?" She'd noted the cameras in the reception area.

"One month."

190

Dead *Pretty*

"You currently have May and June then?" Dak asked.

"Indeed we do. You have perfect timing, Agent Farrell, since May will be deleted in one day."

Newton's sickly sweet smile was making Dak's teeth hurt. "When we're done here, we'd like to quickly check the video against the dates and times of these signatures to ensure Mr. Mitchum was definitely here."

"Of course. Anything for the FBI."

"I know that you're very busy and don't get involved with the daily grind of the home, but did you meet Mr. Mitchum personally?" Dak asked.

"Oh, yes," he said, nodding. "I take all of the initial client meetings, and I check in with them periodically over the first couple of months to ensure their loved ones are settling in and that the family is happy." He leaned across the desk again. "A quality home like this doesn't come cheap, so our clients can expect a high level of service and care for their money."

He was beginning to sound like a cheesy infomercial. Whether they were a top facility for dementia patients or not, his presence would put Dak off from ever placing her mom here, God forbid that need ever arising. The thought reminded her that she still hadn't spoken to her properly since the case had started. She'd remedy that once she finished work tonight.

"Mr. Mitchum and his mom have only been here a couple of months, so you must've spent quite a lot of time with him recently. How does he seem to you?" She didn't want to give him the power of the unreliable narrator but hoped that they could glean something useful from his observations.

Newton smoothed his hair over his ears and smiled, as if he were being given an immense responsibility to play a part in their investigation. "He can be very charming, but a lot of serial killers are, aren't they? That's often how they gain the trust of their victims, so they go with them willingly."

Dak laid her hand on his desk. "If we could just stick to what you've observed in Mr. Mitchum's behavior without labeling it, that'd be great."

He gave an exaggerated wink. "Ah, of course. You have to make sure opinion doesn't color your judgment, don't you, Agent?"

God, this guy had watched way too many bad cop dramas. As if she'd fixate on Mitchum on his say-so. She nodded. "That's absolutely right, Mr. Newton. What else have you noticed about him?"

"He can be gregarious but also very contemplative." Newton tilted his head to the side. "But his mother's condition is very complex, and it's extremely hard for loved ones to handle the changes in attitude and behavior, and the loss of memory, particularly when it comes to their children. Mrs. Mitchum slips in and out of lucid thought, and that's very difficult to witness."

Now he was lecturing on the condition like he was being interviewed by a magazine and showcasing his knowledge. Dak noticed there was no ring on his wedding finger, but a faint white band indicated one had once been there. Whoever it was couldn't have put up with him for long. "Have you noticed anything in his behavior that's alarming or unusual? Is he friendly with your staff?"

"Nothing alarming, no. And no member of staff has reported anything untoward or aggressive. He's a frequent visitor, as you can see. He's exposing himself to an awful lot of emotional stress. That's hard on a person."

Hard, yes, but not a trigger to establish a multi-state reign of terror. Terry Mitchum was looking like as much of a dead end as Billy Taylor. Being charming and contemplative wasn't a crime, and he seemed to be the perfect son, going to extraordinary lengths to ensure his mother was receiving the best available care. If the CCTV provided further proof of his presence here on the nights of each murder, Dak would have no choice but to put aside her gut feeling and go back to looking at the crime scenes. She might be inclined to enjoy the challenge if it weren't for the fact that the killer had threatened CJ. And she was becoming more important to Dak with each passing day in Salt Lake.

Chapter Twenty-Four

CJ SIPPED ON HER wine and tried to focus on the TV program Dak had chosen. On another day, CJ might've been enthralled or at least been willing to engage. But on this evening, she was more interested in the drama unfolding in the kitchen. Dak had said she needed to call her mom and that she wouldn't be long. And that had been thirty minutes ago. A couple of times, Dak had popped her head around the doorjamb and mouthed an apology while pointing at her cell. But CJ's interest level had increased as the minutes without Dak had ticked by, and she'd barely heard Dak speak, indicating that she was probably on the receiving end of a maternal lecture.

Dak had shared her basic family history with CJ, and it had left her wanting to know more and wanting to meet Dak's mom and younger brother. The way Dak had spoken of her dad and the way he'd left such an indelible mark on her made CJ sad that she would never get the chance to meet him. Dak's deep sorrow at not having him around anymore was heart-breaking, and it had played a large part in CJ's decision to attempt to build a better relationship with her own parents. In turn, CJ's willingness to do that had apparently inspired Dak to stop avoiding her living family for fear of confronting her ongoing grief at losing her father way before any child should have a parent taken away from them.

"Sorry about that," Dak said and flopped onto the sofa beside CJ. "I had to talk Mom out of getting on a plane and flying here." She took CJ's hand and kissed her knuckles. "I've got more than enough distraction with you living next door."

CJ snatched her hand away and feigned offense. "Is that all I am? A distraction?" When Dak looked mortified, CJ shook her head and smiled. "I'm teasing. Do you think you'll ever learn to recognize the signs?" Her words spoke of a potential future, of knowing each other over a longer period of time than a vacation romance. She could've held them back, could've censored herself, but it was time to see if this thing between them could be more than a short, very intense, and very sexual, fling. CJ's earlier meeting had blown her mind, and as Paige had detailed every aspect of the Netflix offer, CJ had been surprised by how much she wanted to share the news with Dak. But she'd also wondered how her decision might affect Dak and their fledgling relationship. A serious discussion necessitated itself.

Dak tucked her left leg under her butt and turned to face CJ. "Ever?"

Dak's expression seemed as serious as CJ felt. She could only hope that Dak was ready for this conversation too. Either way, she was about to find out. "Yeah, ever. As in, longer than a couple of weeks' worth of vacation time." She placed her hand on Dak's thigh. "There's some exciting times ahead for me career-wise, and I'm not going to be here for much longer, a couple of weeks, at most." CJ inched closer to Dak and entwined their fingers. "But I don't want to leave you without having 'the talk' and figuring out if this is anything more than a helluva good time."

Dak glanced away briefly, but when she looked back into CJ's eyes, her expression was more soulful and intense than CJ had ever seen. "You want to talk about what we might be to each other if we don't focus on the obvious barriers?"

Dak's focus on the negative hit like a jab, but it wasn't an instant shutdown, so her courage didn't desert her...yet. "Yeah. Yeah, I do. Do you?" CJ took a breath and held Dak's gaze.

Dak uncoupled her fingers from CJ's grasp then clasped CJ's hands between her own. "You've changed your mind about this being just for fun?"

"Have you?"

"Back to answering questions with questions?" Dak laughed lightly. "Okay, I'll go first. Yes, I've changed my mind about us. We started out as a *very* nice way to pass some time, yeah, but somewhere along the line, you got under my skin and made me want more."

Dak's revelation lifted her fear. "I don't want this to end." The gush of emotion caught her breath, rendering her unable to say anything more. Was she about to cry? Jesus, she hoped not. How had she gone from being emotionally unavailable to threatening tears of desperation in two short weeks? Could Dak really be that "someone special" ideal that Hollywood rom-com movies made millions of dollars on? "If we both want it to work, can it be that easy?"

Dak squeezed her hands gently. "I don't think it'll be easy, but very little of worth is ever easy."

Dak leaned in and kissed her. What had been so passionate over the past two weeks was now softer and tasted like sweet promise. The sentimentality of her thought almost made her giggle into Dak's mouth. CJ pulled her hand from Dak's grasp and ran her finger along Dak's jawline. "I can't believe I came home and found you." She felt it. Why not say it? The worst that could happen was that Dak wouldn't say it back. And that wasn't the end of the world. It wasn't like she might never feel it. "I can't believe I fell in love." She swallowed, but it seemed harder than it should be, as if her fear that she might be in this alone had become a physical presence in her throat. Maybe she wasn't ready to *not* hear Dak reciprocate her declaration.

Dak grinned widely. "You're in love with me?"

CJ shrugged. "For now."

"If I said that I was in love with you, might that change into forever?"

CJ traced her fingers down Dak's throat and along her collarbone. Dak shivered. "Are you saying it?"

Dak nodded. "I'm saying it."

CJ didn't answer. She wanted to hear it. She raised her eyebrows and waited.

"I love you, Callie Johnson."

CJ's heart melted. She'd heard the words during sex before, used as a throwaway line after a damn good orgasm. She'd heard her mom and dad say it occasionally, probably more in the last week than in her whole childhood. But she'd never heard it said with such intensity and longing, and she'd never seen that reinforced with an intensity that seemed to dance in Dak's eyes. "Forever might be a possibility," she said and winked. She cupped Dak's face in both hands and kissed her, trying to capture every second of this most perfect moment and convey it in that kiss.

Dak broke away gently. "Would now be a good time to let you know that you're the reason my mom wanted to fly out here or would that be too intense?"

CJ swatted at Dak's chest. "Don't mess with me. You haven't told your mom about me."

"I'm not messing." Dak caught CJ's hand and began to trace a soft line from her palm and along her wrist. "And that's why she was ready to get on a plane tonight. I've never really told her about anybody, and she wants to meet you."

CJ frowned. "You've never told your mom about any previous girlfriends, but you've told her about me?"

Dak shook her head. "Kind of. I've never had a girlfriend to tell her about, and I *wanted* to tell her about you." Dak glanced away and ran her hand over the back of her head. "I can understand why she got so excited—but it's got nothing to do with you being a celebrity. She's way too squeamish to watch your show."

CJ laughed. "No pressure, then?"

"None at all. I think she'd just about resigned herself to the probability that I was never going to have a meaningful relationship. But you've changed everything," Dak whispered and entwined their fingers again.

"We've got no choice but to figure out a future together. It's more romantic than it sounds, right?" CJ leaned closer to Dak and kissed her again. She had a feeling she'd never tire of that sensation. It was a strange but not unwelcome realization that she'd been denying since their first kiss. Talking about the Netflix contract could wait. They'd made a plan of sorts. How hard could it be to work everything else out? "How about we have an early night and I show you how much I love you?"

Dak glanced at her watch and smiled. "I don't think midnight qualifies as an early night, but I'm a big fan of the proposal."

CJ checked the time on her phone. "Why on Earth was your mom still awake? Isn't New York two hours ahead of us?"

Dak nodded. "She said she'd rather wait up for my call than miss out again. It's been difficult to find time to speak to her over the past couple of weeks."

"Mm." CJ ran her tongue over Dak's lips. "You've been too busy seducing me to call your mom. *That's* why she wants to fly over here—so she can personally tell me to stop hogging all your time."

"Let's not talk about my mom anymore." Dak slid off the sofa onto her knees and pulled CJ closer until she wrapped her legs around Dak's waist. "I need to get at least some sleep tonight, but I'm desperate to feel how much you love me." Dak wrapped her arms around CJ and slowly got to her feet.

"Have I told you how much I love that you can pick me up so easily?" CJ put her hands around Dak's neck and sighed at the feel of her sharply cut hair beneath her fingertips.

Dak headed for the stairs. "You can tell me again."

"Just take me to bed."

Dak seemed to climb the stairs with no trouble. They reached the top, and Dak pushed her bedroom door open. At the foot of the bed, CJ slipped to her feet. They undressed each other quickly, and CJ jumped onto the mattress. She was tired too, but her desire for Dak outweighed her desire to sleep. She couldn't help but wish for this damn case to be solved so they could spend some real time together before she had to fly back out to LA to begin preparations for the all-new version of her show.

"I love you, Agent Dak," CJ said and when Dak lay beside her, CJ began to trace a slow line along Dak's body.

Dak lay on her back and placed her hands behind her head. "*Show* me."

CJ nibbled on her lower lip. Oh, she was going to show Dak all right. She was going to show her hard and fast…and maybe forever.

***

CJ woke with a start, her ability to breathe normally impeded. She opened her eyes and tried to move away from the rough, dry cloth that was being shoved into her mouth. She thrashed her arms and legs but found she'd been tied up into a fetal position, and her struggle was useless. Jesus, she knew she was tired but not to wake while she was being bound? That was another level of exhaustion. In the dim light from Dak's digital clock, CJ saw the other side of the bed was empty. Where had Dak gone? And what the hell was going on? If this was Dak's idea of fun, they needed to have a serious discussion.

That distant possibility faded when the person above her came close enough that CJ could feel their hot breath on her neck.

"Struggling only makes the bondage tighter."

A man's voice. And one she had a vague recollection of. She screamed against the material but barely a mumble emerged. He placed his weight on her chest and pinned her down while he pulled something from his pocket. She recognized the unique sound of duct tape being ripped from a roll before he pressed it over the cloth and onto her cheeks. She took in short, panicked puffs of air through her nose and stilled. Her bindings had tightened and were beginning to restrict the normal movement of her chest. Battling against them was futile.

He shifted her onto her side, facing away from the door, and pulled the comforter over her body. "Good decision."

His whispered words convinced her that Dak must be in the house somewhere and that he'd decided to immobilize CJ first. Everything would be fine. Dak would best this asshole. She swallowed against the raspy dryness of her throat as it dawned on her who exactly this asshole probably was: the Artist.

Silently, he moved away from CJ just as she heard Dak's footsteps on the creaky floorboards of the landing. She tried to shuffle onto her back, but the ropes had tightened and made any movement incredibly painful. To Dak, she'd simply look like she was fast asleep.

CJ heard the slap of fist against naked flesh. The thud of a body against the wooden closet. Dak called out. The sounds of a vicious struggle echoed around the room and assaulted CJ's ears. She lay there, helpless and hopeful, waiting out the muffled shouts, the flat packing noise of flesh against flesh, and the TV crashing to the floor.

Then there was the distinct fall of a body to the floor. At the base of the bed, a hand stretched out until a large boot stepped onto it, onto Dak's fingers. CJ's stomach lurched. The Artist dragged Dak along the polished boards. He snapped a handcuff onto her right wrist and fixed the other end to the old-fashioned radiator against the wall. The moonlight shone through the partially closed blinds, and CJ recoiled at the trail of scarlet-red blood trailing along the shiny wooden floor where the Artist had pulled Dak. He got onto his knees and pulled Dak's head up by her hair. He whispered something to her that CJ didn't catch and then he slammed her head onto the floor. CJ yelled against the barrier across her mouth, but her efforts were in vain.

He stood tall and returned to the bed, where he yanked the covers from CJ. A giant blade glistened in the shards of moonlight breaking through the blinds. CJ closed her eyes for a brief moment. If this was the end, if this was her time to die, then her final two weeks had been the best two weeks of her life. But anger rose with that thought. Her life was only just beginning in many ways, and this fuckstick had decided to kill her. That was beyond shit luck.

"Open your eyes, Calista. You don't get to die that easily." He laughed quietly, obviously amusing himself. "I have something very special planned for you."

He lifted her from the bed and threw her over his shoulder as if she were a sack of firewood. The blood rushed to her head, and as he strolled out of the bedroom, CJ caught one last glimpse of Dak, motionless and bleeding, on the bedroom floor. She couldn't be dead, or why would he have bothered to restrain her? The thought comforted her slightly. "I love you, Agent Dak," she tried to say against her gag. The result was muffled and made no sense, but CJ wanted her last words to Dak to be the ones that resounded in her soul for the first—and likely last—time in her life.

Chapter Twenty-Five

DAK WOKE AND TOOK a lungful of air like she'd briefly stopped breathing. She yanked on her right wrist but unsurprisingly, her FBI-issue cuff didn't give under the pressure. Secured to a fucking radiator with her own restraints. If she lived, she wouldn't live this down. She rolled onto her side to assess the damage. The amount of blood was cause for concern, and the white-hot pain that seared through her stomach didn't instill confidence in her overall health. Her white tank was soaked with blood around her wound and being dragged by her assailant had spread it all over her sweatpants.

The Artist had done this, and he'd taken CJ to exact his revenge for her interference in his work. He'd left Dak alive but chained here so she'd bleed out, knowing that she couldn't do anything to save her. That wasn't conjecture. He'd whispered it into her ear before slamming her into unconsciousness. She had to get out of here and go after him...go after who?

She concentrated on his voice and replayed it in her head. Whispered words were harder to assign to a memory of a voice. It wasn't one she'd heard often, that much she did know, but the melodic and menacing lilt had registered in her mind as one she might be able to put to a face.

A sharp sting of pain began in her stomach and spewed along the entry wound until it spilled out into the chilled air of her room, bringing forth a deep and throaty groan. She placed her left palm over the knife wound and pressed hard, sucking in air to dull the agony.

She failed and thought she might pass out if the torturous throb didn't abate. She closed her eyes briefly and tried to reduce her attention to what she could feel in her body. If she could shut that out, she could figure a way out of this. Dislocating her thumb wasn't an option. The movies that showed that as a method to escape handcuffs should be sued, in her opinion. She looked across the floor to the mess she and the Artist had made as they struggled and fought. The cowardly son of a bitch had attacked her from behind when she'd come back from the bathroom, but she hadn't gone down easy. The macho thought flitted through her head, and she dismissed it. It didn't matter how quickly he'd overcome her, or if it had taken thirty minutes. Either way, she was still the one lying on the floor, injured and beaten. Either way, she hadn't been able to protect CJ like she'd promised she would and now CJ was in the hands of a vicious psychopath with a twisted perspective on what was or was not art.

"You offended me, Special Agent Farrell," he'd whispered.

Dak hadn't spoken to the press, so at some point, she must've spoken to the Artist without realizing it, obviously. And in itself, that narrowed her scope considerably. She and Hamilton had interviewed a number of the funeral attendees, staff at the gym, hospital, and Elliott's tech company. For the most part, the conversations couldn't be classed as interrogations and Dak hadn't pulled out any psychological games to play with any of them, because none of them had really been true suspects. She was sure she hadn't offered her personal opinion as to the nature of the Artist's work or talent. Their only real suspect had been Billy Taylor, and it definitely hadn't been his Brooklyn accent rasping in her ear.

Her stomach cramped around another stinging shot of pain from within. She blew out a slow breath and tried to bring her heart rate down. If she could slow her pulse, she could slow the escaping ebb of her life spilling onto the floor beneath her. She shifted her attention to the mess around the dresser she'd smashed him into. An antique jug and bowl had smashed into large pieces and scattered in all directions. If he hadn't found her cuffs and had secured her with some of his shibari rope, a shard of porcelain might've been welcome, but it would do nothing against the hardened steel encasing her wrist.

Among the pieces however, was a dark rectangle that she almost missed, nestled as it was beneath the edge of her bed on top of the clothes she and CJ had discarded in their hurry to get naked and into bed. Her cellphone. She began to shuffle along the floor, extending her right arm as far as the cuff would allow, but each inch she moved resulted in a sharp spasm that shuddered from her stomach and up through her chest to her heart. But she wasn't about to interpret what that might mean.

She stretched her left leg toward the arm of CJ's shirt and tried to grasp it between her toes. The tension shook through her limb, and a cramp threatened, but she ignored them both. After a few moments of trying, she

Dead *Pretty*

resorted to hooking her big toe onto the shirt and finally caught it. She managed to pull it a few inches toward her, and her phone came with it.

But CJ's shirt was lightweight, and as Dak tugged it toward her, her cellphone began to fall in the opposite direction. The pain nagged for her to heed its cry and stretching her body as long as it would go was doing the wound no good at all. She could feel it opening and her blood seeping from it. She shoved away the light-headed nausea. If she didn't acknowledge it, maybe it wouldn't overpower her.

She continued to edge CJ's shirt closer until her sweet scent floated up to her nose and battled with the stench of iron for Dak's attention. God, CJ smelled good. Her perfume and natural scent drove Dak wild. And she wasn't about to let this be the last time her brain got to enjoy it. With renewed focus, she pressed her left hand over her wound and elongated her body as far as it would go. She pulled the material closer until she could touch her phone with her toe.

Pain seared through her whole body, making her curl into the fetal position and yell out. Her hot blood ebbed onto her tank top, and Dak's eyelids felt heavy, like they were trying to close. She fought against the warm pull of darkness and stretched out her left leg again. She hooked her foot around the bottom of the phone and with one monumental effort, dragged it toward her.

It slid across the floor, helped with the slick trail of her blood, and came to rest against her chest. She let out a deep sigh, punched in the security code, and opened her VIP contacts. *Hamilton.* His name was the last thing she thought before she slipped into the welcoming abyss of an involuntary darkness.

***

"Jesus Christ!"

Dak blinked her eyes open slowly and they were flooded with bright light. Someone was over her, shining a flashlight into her eyeballs. She knocked it away with her free hand before she realized her right hand was also free.

"What the hell happened, Farrell?"

Dak blinked again and Hamilton came into a soft focus behind the person and their offending flashlight. "Hey, buddy." She smiled then laughed at his serious expression. It didn't suit him. Her laugh was short-lived when it was accompanied by a pain that racked through her whole body.

"Please stay still."

The disembodied voice came from somewhere behind her, but she knew better than to twist around to see who it was.

"What happened?"

Dak wasn't so far out of it that she didn't catch the fear in his voice.

"Is she going to be okay?"

More fear. She recognized it because she'd had the same tone in her voice when she'd held Ben in her arms as his life slipped away from him. But there was no light beckoning her toward it, and the pain, while excruciating, didn't feel lift-threatening. Though what did she know?

"We have to get her to the hospital." The medic gestured to the floor. "She's lost a lot of blood, and we have to stitch up this wound before she bleeds out."

That seemed a little insensitive. And maybe too much information for her ears. She figured law enforcement officers were supposed to be immune to their own mortality given that they dealt with death on a daily basis. Whatever, she needed patching up ASAP so she and Hamilton could get to CJ before the Artist... She didn't want to complete the thought.

"Whatever you need to do, you should do it fast. He took CJ. I need to find him—" Her eyes fluttered shut and she forced them open again.

"That's who did this? CJ's gone?"

Dak looked to Hamilton, his expression serious and intense almost as if CJ were *his* lover. That's what partners did though, wasn't it? They shared all your burdens and pains like they were their own. She'd all but forgotten that part. "Yeah." She was about to say more, but self-recriminations and her inability to protect CJ when she'd promised she would took up residence in her mind and stopped her words. If they hadn't been together, the patrol would've been present all night. The Artist would've gotten nowhere near CJ's house. She'd be safe instead of in the hands of a murderer—one whose identity remained a complete mystery to them. Darkness tugged at the edge of her vision. The voices around her began to fade into soft, white noise. *You offended me, Special Agent Farrell* played on a loop in her head as Dak lost all sense of feeling in her body and an obsidian blackness enveloped her sight.

Chapter Twenty-Six

"THIS IS CRAZY, T. Why can't we just leave and go somewhere else? I don't want to kill a woman. I've never wanted to kill a woman. That's not what any of this has ever been about."

CJ heard a shuffle of boots across the floor then hushed but harsh whisperings. Great. The guy was more deranged than she thought he'd be, and now he was talking to himself like the guy in that *Primal Fear* movie. She closed her eyes. Stupid, really, since she had a black hood over her head that had already made it impossible to see anything. She could feel though, and the thick ropes she'd been bound in were tight, but she could breathe thanks to the material having been taken out of her mouth. The hard, possibly wooden, chair was making her ass ache though, and he'd secured her to that so tightly, she felt like she'd been glued into it.

She kept her eyes shut in a bizarre effort to hear better. She'd read somewhere that when you lose one sense, the others heightened to compensate. So far, nada, but maybe she shouldn't hear the ravings of this lunatic. He hadn't brought her here for a dinner date, he'd brought her here to kill her so she couldn't "ruin" any more of his work. Listening to what he was going to do to her *before* he did it wouldn't help anyone. But…if he was arguing with himself, maybe she could convince the rational side of him to free her. Damn. She wished she'd paid more attention in psych classes in college. Negotiating with serial killers probably wasn't on the syllabus.

Dak would know what to do and say, but she was lying on the floor of her bedroom, wounded and bleeding. Christ, there'd been a lot of blood. Maybe it looked worse than it was. With spilled liquids, it always seemed like there was more of it than there was if it was in a glass. He'd banged Dak's head hard against the floor, but he hadn't killed her outright. CJ had to hang onto that hope. Dak hadn't wronged him like CJ had. Wronged him. What kind of twisted shithead could believe *she* was the one doing wrong? Maybe that's where the schism in his personality had come from.

Part of him knew he was doing evil, and he was trying to stop himself. What could she do to help that part of him overcome the darkness that drove him to kill?

"This has to be done. She's undoing the artistry of my work. I can't let that pass unpunished."

The Artist was loud and nearby. She shivered. Wherever they were, he hadn't put the heat on. She didn't recognize his voice. Was that a good or a bad thing? If she knew who he was, could she try to reason with him? She heard his heavy footsteps and then she could smell him. Earthy, as if he'd rolled around in the dirt to cover his scent like dogs did.

"We don't want to do this, but you've given us no choice."

His hot breath warmed her ear through the soft material of the cover. "There's always a choice," she whispered, her words harder to vocalize than she'd hoped. She sounded as scared as she was trying not to feel. If she didn't acknowledge it, maybe it wasn't as hopeless as it seemed.

He laughed like a movie villain. Maybe all villains laughed like that, and she'd just been lucky enough not to come across any until tonight. Maybe they learned to laugh like that at villain college. She stifled the urge to laugh herself. She was losing perspective on the situation but that could be a good thing. She didn't want to be completely coherent if she was about to be tortured and murdered by this psychopath.

"What did you say?" he asked.

She swallowed and fought the onslaught of panic that she'd managed to keep down until he started to speak to her. "You said that I've given you no choice, but…but that's not right. There's always a choice."

"That's what I told my mother, but she wasn't strong enough to make a choice."

Mother issues. Was that something to use to connect with him? Lord knows, she had her fair share of parent issues, and yet they'd begun to work them out and were coming out the other side. "My mom wasn't around much. That was her choice, and I hated her for that for a long time. Are you saying you're not strong enough to make a choice, just like your mom?" If she could keep him talking and not slicing her up, perhaps there was hope that she could escape or that Dak might somehow rescue her. She wanted to giggle at the cliché of being a damsel in distress and struggled to retain her grip on reality. She'd have no hope of talking him around if she retreated into her mind.

Dead *Pretty*

"No, that's not what I'm saying. I really must punish you. I don't have a choice, because if I let you live and let you continue to reverse my great works, I'd have no legacy, no catharsis."

Catharsis? "You're giving yourself therapy by using people as your kill canvas?" She chose her words carefully. Antagonizing him wouldn't prolong the conversation or her life. If she could pretend that she understood what she was doing… That was it, let him convince her that what he did was necessary, apologize to him for what she'd done, and promise she wouldn't interfere in his art again. Could that work?

"In a way, yes. Some people don't know why they're driven to do what they do, but I know precisely why." He let out a long sigh.

"If you explain it to me, maybe I could understand why I shouldn't interfere." Her approach was clumsy, she knew that, but she had no fancy psych tools in her kit. All she could do was try to keep him talking. The scraping of a wooden chair being pulled over stone made her jump. She felt his presence closer to her and heard him sit heavily.

"You pose an interesting dilemma for me, Calista," he said. "You're clearly talking to buy yourself time, but I find myself enjoying being able to talk to someone new about my work. That appeals to my ego, and all artists have egos no matter how much we try to deny them."

She jumped again when he touched her knee, even though the contact was gentle. She steadied her voice. "I do want to understand. From a professional point of view, I've been fascinated by your work."

He patted her knee again. "I do promise that your end won't be painful or prolonged. I have no need to experience your suffering."

That was comforting in a way she didn't want to acknowledge. "Is that the same for the men you've…created? That's why you express your art post-mortem, because the killing is a necessity only to give you a canvas?" Her question was bullshit, of course. He had to get something from the murders, otherwise why not just use a life-size mannequin?

"Why do you assume those men didn't suffer? Because there were no signs of physical torture?" He laughed again. "There are more ways of making a man suffer than harming their body, Calista."

"So, you did make them suffer?"

"We did."

"It's not just you? You have a fellow artist?" This was going to be interesting. She knew very little about multiple personality disorders, but it looked like she was about to learn firsthand.

"I wouldn't call Lawrence an artist. And I'm certain he doesn't think of himself as one. No. Our motivations for killing are the same, but I derive something different from the process than he does. Mm, shall we ask him? He doesn't really want to be here. He's not totally onboard with killing you, I'm afraid."

CJ didn't know what to say to that, except that she suspected she was more afraid than he was since she was the one about to die. A painless death, apparently, but he was still quite adamant he was killing her. "But you can get him here even though he doesn't want to be here?" She'd thought there was no control over the other personalities. Christ, this guy was a psychologist's dream patient.

"Of course." He sounded perplexed by her question. "Lawrence, would you come in here, please?" Silence. "Lawrence," he said a few decibels louder. "Get in here."

"I don't want to. I've told you, I want no part of this."

CJ gasped. The second voice came from a completely different direction and from farther away than he was sitting. Either he was exceptional at throwing his voice or there really *were* two of them.

Chapter Twenty-Seven

DAMN IT. DAK STRUGGLED to open her eyes against the pull of an unconsciousness that felt forced. A bright, white light burned her eyeballs when her eyelids finally did as they were told, and when she checked her watch, she discovered it wasn't there. Instead, a strip of white plastic encircled her bare wrist, and a tube taped to her forearm led to a cannula in the crook of her elbow. She followed the tube up to a bag of fluids and inspected the label. It was just saline. She pulled the other end from her arm and pressed her palm over the entry point. After a few moments, she released the pressure on her arm then she pushed the scratchy sheet covering her body down to her waist and tugged her hospital-issue gown up so that she could inspect her wound. There was nothing to see other than a three-inch square bandage with a small circle of brown in the center.

She pushed herself up to a sitting position and grimaced through the sharp pain in her side where the stitches stretched to accommodate her movement. She'd need to keep those knitted together if she wanted to get out here. There was no clock on any of the walls and no sign of her cellphone or watch. How long had she been in here? She swung her legs out of bed and tentatively stood just as Hamilton walked in the room.

He rushed toward her. "Whoa, you're not supposed to be moving yet."

Dak pushed him away. "I can't stay here. I need to find CJ."

Hamilton held up his hands and backed away a few paces. "I get it. But you've just come out of surgery. Let me get a doctor."

"How long have I been out? And where's my watch and phone?"

Hamilton pulled both items from the pockets of his jacket and placed them on the bed beside her. "We're checking CCTV on all the routes from your house right now. He must've used a truck or car to take CJ away. There's not a lot of traffic on the road at that time of night, so it shouldn't take long before we get something to go on."

Dak put her watch on. "Fuck, Hamilton. It's been three hours. She could already be— Did you bring any of my clothes?"

"I grabbed a few things and stuffed them in that bag." He pointed to the battered, FBI-branded roll bag she'd had since training at Quantico.

"*Special Agent Farrell*," the doctor said as she entered the room, "what do you think you're doing?"

You offended me, Special Agent Farrell. The memory clicked into place like her brain had just cracked a safe. "Terry Mitchum."

"What about him?" Hamilton frowned.

"Before he smashed my head into the floor, he said I'd offended him as if we'd had a conversation. The only person I spoke to that I ever passed a judgment on the Artist's work was Terry Mitchum. Outside the Bryan's Funeral Home, I said something about how people would celebrate when the killer was dead, and that no one would celebrate his work." She shook her head. "He laughed but obviously he took it to heart."

"Agent Farrell, I need you to get back into bed. You have to rest." The doctor stepped between the two of them and gestured toward the bed.

Dak waved her away. "Just a second, doc."

Hamilton looked unconvinced. "He came up totally clean, Dak. And his alibis checked out—you saw the footage of him going into his mother's nursing home yourself."

"It's the only thing that makes sense to me, Hamilton. There was something about him that was off. The way he offered his boot print and how he told me all about moving to the city…it was like he was pre-empting my suspicions. This killer is super intelligent, and he's been ahead of us the whole game. I don't know how he got his alibi to work, but he's our guy. I recognized his voice." Dak tried to step around the doctor to get to her bag of clothes, but she held out her arm.

"Agent Farrell. You've just had surgery and a blood transfusion. You need to rest."

Dak shook her head. "I'll rest when I'm dead, doc. We've got a killer to stop."

"You might be dead sooner than you want to be if you tear those stitches."

What was it with health professionals and their lack of tact? "Did you perform the surgery?" Dak asked.

"Yes."

"Are you confident you did a good job?"

The doctor nodded. "Yes, but—"

Dead *Pretty*

Dak put her hand on the doc's shoulder. "The Artist has kidnapped someone very close to me, and I need to stop him from harming her. When I've done that, I promise I'll come right back for you to check me over. Okay?"

The doctor arched her eyebrow but stepped aside. "You better be, Agent Farrell. I don't want a dead FBI agent on my record." She walked out without a backward glance.

Yet another example of a fine bedside manner. "Lovely." Dak pulled the clothes from her bag and tossed them on the bed. "Call the captain and tell him we're headed to the cemetery. Mitchum lives in a ground floor apartment with no basement and no garage. There's no way he'd take her there but get them to send a team just in case."

"On it." He headed out the door and closed it behind him.

Dak yanked off her paper-thin gown and began to pull on the clothes Hamilton had brought her. She resisted checking her watch again. She had to believe that whatever Mitchum had planned for CJ, he hadn't already done it. Dak couldn't lose the woman of her dreams now that she'd finally found her.

Chapter Twenty-Eight

THE ARTIST AND LAWRENCE argued for quite a while in the same room as CJ before it sounded like the Artist dragged Lawrence away and slammed the door behind them. She had zero concept of time. It could've been forty-five minutes, or it could've been fifteen. She'd never been good at telling the time without the aid of a watch. She hoped it had been a long disagreement. She was playing for time, just as the Artist had pointed out, but she had no idea whether it was worth doing or not. For all she knew, Dak might still be unconscious on the floor of her bedroom. And even if she had come around, how could she have gotten free from her cuffs? It wasn't like she would have a spare key concealed in her boxer shorts or tank top. CJ tried not to think about the amount of blood she'd seen. Dak was tough. She was a Federal Agent, and she'd been trained for physical altercations. CJ was certain that once Dak did wake up, she would've been able to stem her bleeding somehow. She had to believe that. She had to believe in something right now.

CJ also tried not to think about the fact that Dak's investigation was no closer to a suspect than they had been two weeks ago. So, even if Dak had managed to get free somehow, she wouldn't have a clue where to look for CJ. Damn it. She needed to stop thinking about what may or may not be happening outside these walls. She had to figure a way out of here herself, and with the way her two captors had just acted, maybe that wasn't such a far-fetched concept. She still hadn't seen their faces, which was a good thing. They'd never let her free if she could identify either of them. And though the more the Artist talked, the more familiar his voice became, she couldn't place it definitively. Whoever he was, if she'd spoken to him at all, it had been brief and not memorable.

She hung her head toward her chest and blew the material of the hood away from her mouth in an effort to see how she was bound to the chair. She couldn't see a thing. However the Artist had secured her, her restraints weren't biting into her wrists or ankles. Yet. Recalling the way they'd tightened against her struggle at Dak's, she attempted to gently lift her wrist from the arm of the chair. As she suspected, the slack disappeared and pulled her arm back in the opposite direction. Just as before, struggling would only hurt. Talking her way out of this remained her only option.

The door opened and someone entered. Could she dare to hope that Lawrence had overpowered the Artist and come to release her? Lawrence had been clear that he wanted no part in killing her, but the Artist had been more concerned in whether or not Lawrence thought of himself as an artist too. It was obvious he wanted that title all to himself, making CJ wonder about a sibling rivalry. Two people working together to kill people had to have a very strong bond, and there was no indication that they might be lovers. Brothers seemed like a logical conclusion.

She concentrated on the footsteps but couldn't tell whose they were. Her hearing hadn't improved with the temporary loss of her sight. So much for that theory.

"What do you think? Is Lawrence an artist or not?"

CJ sighed. "What exactly is it that Lawrence does to your...canvasses?" Victims was the word she'd nearly said, but that wasn't how he viewed the dead men. If she was to have any hope of convincing him to let her go, she had to make him think that she understood his work.

"He ends their life and drains their blood."

The matter-of-fact way in which he said it made her teeth tingle. He was so incredibly blasé about the murders. She paused before answering. Was Lawrence standing in the doorway listening? He was already on her side and wanted to release her. If she angered him by belittling his contribution, it could tip him toward the Artist's perspective. But if she didn't say the words the Artist clearly wanted to hear, she wouldn't convince him to let her go either. "Art is very subjective though, isn't it? An unmade bed sold for over four million dollars once."

"Mm, I suppose I hadn't thought of Lawrence's work in that way before. You're right."

A short silence followed, and her own breathing was the only thing she could hear. "Would you be willing to tell me why you've chosen to express your creativity this way?" CJ almost smiled. If she got out of here, maybe she could consider a career in journalism. No doubt Paige could make it happen. If she *did* survive this, Paige would probably have a book deal secured within the day too.

"What a great way of putting it," he said. "This feels like one of those moments in a Bond movie where the villain reveals his plan, but I really don't see the harm in discussing it with you. And as I said, I really am enjoying talking to someone else about what we do."

There really was no harm. She couldn't do anything about the murders he'd already committed, and all she could think about right now was saving her own ass. "There's something very controlled and deliberate about every one of your strokes…"

"That seems to have baffled everyone, hasn't it? People are so used to slashers and smashers, as I call them. But there's nothing manic about what I do. The men *must* die. Lawrence is driven to do that. In the beginning, so was I, but as we killed more men, my need for that waned, and I began to find my creative expression."

She felt him close by again and figured he'd sat back in a chair close to her. "Had they all wronged you in some way?"

"Not these men, no. One man." He sighed deeply. "It's a shame you chose the career you did—though your talent is impressive—you would've made a good therapist. I find myself wanting to tell you everything, and yet, this is something I've never spoken of before."

She doubted that. The guy had an ego the size of the Grand Canyon and was clearly desperate to talk about himself. He'd just not had the opportunity to do so freely before, and he was grabbing it with both hands. Which, of course, she should be grateful for because it kept her alive. And the longer she was alive, the more chance she had of surviving. Maybe. "I'm starting to wish I'd chosen a different career too. I wanted to go to art school to become a sculptor, but my parents wouldn't allow it. They said I'd never make a living from it." She laughed. "Funny that they've just converted my dad's old office into a studio for me. That's definitely too little too late."

"Perhaps. But to answer your question, no, these men hadn't wronged us. They're just suffering the consequences of one man's actions."

He took a deep breath and as he released it, the material of her hood swayed. A hint of peppermint permeated the cotton, and CJ idly wondered if that would be the last time she'd be exposed to that smell. "Your father?"

He made a noise like a gameshow buzzer that indicated her guess was incorrect.

"Close. Our stepfather. Our real father died in a roofing accident.

But the man Mother replaced him with was no man at all. I won't feed your nightmares with the harrowing details, but suffice to say, Lawrence and I have many, many scars to show just how much he delighted in our suffering."

"He beat you?"

The Artist let out a mirthless laugh. "That was part of it. If you saw Lawrence and me naked, you'd see a whole canvas of torture. The men we choose closely resemble him. They're unfortunate that way, I suppose. If they weren't vain, and rich, and in peak physical condition, they would've been perfectly safe."

That seemed like a massive understatement. "Like the majority of American males." She laughed, and he joined her. Could she dare to hope she was gaining his favor?

"Exactly. As a nation, we do have an overabundance of ordinary men, don't we?"

CJ felt a rush of air as the door burst open and smashed against the wall, startling her.

"Someone's here. I think it's the police. I told you we shouldn't have taken her, Terence."

Terence? Her memory of his voice slipped into place. Terry? The gentle giant who was dating Beth at the funeral home? She'd said how wonderful he was. Cool air blew across her face as her hood was lifted. She squeezed her eyes tight, and her heart pushed hard against her chest. "I'm not looking at you."

His rough hand held her chin, and he forced material of some kind into her mouth. "I'm sorry to have to do this."

He released her, and she heard the tell-tale rip of duct tape before she felt it pressed over her lips, and the hood covered her face once more.

"Lawrence, you know what to do."

CJ fought to control a rising panic and her suddenly labored breathing. The material of the hood sucked up against her nose, making it even more difficult. Every instinct urged her to fight against her bindings, but she knew it was no use. Praying for rescue seemed like her final option.

Chapter Twenty-Nine

HAMILTON PARKED THE CAR at the end of the cemetery driveway, and Dak got out. She grunted when pain shot from her wound down her left leg, almost taking it from under her.

"You okay?"

She nodded at Hamilton as he emerged from the car, concern etched on his expression. She opened the back door, and Davis and Earl got out from the rear seats. Burnett hadn't been convinced by Dak's argument that Terry Mitchum was their killer, so Davis and Earl were all they had to work with. Burnett had also been disinclined to send a unit to Mitchum's house, but Marks and Williams had been working the case long enough to pin their hopes on whatever Dak advised and were happy to check it out.

"We'll go around the back, and you take the front entrance." Dak looked at the two-story building, wishing they had more back-up. She'd be taking this up with Walker however this played out. Burnett had pulled in a favor to keep Dak for this investigation, but his lack of faith in her right now had her pissed. "Stay in radio contact, and don't take any chances." *Especially if Mitchum is anywhere near CJ.* She kept that thought to herself. They were all aware she had a personal stake in this now, and they'd promised her everything was going to be all right. She'd rather they hadn't made a promise they couldn't be sure of keeping. She knew just as well as they did that the odds were 50/50 on surviving a regular kidnapping, let alone one where the victim had been specifically targeted by a psychopath with a grudge.

Regardless, she was glad the three of them were by her side and she wasn't attempting a rescue alone. Her wound was already seeping, and she felt like she might collapse at any given moment. But she was convinced Mitchum was their guy, and she couldn't leave CJ in his hands a second longer. He'd already had her way too long.

The four of them edged toward the building, trying to stay out of sight by moving from gravestone to tree to tomb. At the main entrance, Dak saw a dark panel van, a perfect vehicle to kidnap someone in. She glanced over her shoulder at Hamilton and motioned toward it. He followed her finger, nodded, and looked hopeful. If Mitchum had brought CJ here in that van, she must still *be* here, and he hadn't… The vocab she used for these cases seemed too distant and dismissive, disrespectful even. Dumped. He hadn't dumped her body yet. Dak choked down a wave of nausea. She couldn't think like that. And a little distance would be a good thing. She didn't want to freeze if it came to a confrontation between her and Mitchum, though something not so deep inside her was willing that confrontation to happen.

They reached the outer walls of the main building, and she and Hamilton peeled off toward the back entrance. As they turned the corner, she glanced back to see Marks knelt at the door, picking the lock. A surprise approach was vital if they were to get anywhere near CJ without putting her in danger. She steeled herself and continued around the edge of the walls with Hamilton creeping along quietly behind her.

When they got to the back entrance, Dak tried the handle and found it unlocked. She pulled out her Maglite, and Hamilton unholstered his weapon. It had never been her first instinct to shoot someone, so she avoided drawing her gun as much as possible, and right now, as woozy as she was, she wouldn't be sure to aim properly. She pushed the door open slowly and flicked the flashlight on, illuminating the way. Hamilton closed and latched the door behind them, and they moved forward through the corridor. Dak signaled for Hamilton to stop when she saw another light source at the end of the corridor. She leveled her weapon and waited. Davis and Earl came into view and headed up the stairs.

Dak blew out a quiet, long breath and continued along their trajectory. At the far side of the corridor, a strip of light showed beneath a large wooden door. She temporarily pocketed her Maglite and slowly twisted the handle. She pushed the door open slightly, and the hinges creaked like all hinges did in horror movies.

"Shit," Hamilton whispered.

Dak flashed him a warning look for him to keep quiet. She held the edge of the door and shoved it all the way open in one swift motion, making minimum noise. A long set of wooden steps were partially lit before they plunged into darkness beyond. She looked down at her shoes and then at Hamilton. Why hadn't he brought her trainers and jeans instead of brogues? He shrugged and looked vaguely apologetic.

Dead *Pretty*

Dak retrieved her flashlight, and they made their way as quietly as possible down the stairs. At the base of the stairs, another strip of light garnered Dak's attention. She pointed toward it, and Hamilton nodded. They walked side by side toward the door at the end of the corridor. Dak crunched a stone underfoot and it sounded like a firecracker in the silence. She lifted her foot carefully and continued on.

She looked for any sign of movement or shadows in the dim light, but nothing stirred. Behind her, the sound of a stone crunched onto the concrete floor echoed. In one fluid motion, she turned and dropped to her left knee before throwing a hard right jab straight out in front of her. Her fist connected with something soft, and the ensuing howl convinced her it wasn't a beer belly she'd struck. She lunged up with all her force and drove her elbow upward to strike beneath the chin of their would-be attacker. He hit the floor with a heavy thud, and Dak jumped onto him. She twisted his arm around and behind his back, and he yelled out for her to stop.

Hamilton stepped alongside her. "Now I see why you don't bother with your gun. *You're* a weapon."

She pressed the guy's hand into his back and shone her flashlight in his face. *It was him.* "Terry Mitchum. Where's CJ?" She didn't acknowledge that his mere presence here wasn't any kind of proof of him having kidnapped CJ. When he didn't answer, she forced his hand a little further up his back. Pain shot through her torso instead, however, and she sucked in a breath. He still remained silent, but his eyes glittered as he stared at her, a malevolent force of evil behind them.

Hamilton knelt beside them and pressed his gun to Mitchum's temple. "Don't do anything stupid." He slowly pulled Mitchum's other hand out from under his body and swiftly cuffed his wrists.

When Hamilton stood and pulled Mitchum upright, Dak searched the floor beneath him, and the beam of her flashlight fell on an automatic pistol. Hamilton shoved Mitchum face first into the wall, and Dak retrieved the gun after pulling on a latex glove.

"Davis, Marks. We've got our guy down in the basement. No sign of Callie Johnson." It seemed strange to use CJ's full name but using her nickname would have been inappropriate.

"On our way," Davis said through Dak's earpiece.

She exchanged a look with Hamilton before they both glanced toward the light at the end of the corridor once again.

Robyn Nyx

"Do you want to wait here for Davis and Earl while I check that out?" Hamilton asked.

She shook her head. Whatever lay behind that door, Dak wanted to be the first to open it. She clenched her jaw and took a deep breath to steady her nerves. "I've got it."

Hamilton shoved his shoulder into Mitchum's back, knocking his head against the wall. "If you've done anything to Callie, we'll make you pay, you son of a bitch."

Dak swallowed. She appreciated Hamilton's support, but she had no idea *what* she'd do if Mitchum had hurt CJ. Her legs already felt like they might give way, and the wetness around her wound indicated she'd managed to tear her stitches. None of that mattered right now. She had to see what was beyond that closed door, whether her future had been taken from her before it had really even begun.

She tried to stride out to the door and not reveal her weakening physical state. She'd happily go back to the hospital and spend all the recovery time she needed to—as soon as she knew that CJ was in one piece. She retched as she reached for the door handle. The Artist hadn't cut anyone into pieces, but his handiwork had been sickening. What if he'd already used CJ as his next canvas?

She turned the handle and pushed the door open with the little strength she had left. The tension flooded from her body when she focused her Maglite in the center of the room and saw CJ, bound to a chair but alive and breathing rapidly. And there was no sign of blood on the floor. Dak ran to CJ and pulled the hood from her head. Her eyes were wild, and she shook her head frantically. "It's okay, baby. We've got him. You're safe now."

CJ was trying to get something out, but the tape across her face stopped her from vocalizing it.

"This might sting a little," Dak said as she began to peel the edges from CJ's cheek.

"Not as much as this will sting you."

Dak turned swiftly at the sound of the voice that had whispered in her ear a few hours ago. It couldn't be. As the figure behind the voice came into focus, Hamilton came into the doorway on the opposite side of the room. Dak saw the glint of a gun barrel as Mitchum swung his arm toward Hamilton. She took one step and jumped toward Mitchum in an attempt to grab at his gun. The crack of the firearm echoed around the small room as Dak tumbled to the ground with Mitchum. Agonizing pain blossomed throughout her body, and darkness crept around the edges of her eyesight. Her hands burned, and she found she was still grasping the barrel of his gun. She rolled away from the business end and used every iota of her strength to twist the gun away from her and out of his grip. She lifted the gun and slammed it and Mitchum's hands against the unforgiving concrete floor, over and over until he released the gun. Hamilton came up beside them and kicked the gun away before he leaned down and punched Mitchum in the face to knock him unconscious.

Hamilton pulled out his phone. "Officer down. Officer down. Immediate assistance required at High View Cemetery."

Dak dragged herself off Mitchum's body and flopped onto her back, unable to find the fortitude to do anything more. "You let him go?" Dak stammered and gripped her gut. Warm blood oozed all over her hands. *That* wasn't just the original wound. She must've taken the stray bullet. Someone flipped the switch, and the room flooded with light. She lifted her head and looked back across the room to see Marks removing the tape from CJ's mouth. CJ's eyes were wide, but she was okay. At the doorway, Davis held Mitchum by the crook of the elbow. *What the hell?* She looked to her side at the guy she climbed away from. *Mitchum.* Twin brothers.

"Now that you've taken a bullet for me, you're my partner for life, you know that, right?"

Hamilton's face filled her view and she laughed, though it hurt to do so. "You're dreaming if you think that's ever happening," she said, struggling to speak through the pain. She coughed and spat out the thick liquid in her mouth. Hamilton glanced at it, and she recognized the fear in his eyes. She imagined she'd had that very same expression when she was hovering over Ben's body after he'd taken the bullet meant for her.

"Don't punch me," he said as he pulled her shirt from the waistband of her trousers. He clenched his jaw, replaced the material, and pressed his hand onto her stomach.

She let out a long breath through clamped teeth when the pain fizzed through her like she'd been shot for a second time. The adrenaline of the past hour began to fade, and she became aware of a cold that seeped into her and chilled her bones. She began to shiver, and something heavy tugged on her eyelids, drawing her to sleep. Her eyes flickered. Hamilton's mouth moved, but she couldn't hear his words. Light and sound drifted in and out of her consciousness until she heard and saw nothing. Darkness beckoned, and she fell gladly into its arms. *Time to rest.*

Chapter Thirty

CJ RAN HER FINGERTIPS up and down Dak's arm as she lay unconscious in the hospital bed. It had been over fifteen hours since she'd been rushed into emergency surgery for her bullet and knife wounds. The doctor had told CJ the bullet had nicked Dak's lung and that she'd been lucky it hadn't pierced it completely. CJ thought Dak probably didn't feel too lucky and would say so when she awoke. *Please wake.* Hamilton had assured her Dak would be fine. The surgeon had said Dak was strong and there'd been no complications. She'd wake when her body was ready.

CJ dropped her head onto Dak's forearm. "Wake up," she whispered. She was sick of being told things by everyone else. The only person she wanted to hear from was Dak. She knew that the longer someone was unconscious, the less likely they were to ever wake, or if they did, there was brain damage, and they simply weren't the same person they'd been before.

"Excuse me."

CJ looked up to the doorway to see an older woman who looked vaguely familiar. "Yes?"

The woman nodded and strolled in. She took the other seat beside Dak's bed and held Dak's hand. CJ waited for an explanation, but the woman seemed to ignore her and concentrated on Dak.

"Come on now, Daniella. It's time for you to rejoin the land of the living," she said. She stroked Dak's cheek then finally looked at CJ. "I'm Daniella's mom. You must be CJ."

CJ nodded. "It's lovely to meet you." *Really?* That's the best she could come up with?

Dak's mom offered a tight-lipped smile. "I've been looking forward to meeting you..." She looked at Dak and exhaled loudly. Tears edged into her eyes. "But not like this."

CJ reached over Dak and held her mom's hand. She felt cold, and CJ suppressed the urge to gently rub it. That seemed way too familiar for someone she'd just met. "She's going to be okay." If she repeated what everyone her was saying, maybe it'd be a self-fulfilling outcome.

The sorrow of a mother whose child's life hung in the balance rippled from her eyes and streaked her cheeks. "I lost her father too soon." She swallowed. "I can't lose my Daniella." She pulled her hand from CJ's grip and wiped her tears away. "She mustn't see me like this."

Dak's mom blinked rapidly and looked up at the ceiling. CJ couldn't help wondering why tears were seen as such a negative thing, a sign of weakness when they were evidence of the strength of someone's feelings. Her own liquid emotion simmered behind her eyes, begging for attention.

Dak's mom fell silent, and CJ flicked through her mind for something to say. She came up empty and pulled her hand back so she could keep stroking Dak's arm. Dak was so strong. Even in repose, her muscles bunched beneath her skin and evidenced her physicality. Those same arms had felt so good wrapped around CJ's body, made her feel safer than ever before, like nothing could hurt her. She shuddered at the thought of her recent experience. She'd come close to death, though she'd hoped she might've talked Mitchum out of it. But it was possible he was simply playing along just so he could talk to her about his psychopathic inclinations. He'd only begun to scratch the surface of why he and his twin brother killed those men, and who knew how many more they'd murdered in other cities around the country. Her heart ached for their mother, isolated and alone in the nursing home with no one to visit her. Would she even understand what had happened? Would she remember if they told her? Maybe not remembering would be best for her, in this instance.

She looked up at Dak's face, and her heart caught in a vice. She couldn't lose her. CJ loved her, she knew that with certainty. She'd never experienced love before, but she didn't need to. This all-consuming range of emotions she was swept up in, the irregular beat of her heart when Dak looked at her a certain way, the racing of her pulse in the aftermath of their love-making—they were everything she'd seen in movies and so much more.

CJ had faced death and survived. It had to be for a reason. It had to be so she and Dak had a chance at a happy ever after. CJ would give up her new Netflix deal in a New York minute if it meant Dak would wake and love her forever. *Forever*. She wasn't offering enough, but what else did she have to barter with for Dak's life? She closed her eyes and prayed, something she hadn't done since she was a kid in Sunday school. She'd do anything He wanted if He'd just let Dak live.

"Was she happy?"

The strange question from Dak's mom startled her from her deep thoughts. Dak had said she should've spent more time with her mom. CJ didn't want to contemplate the possibility that the chance was lost to them both now, but it gnawed semi-silently at the back of her mind. "I think so." CJ had seen nothing but positivity and enthusiasm from Dak for each day. It was bothering her that she couldn't break the serial killer case, but she'd never seemed unhappy—except when CJ had insisted on going out with Emily. But that night had turned out very nicely when they got home.

CJ let her tears fall onto their entwined hands. They'd been too together such a short time but had experienced so much. It couldn't be over already.

"She sounded happy."

Of course. Dak and her mom had spoken last night before CJ and Dak had gone to bed. "She said you wanted to get on a flight to see her."

Dak's mom pressed her lips together and a desperate sadness flickered across her expression. "I wanted to see you both. She's never talked to me about a partner before and I got a little over-excited, I'm afraid. Daniella's always been quite alone in the world since her dad died." She looked across at CJ and shook her head. "She wasn't *actually* alone. She still had me and her younger brother, Ward, but we couldn't fill the hole in her heart that her father left her with." She reached up and stroked Dak's cheek with the back of her fingers. "She was always such a daddy's girl. The bottom of her world fell out when he died, and she's never been the same since."

"I can't imagine." And she couldn't. She'd tried hard to be the child her parents wanted around and had failed, so her connection to them had been blood alone. They were working to change things now, sure, but the early years when that strong bond was developed was lost. And while she would mourn her parents if they died, her life would go on pretty much the same as it had before. She'd had to survive without them so long, she'd be able to do so again.

"I don't think I've seen her happy for twenty years." She gave a small laugh. "Well, I haven't seen her much at all for twenty years."

Sorrow for Dak's mom's loss settled like a heavy mass in the pit of her stomach. Anything CJ thought of saying seemed trite. She couldn't fathom Dak's reaction to her father dying or how she'd isolated herself from the rest of her family. Only Dak could explain that, and even she might not be able to. CJ had nothing to offer Dak's grieving mom other than patronizing platitudes. "I know she was looking forward to seeing you."

Dak's mom nodded. "I always love when she comes home, but I don't think it feels like home without her dad." She sighed deeply and squeezed Dak's hand then wiped her face dry of tears. "Anyway, I shouldn't be so maudlin. She won't want to wake up to another guilt trip." She reached over and patted CJ's hand. "It's wonderful to meet you, CJ. I can't wait to get to know you."

"Me too." CJ looked back at Dak, motionless on the bed. She looked so helpless, but she was anything but. She'd saved her partner's life, and she saved CJ from an ugly death. *Please wake up.* CJ wanted to spend the rest of her life loving the hero who'd gifted that life to her.

Chapter Thirty-One

DAK SLOWLY BECAME AWARE of her surroundings and opened her eyes. On either side of her bed were the two people she loved most in the world, deep in conversation and laughing. Her hearing seemed muffled for a moment but when it came around, she registered her mom regaling CJ with one of the many childhood tales she remembered. Dak always marveled at her mom's memory for the tiniest of details. "Please don't tell her any more embarrassing stories, Mom, or she's sure to leave me."

CJ and her mom pushed up from their chairs and drew her into a group hug.

Dak grimaced when one of them squeezed a little too hard. "Ow."

They released her with a chorus of apologies.

"Let's get the doctor in here." Her mom pressed the call button and sat back in her chair.

CJ remained standing, her gaze fixed on Dak. "It's about damn time."

Dak raised her hands. "You want me to apologize for getting shot in the line of duty?" She dropped her hands back to the bed when a shooting pain spread across her chest.

"I want you to apologize for thinking about leaving me—us." CJ leaned in and gently kissed her.

Dak lifted her hand to CJ's cheek and ignored the sharp, pulling pain in her stomach. "I *never* thought about leaving you. I've been fighting my own little battle with Death and trying to convince her I wasn't ready to go with her yet. I don't care how tricked out the afterlife is, I'm not done with this one." She kissed CJ again. "I'm not done with *you* by a long shot."

"Agent Farrell, it's nice to have you back. How are you feeling?" She practically shoved CJ out of her way.

The question came from the surgeon who'd tried to keep her from leaving the hospital with Hamilton after she'd been stabbed. "I feel like I've gone a few rounds with an angry bull. My chest and stomach are on fire." She didn't expect any sympathy, but she said it anyway.

The doctor laughed. "That's no surprise. At least you didn't die from the original wound," she pulled back Dak's covers, lifted her shirt, and pressed the flesh around her gunshot, "or your new one."

Dak grunted at the touch of the doctor's cold fingers. "I took your threat very seriously, doc. I didn't want to spoil your record."

The doctor smiled briefly and flicked a glance toward CJ. "And is this the kidnapped person you risked your life for?"

Dak looked across at CJ, and an unfamiliar feeling flooded her mind. A chill enveloped her, and icy fingers wrapped around her heart as realization hit that she'd almost lost CJ, almost lost the chance to see if their new love would endure. Fear burned hot behind her eyes, and she looked up at the ceiling, blinking it away. "She is," she whispered, struggling to vocalize the words. Dak *had* risked her life, but she'd do it again every day and twice on Sundays if it meant they could be together.

"I hope you realize how dangerous it was for Agent Farrell to discharge herself from my care to come to your rescue."

CJ frowned, clearly confused by the doctor's challenge. "I didn't at the time I was *kidnapped*, but I do now." She repositioned herself opposite the doctor and held Dak's hand. "Perhaps true love is a hard concept to understand for a woman of science."

Dak suppressed a small smile at the tone of CJ's response. She was obviously unimpressed by the doctor's inference and wasn't about to cower away, mouse-like, in the face of a confrontation.

The doctor gave a short laugh. "Absolutely. It's all biochemistry and basic drives as far as I'm concerned." She checked Dak's pulse and studied the monitors before scribbling on Dak's notes. "But sometimes people don't appreciate the self-sacrifice of others until it's too late." The doctor turned from the bed and headed for the door. "You're going to be fine, Agent Farrell, if you rest up and don't go being all heroic in a hurry." She winked and left.

"What was all that about?" her mom asked.

"I have no idea," Dak said. "Maybe she thinks of herself as a therapist as well as a surgeon." Dak tugged down her shirt, as baffled by the doctor's bedside behavior as everyone else. "But..." She held out her hand and her mom took it. "I want you to know that I love you, Mom." Dak had already been thinking about changing the way she treated her mom and her brother, but her brush with death solidified the need to make things

Dead *Pretty*

right.

"I know you do, Daniella." Her mom sighed and patted the back of Dak's hand. "Ward wanted to come, but he couldn't—"

"It's okay, Mom. Now that this case is over, I'll come home and spend some time with you both."

Her mom nodded. "That would be lovely, Daniella, but there's no pressure."

Her mom's expression indicated skepticism. It wasn't surprising, but it still hurt to see. Dak had been trying to stay blind to the hurt she was causing by being distant and unreachable. She'd been eager to give advice to CJ about spending time with her parents but for a long time hadn't practiced what she'd been preaching. Dak turned her hand over and took her mom's hand. "I mean it, Mom. A lot has happened over the past few weeks." Dak glanced at CJ and her heart threatened to explode. Of all those things, meeting and falling in love with CJ had blown her away and reframed her whole perspective on life. "And I've realized I haven't been a great daughter. Things are going to change."

"Don't be silly, Daniella. You're a wonderful daughter."

Dak shook her head. She knew damn well she didn't deserve that title, but she was going to change that. "I'll be better."

Her mom tapped her handbag. "I'm going to call your brother and tell him you've come around." She took out a pack of Camel Lights and the Zippo Dak's dad had used. "And I'll get some fresh air at the same time."

"Okay, Mom." Dak waited until she was gone and turned to CJ. "Are you okay?" She looked CJ over but couldn't see any bandages or obvious injuries. "He didn't hurt you?" Her blood boiled with the thought that Mitchum had laid his hands on CJ at all.

"No. Neither of them did," CJ said. "I'm fine, thanks to you."

Everything came back to her. There were two Mitchums. "Twins?" When CJ nodded, the alibi made sense, but they were both there with CJ, so she assumed they were both involved in the murders somehow. She knew better than to quiz CJ about it now. That would have to be done in an official capacity, and better Hamilton than Dak, if CJ hadn't already made a statement. "I should never have let them take you. I'm sorry."

CJ leaned over and kissed her again. "You have nothing to apologize for. You saved me from them, and you've saved a whole lot of other lives in the process." CJ pressed her hand over Dak's chest. "And when I

get you home," she whispered, "I'm going to show you that I *do* realize exactly how dangerous it was for you to risk your life to save me and then I'm going to show you just how grateful I am."

Dak chuckled. "It's the doc you need to prove it to, not me."

CJ raised her eyebrow and harumphed. *"Her* opinion doesn't interest me."

"But it is true love though?" Dak asked. CJ's retort to the doc had stuck in her mind.

CJ dragged her nail across Dak's lips before she kissed her again. "You're my prince and my hero. Yes, this is true love."

"And true love conquers all?" Dak couldn't deny she had concerns about how they might navigate their future without either of them having to sacrifice anything. Somehow though, Dak's own career felt far less important to her than it ever had, like a pressure had been lifted from her shoulders and she no longer had the unforgiving drive to push forward. In the face of death, love and family had trumped ambition. And faced with losing CJ, everything else had lost all its importance. She was Dak's everything.

"It does."

"I'll do whatever it takes to make this work, CJ. I love you so much, it hurts." Dak tried to push up from her bed, but CJ stopped her.

"If you try to 'love' me now, it will actually hurt. Remember what the doc said? You have to rest."

Dak rolled her eyes. She didn't want to rest. She wanted to take CJ in her arms and enjoy a hero's prize of true love. "What's the point in getting the girl if you don't actually *get* the girl?"

CJ cupped Dak's face. "Don't worry, you've got all the time in the world to get this girl."

Dak craned her neck and kissed CJ with all the passion and strength she could manage. Every inch of her body seemed to hurt, but she didn't care. All she cared about was CJ and the road ahead.

Epilogue

Two months later

"THE D.A.'S OFFICE WANTS the death penalty for both brothers," Hamilton said. "If they get it, it's going to be the first one in over ten years."

Dak wasn't a supporter of that outcome, but she wasn't surprised the D.A. was going for it. The murders had rocked the city and its people. They were baying for what the media had called "God's retribution." Dak glanced across the room and saw CJ tapping her watch. She held up one finger to indicate she'd be just another minute. "Everything Lawrence gave you was true?"

"Yep, everything the younger brother told us about our murders and the ones in other cities checked out. They were in Quebec and Ontario before they moved to Chicago. We're looking at another fifteen murders on top of what we have."

Being twins covered the ease of their alibi for the Salt Lake murders, but what about Chicago? "How did they manage the Chicago murders when they were in Virginia?"

"Terry was living there while Lawrence was in Virginia with their mother. No one in any of the cities knew there were two of them. Their mother having dementia and not communicating with anyone outside the nursing homes made it easier for them. They were really good at covering their tracks."

Dak agreed with that assessment. She had never come across such careful killers, and she didn't want to again. Two months had passed since the night they caught the Artist and got two for the price of one. Dak was still signed off from active duty and had been pushing paper since she'd been well enough to return to work, but she was beginning to think about getting back in the field—she just wasn't certain which field that might be.

"Have you thought about Burnett's offer?" Hamilton asked when she said nothing in response.

Robyn Nyx

Dak heard the hope in his voice. Burnett wanted her to stay on with Salt Lake and partner Hamilton. But Walker wanted to promote her within the FBI. In truth, though she had a soft spot for Hamilton, she didn't like working with either Burnett or Walker, but she didn't know where that left her. For now, she was happy being the supportive partner of a reality TV superstar and given how much CJ was enjoying the filming of her new show, Dak was more than happy to sit back and watch. Living with CJ in LA wasn't exactly a hardship, either, and they'd settled into a sensual domesticity that suited her perfectly. Occasional dinners out and plenty of quiet nights in seemed to be suiting them both. Whatever professional choice she made, she wouldn't be giving that up.

"It's not much of an offer, Hamilton." Less pay, less variety, less autonomy. The only plus side would be working with Hamilton. She caressed the new stone sculpture CJ had finished last month. The woman's back arched much the same way CJ's did every time she orgasmed, and it never failed to make Dak smile.

"I'd be offended, but I get where you're coming from," he said. "I've made a necklace from the bullet you took for me."

He laughed but she suspected he wasn't joking. "Maybe you should be looking at applying to the FBI. Salt Lake is a little too pedestrian for a talent like yours." In the pause that followed, Dak could imagine him puffing out with pride at her praise. It wasn't something she gave out often.

"You think I've got what it takes?"

"I wouldn't say it if I didn't believe in you," she said. Dak looked up when a shadow blocked the sun. "Hamilton, I have to go. Keep me posted about the case." She hung up and smiled at CJ. "Hey, beautiful. Are you done for the day?"

"Yep. Do you want to get something to eat?"

Dak rose from the bench and took CJ in her arms. "Are you on the menu?"

"I can be your dessert." CJ placed her hand on Dak's stomach gently. "If you're up to it, I've been thinking about you strapping on your silicone buddy. I've missed her while you've been resting."

Dak kissed her and slipped her tongue inside CJ's mouth, deepening the connection. "She's missed you."

CJ pressed her hand against Dak's chest. "What did Hamilton want?"

"He was just updating me on the case." She shrugged. "And Burnett

232

asked him to push for my answer on their offer."

CJ looked pensive. "And?"

"And I'm very happy being your groupie right now. But whatever I end up doing, it'll be a joint decision. You're the most important thing in my life, and whatever's next for me, it has to work for both of us."

"And we're still flying up to see your family this weekend?"

"We are," Dak said. "Ward can't wait to see you again. I think he's got a crush on you. Mom says he's always talking about you and has all your shows recorded." She held CJ a little tighter. "I'm going to have to keep an eye on him when we're there. Now that I've found the love of my life, I can't have you swept away by my sneaky little brother."

CJ shook her head. "An army of wild horses couldn't drag me away from you, my love."

Dak grinned and kissed CJ's nose. "I hope not." She took CJ's hand and led her toward her car. Dak stuffed her other hand into her pocket and wrapped her fingers around the ring box nestled in there.

Their forever started tonight.

What's Your Story?

Global Wordsmiths, CIC, provides an all-encompassing service for all writers, ranging from basic proofreading and cover design to development editing, typesetting, and eBook services. A major part of our work is charity and community focused, delivering writing projects to under-served and under-represented groups across Nottinghamshire, giving voice to the voiceless and visibility to the unseen.

To learn more about what we offer, visit: www.globalwords.co.uk

A selection of books by Global Words Press:
Desire, Love, Identity: with the National Justice Museum
Aventuras en México: Farmilo Primary School
Life's Whispers: Journeys to the Hospice
Times Past: with The Workhouse, National Trust
Times Past: Young at Heart with AGE UK
In Different Shoes: Stories of Trans Lives
From Surviving to Thriving: Reclaiming Our Voices
Don't Look Back, You're Not Going That Way

Self-published authors working with Global Wordsmiths:
E.V. Bancroft
Addison M. Conley
AJ Mason
Ally McGuire
Emma Nichols
Helena Harte
Iona Kane
James Merrick
Karen Klyne
Robyn Nyx
John Edward Parsons
Simon Smalley
Valden Bush

Other Great Butterworth Books

The Copper Scroll by Robyn Nyx
When love and ambition collide, will Chase and Rayne's fledgling relationship survive the fallout?
Available on Amazon (ISBN 9798711238386)

Scripted Love by Helena Harte
What good is a romance writer who doesn't believe in happy ever after?
Available from Amazon August 2021 (ASIN B0993QFLNN)

Caribbean Dreams by Karen Klyne
When love sails into your life, do you climb aboard?
Available from Amazon (ASIN B09M41PYM9)

Nero by Valden Bush
Banished. Abandoned. Lost. Will her destiny reunite her with the love of her life?
Available from Amazon (ASIN B09BXN8VTZ)

Warm Pearls and Paper Cranes by E.V. Bancroft
A family torn apart. The only way forward is love.
Available from Amazon (ISBN 9781915009029)

The Helion Band *by AJ Mason*
An all-powerful band, a maniacal queen, a rascal pilot, and an escaped servant. The galaxy isn't ready for this fallout.
Coming in 2022

That Boy of Yours Wants Looking At by Simon Smalley
A gloriously colourful and heart-rending memoir.
Available from Amazon (ASIN B09HSN9NM8)

Judge Me, Judge Me Not by James Merrick
A memoir of one gay man's battle against the world and himself.
Available from Amazon (ASIN B09CLK91N5)

LesFic Eclectic Volume Three edited by Robyn Nyx
A little something for all tastes.
Available free via BookFunnel (ISBN 9781915009135)

Made in United States
North Haven, CT
27 February 2022

16573827R00141